"What do you want, Zachary?" she demanded.

He replied quietly. Solemnly. Honestly. "I want you."

Beth stared at him. She'd heard the words from other men. But coming from Zachary, they meant something entirely different. Not mere physical pleasure. Not a few hours tonight that would be forgotten tomorrow.

He was talking about making love. About sharing. About caring.

About things she'd sworn she didn't want in her life.

About things she wanted so badly right now that she ached.

"Beth?" His whisper was raw, and he searched her face for a clue to her feelings.

She had no answers. Only questions. Could she survive loving him tonight, knowing he would soon go back to his life without her?

But could she pass up the opportunity to be Zachary's lady, even if only for a little while?

Dear Reader,

I'm really excited about the books I'm bringing you this month. I think every one of them is a winner. Marilyn Pappano checks in with *Somebody's Lady,* the sequel to her ultra-popular *Somebody's Baby.* Lawyers Zachary Adams and Beth Gibson met as adversaries in that first book, but this time they're on the same side of a difficult case, one that tests all their professional skills as they work side by side. Of course, emotions have a habit of coming to the surface in such situations, and this one is no exception. Can "city" and "country" meet and make a match? If you know Marilyn's talents, you'll know this book is a must read.

Paula Detmer Riggs will also put you through an emotional wringer in another must read: *Paroled!* When Tyler McClane got out of prison, all he wanted was to forget his ex-wife's unjust charges, charges that had destroyed his career and torn his daughter from him. But Caitlin Fielding wasn't about to leave the past alone, not when she knew her sister had wrongly sent a man to prison—with her own unwitting help! Not when a little girl's future happiness depended on setting things straight with her daddy. I don't want to tell you any more, because you should experience this wonderful book for yourself.

To complete the month, we have Mary Anne Wilson's *Echoes of Roses,* a beautifully wrought story of a man who's the idol of millions, but wants only one woman, a woman with a secret she's sure he'll never understand. And welcome new author Sally Tyler Hayes. In *Whose Child Is This?* she has written a stunning debut book filled with characters who will touch your heart.

Next month, we have a very special book from Joyce McGill, but that's all I'm going to say for now. I hope you'll join me then to hear all about it.

Yours,

Leslie Wainger
Senior Editor and Editorial Coordinator

MARILYN PAPPANO

Somebody's Lady

SILHOUETTE·INTIMATE·MOMENTS®

Published by Silhouette Books New York

America's Publisher of Contemporary Romance

SILHOUETTE BOOKS
300 East 42nd St., New York, N.Y. 10017

SOMEBODY'S LADY

ISBN: 0-373-07437-9

First Silhouette Books printing July 1992

All the characters in this book have no existence
outside the imagination of the author and have
no relation whatsoever to anyone bearing the same
name or names. They are not even distantly
inspired by any individual known or unknown
to the author, and all incidents are pure invention.

Books by Marilyn Pappano

Silhouette Intimate Moments

Within Reach #182
The Lights of Home #214
Guilt by Association #233
Cody Daniels' Return #258
Room at the Inn #268
Something of Heaven #294
Somebody's Baby #310
Not Without Honor #338
Safe Haven #363
A Dangerous Man #381
Probable Cause #405
Operation Homefront #424
Somebody's Lady #437

Silhouette Books

Silhouette Christmas Stories 1989
"The Greatest Gift"
Silhouette Summer Sizzlers 1991
"Loving Abby"

MARILYN PAPPANO

has been writing as long as she can remember, just for the fun of it, but a few years ago she decided to take her lifelong hobby seriously. She was encouraging a friend to write a romance novel and ended up writing one herself. It was accepted, and she plans to continue as an author for a long time. When she's not involved in writing, she enjoys camping, quilting, sewing and, most of all, reading. Not surprisingly, her favorite books are romance novels.

Her husband is in the Navy, and in the course of her marriage, she has lived all over the U.S. Currently, she lives in North Carolina with her husband and son.

Chapter 1

Zachary Adams leaned back, his feet propped on the only clear spot on his desk, his chair tilted as far as it would go, and mentally reviewed the day's schedule. Patricia and Darren Thompson were due at one o'clock to begin work on their divorce settlement. Mattie Ferguson wanted to draw up a new will, probably to reinstate the daughter she'd disinherited four—no, five—times in the last three years. Bill Henry's kid had scheduled an appointment after school for an interview for the careers section of the school paper. And Daniel and Sarah Ryan wanted to legally change their daughter Katie's name from Lawson to Ryan.

All in all, not a bad schedule, he thought with a grin. If the rest of the week stayed like this, he could do all his work, earn a little money and still have plenty of time to putter around the farm up on Laurel Mountain.

He felt a momentary twinge of guilt for agreeing to talk to Henry's kid. Being a lawyer in the real world was something Zachary knew little about. It had nothing in common with being a lawyer in Sweetwater, Tennessee. His practice here was part-time at best, consisting primarily of divorces, wills, probates and contract law. There were occasional criminal cases, but rarely anything more serious than vandalism, breaking and entering, or public drunkenness.

And if his caseload was nothing like his big-city counterparts', neither was his income. He earned enough to get by, but only because he owned this building, and the rent from the other tenants—the bank next door and the dentist upstairs—was steadier than his own income. If he hadn't inherited that twenty acres on the mountain from his grandfather, he never could have afforded it, and if he weren't clearing the land and building the house out there himself, he could never have afforded that, either.

So there were trade-offs. He carried a light caseload, and he earned less money. He also faced less stress, knew all his clients personally, took time off whenever he wanted and went fishing every Tuesday morning with the mayor and the sheriff. He would never get rich, but he would never burn out, either.

He glanced at his watch, then at his desk, which desperately needed cleaning. Since his sister Alicia had quit a few weeks ago for a better-paying job in the insurance office down the street, he'd let his paperwork slide. His filing system consisted of stacking records on his desk until they threatened to topple over; then he simply divided them into two smaller stacks, repeating the process as necessary. He could spend the three hours until Patricia and Darren were due sorting through all those files and notes . . . or he could drive up the mountain and cut down that dead pine that threatened to block his driveway when it inevitably fell.

It was no contest. He swung his feet to the floor, the rubber soles of his tennis shoes squeaking against the wooden planks when they hit. He picked up the sheepskin-lined coat he'd tossed over one chair, grabbed his keys from their place in the ashtray and started out the door.

He hadn't gone more than ten feet from the building when someone called his name. Zachary paused in the act of buttoning his coat and looked up to see Dutch Morris and his wife Ruth hurrying toward him. They both looked as if the ky had opened up and fallen in on them. So much for chopping wood, he thought philosophically.

"How are you today, Dutch? Miss Ruth?" he asked with a friendly smile.

Dutch, a big, burly, hard-luck sort of person, shifted uncomfortably before asking, "Can we talk to you in your office, Zach?"

With only a twinge of regret at this change in plans, Zachary led the way back inside, unlocking the outer door and showing them through the empty reception area to his office. He removed his coat once again before taking a seat behind the desk. "What can I do for you?"

He watched the couple exchange worried looks and saw the evidence of recently shed tears on Ruth's face, and he wondered what had happened this time. Dutch and Ruth had shared more trouble in their lifetimes than any two people deserved. No matter how hard they worked or how hard they tried, something always went wrong. This time, if it was enough to make Ruth cry, it must be serious.

It was. She pressed a handkerchief to her mouth and lowered her gaze to the floor, leaving the task of answering Zachary's question to her husband. For a moment Dutch searched for the right words; then he simply blurted them out. "Carrie, our oldest girl, killed her husband last night."

It was a three-hour drive to Nashville, where Carrie Lewis lived. Zachary got an early start Tuesday morning, pulling out of his driveway while the sky was still dark except for a faint rosy hue to the east.

He'd told Dutch and Ruth that he couldn't handle their daughter's case. Not once in all the years he'd been practicing law had he ever turned down a client based on money—more times than he could count, he'd been paid in favors or services rather than cash—but he'd had no choice this time. A murder trial was expensive, and Carrie's would be held in Nashville. He would have to live there until the trial was over, he had explained to the Morrises, and he simply couldn't afford that.

Added to that very real consideration was the fact that he
didn't have the experience to handle such a case. The minor
infractions of the law that he'd dealt with in the past had in
no way prepared him for a murder trial. It would take a lot
of hard work and talent to undo the damage of Carrie's
confession. The hard work he could handle. The talent, he
was honest enough to admit, he didn't have.

So why was he going to Nashville to see the client who
wasn't *his* client, to work on the case that wasn't *his* case?
he asked himself dryly.

Because he hadn't been able to leave the Morrises out in
the cold. Because as little as he knew about capital crimes,
it was more than they knew. Because their grandchildren—
the oldest fourteen, the youngest three—had been placed in
temporary foster care and had to be scared half out of their
minds with their father dead and their mother in jail. Because Carrie needed a lawyer—not a country boy like him
and not a public defender who was overworked and underpaid, but a bright, dedicated, passionate, tough, intelligent
lawyer.

And because he knew a lawyer in Nashville who fit that
description perfectly. Along with beautiful, intriguing and
sexy.

Beth Gibson was a partner in one of Nashville's largest
firms, a firm filled with names that were found in Tennessee history books. Old South. Old money. Incredible power.
It was a firm not known for doing anything out of the
kindness of its heart, not without a six-figure retainer in return.

Still, Beth *had* represented Sarah Ryan in her divorce from
her first husband and in the custody arrangement with
Daniel, and no one could have been poorer than Sarah was
then. Maybe she would extend that generosity to another
unfortunate woman in trouble.

Reaching the interstate, Zachary turned toward Nashville, then turned his thoughts back to the day he'd met
Beth. She had come to his office with Daniel Ryan one
pretty September day. He couldn't remember which had

surprised him most: his instant attraction to the red-haired lawyer or the reason for her visit. It was a custody case, she had announced in that thoroughly efficient, all-business voice of hers. Daniel had fathered her client's daughter, and the mother wanted him to take temporary custody.

In the first few moments Zachary hadn't believed her claim. Daniel was a good man, but he was practically a hermit. Zachary had never met anyone less comfortable with people, particularly women, than Daniel. He'd never known anyone less likely to indulge in a one-night stand—or, in this case, two nights—than Daniel. And frankly—shamefully—he had wondered what kind of woman would be attracted to Daniel. What kind of woman would be intimate with the big, withdrawn, hard-looking man?

But Daniel had verified Beth's story. Yes, he'd had an affair with Sarah Lawson, and yes, he wanted the one year's custody of three-month-old Katie that Sarah was offering.

Zachary and Beth had handled all the paperwork, and a few days later she had brought Daniel's daughter to him, a sweet, adorable baby with her father's eyes and her mother's delicate beauty.

That had been the last he'd seen of Beth for nearly a year. Then Sarah had come for her baby, and Daniel hadn't wanted to give her up. That had brought Beth back into Zachary's life, and his attraction to her had been even stronger. No woman had ever drawn him the way she had. No desire had ever gripped him the way this one had. No prospective relationship had ever seemed so impossibly right the way this one had.

But fairness had dictated that as long as matters remained unsettled between Sarah and Daniel, the only relationship Zachary could consider with Beth was a professional one. And once the case had been settled? Once Daniel and Sarah had gotten married? Why hadn't he made a move—called her, asked her out, done anything to establish contact between them?

Because he was a coward, Zachary readily admitted. He didn't like challenges—if he did, he would be practicing law in the city and earning big bucks like everyone he'd gone to law school with—and Beth was sure to be a challenge. The only thing they had in common was their profession, and law the way he practiced it was only a poor relation to the way she did. In everything else—tastes, backgrounds, ambitions—they were complete opposites.

And while opposites might attract, he acknowledged with a humorless smile, they didn't often make for lasting relationships.

But that wouldn't stop him from going to Beth's office after he saw Carrie. It wouldn't stop him from asking for her help.

And it wouldn't stop him from wanting her.

Restlessly he turned on the radio, tuning it to a Nashville country station. The music and frequent traffic updates kept him distracted all the way into the city and downtown to the detention center. There he identified himself and was shown into the interview room, where he waited for Carrie.

After the Morrises had left his office yesterday, he'd found their daughter's picture in an old high school yearbook. She was two years younger than he was, and, in spite of the small size of the school, he hadn't known her very well. She'd been painfully shy and withdrawn, a poor student with few interests and fewer friends.

She'd had long, straight brown hair that was parted in the middle and anchored behind her ears, and she'd worn a plain white shirt and no makeup, no smile. He recalled that her eyes were also brown, like her mother's. In the sharp black-and-white picture, they looked vacant, as if there were a body there but no mind. No heart. No soul.

After high school she had stayed on the farm and worked alongside her father, he remembered, until she married a farm boy in the next county by the name of Lewis. But neither the Lewis nor the Morris farm could feed two mouths, so Delbert Lewis had gone off to find a job elsewhere. Once Carrie had joined him, Zachary hadn't seen or heard anything about them except the news of each of their children's births. There were four kids, Ruth had told him, and another one on the way. Seven lives, counting the baby's, shattered in one night.

The opening of the door interrupted his thoughts, and he looked up to see Carrie Lewis. Next to the muscular woman escorting her, Carrie looked thin and insubstantial. The uniform she wore was too big and added to her waifish appearance. The sleeves fell past her elbows, the skirt hid the curve of her belly, and the hem ended at her knees, revealing legs that were marked with bruises in varying stages of healing.

She shuffled across the room, her head bowed, her hair falling forward to hide her face. Her hair was still long and straight, still mousy brown, limp and lifeless. Zachary instinctively knew that her brown eyes would still be vacant, that she was still painfully shy and probably more withdrawn than ever.

As he stood up, she stopped beside the empty chair across from him and simply stood there. Zachary extended his hand, but her own hands hung motionless at her sides. He withdrew his and said, "Carrie, I'm Zachary Adams. Do you remember me from Sweetwater? I was two years ahead of you in school. I'm friends with your parents."

No response.

"Sit down, will you?" he invited as he seated himself once again.

She hesitated a long time, then slowly slid into the chair. She didn't settle comfortably or rest her arms on the tabletop or look at him. She didn't show any interest in him or their surroundings at all. She simply sat there, her head ducked so low that all he saw was the crooked part in her hair.

"Your folks asked me to come and see you. They're worried about you."

Still no response.

"They're worried about your children, too." There, he thought with a small measure of satisfaction. Mention of her kids had caused her to stiffen. Maybe that was the way to get through to her. "You know your kids have been placed in foster care, don't you?"

She raised her head a fraction of an inch. He could feel her narrow, flat, empty gaze on him.

"Your parents would like to gain temporary custody of them, and they need your permission. Do you have any objections?"

The slight shake of her head set her hair swinging.

He opened his briefcase and withdrew the forms he'd prepared the day before. "I'd like you to sign these papers. They say that you want your parents to take care of your children while you're in jail. When you get out—" *if* you get out, he thought privately "—you'll be able to regain custody of them."

He slid the papers and a pen across the table to her and watched as she painstakingly signed her name on the lines he'd marked. She clutched the pen in her fist and formed each letter carefully, clumsily, reminding him of a child attempting cursive writing for the first time.

Wordlessly she returned the papers to him, and he slid them back into his briefcase, closed it and set it on the floor. "I'm not representing you in court, Carrie," he explained. "I'm here for your parents. But while I'm in Nashville, I'm going to try to find an attorney who will take your case. Is there someone you prefer?"

She shook her head.

"For the record, do you have any money? If the court will set bail, can you pay it?"

"No." Her whisper was so soft that he could barely make it out. But at least it was a start.

"Your father said you confessed to the police. Is that true?"

Another tiny, formless whisper. "Yes."

"You told them you killed your husband."

"Yes."

"Why? Why did you do it?"

Finally she looked up, and he saw her face. He saw her swollen lip, her black eye, her crooked nose. He saw the bruising and the scarring and the missing tooth, and the muscles in his stomach tightened.

That—that single long look—was her only response. It was the only response Zachary needed. "There shouldn't be any problem getting your children released," he said, hiding his revulsion at what she had suffered. "They should be spending tonight with your family. And as soon as I can get you a lawyer, we'll be back. You'll have to tell her—or him—everything about your husband and your marriage and what he did to you. Do you understand?"

Bowing her head once again, she nodded.

Zachary stood up and picked up his briefcase, then waited for Carrie to rise. She did so slowly, wearily, and crossed to the door with that same uncaring, beaten-down shuffle. He followed her, pausing in the hall to watch the guard lead her back to the cell where she'd spent the last thirty-six hours. The cell where she would spend the next weeks or even months until her trial. Instinctively he pitied her, but realistically he knew she was probably better off in that cell than she'd been in her own home. She was definitely safer.

Outside he paused on the sidewalk to breathe deeply, replacing the stale, recycled atmosphere of the jail with the cold, clean November air. The only other jail he'd ever been inside was Sweetwater's, and that was a world away. The cells there were empty more often than not, sunshine reached into every corner, and they smelled of Sheriff Tomlinson's wife's apple pie and homemade bread. Not despair. Not hopelessness.

He glanced at his watch. It was only nine-thirty, and he was starting to feel hungry. He'd skipped breakfast this morning, intending to stop someplace on the road. Now he might as well wait until lunch. If matters moved quickly enough at Social Services, maybe he could persuade Beth Gibson to join him for lunch. That would certainly brighten his day.

But first things first. If the state would release the Lewis children today, he needed to know in time for Dutch and

Ruth to drive into the city and pick them up. Gaining their release was his primary goal.

Then he could see Beth.

Although her schedule was full, as usual, and she would be lucky to get out of the office before eight, Beth Gibson was indulging in the purely wasteful endeavor of loafing. She had kicked off her shoes and drawn her feet onto the seat of her leather chair and was rocking slowly back and forth while staring out the window at the city twenty stories below. She was ignoring the pile of letters that had to be answered, as well as the stack of current cases that filled one corner of her teak desk. She was doing absolutely nothing but brooding.

She was dissatisfied, she admitted as she wound a strand of sleek red hair around her index finger. Dissatisfied with her twelve-or-more-hours-a-day job. Dissatisfied with handling fifteen to twenty high-profile, high-income cases for every one case that she enjoyed. Dissatisfied with devoting herself one hundred percent to her career and dissatisfied with what was left over—exactly nothing—for her personal life.

When she'd graduated from law school ten years ago—at the top of her class, naturally—she had set some pretty lofty goals for herself. Full partnership in the state's oldest and most prestigious firm. A ninety percent or better success rate. Financial independence. The respect of her fellow attorneys. An outstanding reputation as one of the best and the brightest.

With the partnership that had been offered last year, she had achieved all her goals before the age of thirty-six. Even in this male-dominated profession, she had earned the respect, though sometimes grudgingly given, of every lawyer she'd ever beaten and every judge she'd ever appeared before. In the process, she'd earned enough money that, if combined with Great-Grandmother Townsend's trust fund, she could quit working today and never lack for anything as long as she lived.

Except satisfaction.

The frustrating part was that she didn't even know what was missing from her life. In spite of her earlier lament, it wasn't personal relationships. She'd never included those in her career plans. After eighteen years spent ducking the fallout of her parents' turbulent marriage, she'd never wanted a husband, and she felt not the slightest desire to experience motherhood. There were enough children in this world already; she didn't need to contribute her own for simple ego gratification.

So what did she need? She chose her own cases and set her own hours. She did nothing in or out of the office that she didn't want to do. She was in total control of her life.

But something was still missing.

When the knock sounded at her door, she quickly slid her feet to the floor and into the three-inch heels she'd discarded. It wouldn't do for Loretta, her secretary, or anyone else to find her lazing comfortably. She'd put too much time and effort into constructing an appropriate image. No need to tarnish it now.

After waiting a suitable moment, Loretta opened the door and slipped inside. "There's a gentleman here to see you, Ms. Gibson," she said in her brisk, efficient manner. "His name is Zachary Adams. He doesn't have an appointment, but as he said it was quite important, I told him I would check with you. You do have a little free time before your appointment with..."

The woman continued, but Beth had stopped listening. She knew her schedule for today better than the secretary did, and she didn't need reminders. Instead she concentrated on Loretta's earlier words. *His name is Zachary Adams.*

Zachary. She hadn't seen him since Sarah and Daniel's wedding. She had rather vainly thought he would ask her out once their clients' custody case had been resolved in church rather than in court. She had even decided that she would turn him down on the grounds that he wasn't her type. The men she dated were all intelligent, successful and ambitious. They ranged in age from late thirties to mid-forties. They were, for the most part, divorced. They generally had a good deal of money and even more ego. They were satisfied with being seen in the right places by the right people with Walter Gibson's daughter and Bill Townsend's granddaughter. They expected little from her on a personal level.

More importantly, they didn't threaten her. They didn't tempt her. They left her cold.

They were safe.

And none of those words fit Zachary Adams. There was no denying he was intelligent, and she supposed in his own way he had achieved success. He lacked ambition, though, and money, and, from what she'd seen, ego. He was satisfied with his little practice in his little hometown, handling little cases and giving little bits of legal advice to people he'd known all his life. She doubted that he even knew she was Walter Gibson's daughter and Bill Townsend's granddaughter, and he wouldn't be impressed if he did.

He didn't even fall into the proper age range. He couldn't possibly be older than thirty-three, and she did not date younger men. Not even only-three-years-younger men.

And he tempted her. He tempted her to forget all the rules she'd lived by. He tempted her to forget about logic and caution and replace them with emotion. With passion.

He wasn't the least bit safe.

So she had prepared all sorts of polite, socially correct excuses for not beginning a relationship with Zachary—but he had never called. After Sarah's wedding, where she had been the maid of honor and Zachary had served as best man, she hadn't heard from him again. So much for her ego, she'd thought.

But now he was here, waiting to see her.

"Ask him to come in, Loretta," she said when the secretary finished speaking. As soon as the door closed behind the other woman, Beth raised her hand to smooth her hair. It was simply a desire to appear thoroughly professional, she told herself. It *wasn't* feminine vanity.

A moment later the door opened again, and Loretta stepped aside to allow Zachary to enter. He was just as she remembered, Beth thought as she rose to her feet: blond, blue-eyed and *handsome.* Not attractive, not good-looking, but drop-dead gorgeous.

He was dressed as formally as she'd ever seen him, with the exception of Sarah's wedding, when he'd actually worn a suit. His jeans were faded but neatly pressed, his shirt a subdued plaid, his sport coat a soft, buttery tan corduroy. The tie knotted loosely around his neck lent a touch of convention to the outfit, but only a touch. Now that he was in front of her desk, she couldn't see his feet, but she would wager he wore boots, something suitable for traipsing around his southeast Tennessee mountains.

She would also wager that this was the first time in history that so casually dressed a lawyer had appeared within these hallowed halls.

"Hello, Zachary." She offered her hand, and he accepted it for the briefest of handshakes.

"Thanks for taking time to see me." Without waiting for an invitation, he sat down in the chair closest to her desk, and Beth followed his lead.

"What brings you to Nashville?"

"I have a favor to ask of you on behalf of a client."

Business. Somewhere deep down inside, she felt a tiny rush of disappointment. She would have liked... She wasn't sure exactly what. *More.* A little personal attention. A friendly exchange before getting down to business. Some hint of the interest that had been in his eyes the last few times she'd seen him.

She forced away the disappointment, replacing it with cool professionalism, and gestured for him to go on.

"The daughter of one of my clients back home was arrested here in Nashville Sunday night for murdering her husband. She stabbed him while he was asleep on the sofa." He paused, stroking one fingertip along his jaw, then went on. "She confessed to the police. No excuses, no explanations, just, 'I did it.'"

"Are you going to plead her guilty?"

"*I'm* not going to do anything. I can't take the case." He smiled, a shadow of the boyishly charming smile she remembered so well. "She can't plead guilty. She's got four kids and is pregnant with the fifth."

"But if she confessed—"

"Don't you want to know why she did it?"

Again she silently gestured for him to continue.

"He'd beaten the hell out of her. And this wasn't the first time. Some of her injuries were recent, the others were almost healed." He crossed his legs, resting one foot on the other knee, and Beth saw that she'd guessed right. He had on hiking boots, sturdy and worn and somehow right with the jeans and the coat and even with the tie.

"Even with a confession," he said, "a good lawyer might be able to get her off. Battered woman syndrome is being used successfully as a defense all across the country. A good lawyer could use it in this case."

Beth felt an uncomfortable tingle down her spine. The first time he'd said "a good lawyer," she had known immediately what he wanted from her, and it was a lot. Too much. "That's a hell of a favor, counselor," she said softly.

He smiled again, but said nothing.

"Do you know how much it costs to defend against a murder charge?"

"Not to the penny, but I can guess at the range." Then he turned the question back on her. "Do you know what it'll cost those five kids to lose both their father *and* their mother?"

That was unfair, she thought. She might not have any desire for children of her own, but well hidden somewhere inside her was a soft spot for the kids already on this earth. "I take it she has no money."

He shook his head. "She stayed home with the kids while her husband worked. With him gone, there's no income."

"I don't think the partners would approve." That was an understatement, she thought silently. It wasn't a love for the law that drove her associates, but money. They wanted their share of it, along with everyone else's. If she went to the next meeting and told them that she'd taken on a pro bono murder case, their rumbling and grumbling would be heard down in the streets.

"Your name's on that letterhead, too," Zachary reminded her. "Doesn't that give you some measure of authority? Or do you have to ask their permission before you take on a new client?"

She gave him a long look that let him know she found his suggestion insulting; then she asked, "Why don't you want to handle this?"

"I've never handled a felony case before. I'd be willing to learn, but a case where someone's life is at stake is too important for me to use for on-the-job training." He rose from the chair and wandered over to the full bookcases that lined one wall. "And... I can't afford it."

"*You* can't pay the cost yourself, yet you have no qualms about asking *me* to?" she asked dryly.

"Not you. Your firm." He turned to look at her. "Come on, Beth, you people are experts at making money off people in trouble. You can afford to give a little of it back. I don't have your resources, your background, your expertise or your reputation. If anyone can help Carrie, it's you. Maybe it means you earn a little bit less this year. From the looks of things around here, you won't even miss it."

She certainly couldn't argue that point with him, not sitting here in an office that cost more to decorate than he probably earned in a year. But to accept this case, to commit not only herself but also the firm to such an outlay of time and money when she couldn't even guarantee a victory...

Still, murder cases were always a challenge, and this one, which on the surface seemed a sure loser, would be even more so. And hadn't she just been complaining not ten minutes ago about how rarely she got to handle a case that she cared about? Arguing for some poor, abused victim's life in court had to be more interesting than the cases already stacked on her desk. And wouldn't it be nice for once to feel that she had really made a difference in someone's life? To know that she had accomplished something that none of her associates could have done for the simple reason that they didn't defend people without money?

She had learned in law school that everyone, guilty or not, was entitled to the best defense. But the real world had revised that tenet: everyone was entitled to the best defense that money could buy. Poor people went to jail all too often because they couldn't afford a good lawyer, and rich people got away with all sorts of crimes because they could hire the best. Like her.

Wouldn't it be nice to turn the tables for once?

"I'm not sure I even believe in the battered woman syndrome defense," she stated evenly. "I have no doubt that this woman deserves our sympathy. There's no question, either, that while her husband was alive, she deserved help and protection under the law that probably wasn't forthcoming. But does she deserve permission to kill? To take the law into her own hands and murder the man who hurt her?"

"Since no one else was protecting her, didn't she deserve the right to protect herself?"

"Of course. So why didn't she exercise that right by leaving him?" Beth countered.

"Maybe it wasn't that easy." Zachary was watching her thoughtfully from across the room. "Before you make a decision either way, will you at least meet Carrie—talk to her, see what he did to her?"

He thought she was going to turn him down—Beth could see the resignation in his eyes even from this distance—and he was probably already thinking ahead to what his next move would be. And most likely she *would* turn him down. But she could give him something. She could talk to this woman, could listen to the details of her particular case, before she rejected it. "All right. I take it she's still in jail?"

He nodded.

She stood up and slipped into her jacket, then picked up her briefcase from the credenza. "I have an appointment in court at three. If we hurry..." She hesitated, considering what she'd been about to say, then, against her better judgment, said it anyway. "Maybe we can find time for lunch after we see her."

After another nod from Zachary, she led the way from her office, pausing only briefly at Loretta's desk to instruct the secretary to rearrange her schedule.

It wasn't far from her office to the jail; within fifteen minutes they were seated in the interview room and waiting for Carrie Lewis. Beth drew a yellow pad and a pen from her briefcase, then glanced covertly at Zachary. She knew intuitively that he would have been disappointed if she'd turned him down cold—not just disappointed for Carrie's sake, but disappointed in *her*. She knew, too, that that would have disturbed her. It didn't make sense—caring what this man thought of her—and if she spent any time analyzing it, she was quite sure she wouldn't like her conclusions, so she pushed it out of her mind as the guard escorted the prisoner inside.

The first word that came to Beth's mind when she saw Carrie Lewis was *pathetic*. She was a pathetic figure: thin and battered, helpless and hopeless and lost. There was no doubt in Beth's mind that this woman was a victim—of her husband, of the legal system and of society as a whole. But enough of a victim to literally get away with murder?

Zachary introduced them, and Beth offered her hand, deliberately waiting until the other woman took it in a cool, limp handshake. Then she picked up the pen, braced the pad against the edge of the table and politely said, "Tell me why you killed your husband, Carrie."

The words came haltingly, emotionlessly, filtered through a curtain of mousy brown hair, and they wove a story that Beth had heard countless times before. Only the ending was different.

Delbert Lewis had beaten his wife when he was angry, when he was drunk and when he was bored. With no place to go, no one to turn to for help and feeling that she somehow deserved his abuse, she had tolerated it until something inside her had shattered. Something had said *never again,* and she had taken the only action that she knew beyond a doubt would protect her. Maybe she had simply tired of being his victim. Maybe she had feared for the safety of the baby she was carrying. Maybe she had suffered too much shame or helplessness or pain, or maybe his threats against the children had been more than she could endure.

Whatever the catalyst, she had chosen her moment carefully. She had waited until he was asleep, relatively harmless, unable to hurt her. Unable to stop her. And she had resolved the problem herself. There would be no more beatings. No more fear. No more pain. No more threat.

And possibly no more freedom.

"Why didn't you call the police?" Beth asked, looking up from the notes she'd jotted down.

Carrie also looked up. Her face was painful to look at. "What could they do?" she asked dully.

"If you'd pressed charges, they could have arrested him."

"And held him how long?" Zachary asked. It was the first time he'd spoken, and Beth turned to look at him. "A few hours? Maybe one night? Certainly no more than that. And then what?"

"Why didn't you leave him?" Beth asked, turning her attention back to Carrie. "Why didn't you divorce him and get a restraining order against him?" Silently she acknowledged that the questions sounded naive. She knew the reasons as well as anyone. Women who left their husbands were all too often found, and the punishment was severe. To men like Delbert Lewis, their wives weren't their partners, they were property. Divorce meant nothing, and restraining orders weren't worth the paper they were written on.

But she wanted to hear Carrie's answer. She wanted to hear why *this* woman had chosen to stay in an abusive marriage. She wanted to know why she'd chosen murder instead of divorce.

"He told me if I ever left him," Carrie whispered, "he would kill me."

"And you believed him."

She looked up again, her face marked with the colors of violence. With a quiet certainty that had been absent throughout the interview, she softly replied, "Yes. I believed him."

Chapter 2

Over lunch in a nearby restaurant, Zachary asked the question that had been nagging at him since Beth had begun to interview Carrie. "Will you take the case?"

Beth fingered the delicate stem of her water glass for a long moment before looking up at him. "I don't know."

"Do you think locking her away in prison is the proper punishment for what she's done?"

"Do you think a butcher knife through the heart was the proper punishment for what Delbert Lewis did?"

He started to respond, then gave a rueful shake of his head. Carrie was so easy to pity. She fit the image of a victim so well, and Del was so easily cast as the villain. The big, violent bully and the fragile, defenseless woman. "I don't know," he replied with a sigh. "But I do know Carrie was in a desperate situation."

"But murder wasn't the solution."

"Maybe it wasn't the right solution," Zachary countered. "It's certainly not the one I would have chosen, or you. But neither you nor I would ever be in her situation. For Carrie, killing Del might have been the only way to escape, the only way to stop *him* from killing *her.* How many women live their entire lives in fear of the men who are supposed to love them? How many women are killed by those men? The courts don't offer much in the way of help. The cops' hands are tied by the system. Social Services doesn't have the resources to handle every single case. What's a woman supposed to do? Just sit back and wait to die?''

"She's not supposed to commit murder," Beth said dryly.

"According to the battered woman defense, it's not murder. It's self-defense."

She leaned toward him, her green eyes fired with passion. "Delbert Lewis was *asleep* when Carrie killed him. He didn't present a threat to her or the children. He wasn't capable at that moment of harming her. She wasn't defending herself from anything." Then the heat faded away, and she frowned distractedly. "If she had killed him during their fight, in the midst of his rage, there wouldn't even be a case. The district attorney would have taken one look at her, and he would have declined to bring charges against her. Her husband's death would have been a clear-cut case of self-defense."

"If she had tried to defend herself then," Zachary pointed out, "there would still be a case, only the defendant would be Del, because Carrie would be dead."

Beth acknowledged his statement with a slight shrug as the waiter served their meal. When he was gone, she asked, "When is her arraignment?"

"Thursday afternoon."

"Does her family have any money?"

"To pay for a murder defense?" Zachary didn't try to temper his skepticism. After seeing her firm's offices, the issue of money seemed a petty one.

"To pay her bail, on the off-chance that the judge grants it."

"No, the Morrises don't have any money." Ignoring the food in front of him, he rested his arms on the table and asked once more, "Are you going to take her case?"

"There are a dozen reasons why I shouldn't."

"Because it will be controversial."

"To say the least."

"And expensive."

Beth nodded.

"And you're not totally sure Carrie should go unpunished." He knew that was the most important objection, the strongest one. She couldn't commit herself. She couldn't say yes, even though Carrie had murdered an unarmed, sleeping, defenseless man, she should go free. Yes, she should be given the chance—the same chance *she* had chosen to deny Del—to live the rest of her life as she pleased.

"I believe in self-defense," Beth said slowly. "But I don't believe in disguising murder as self-defense."

"You're not the judge and jury, Beth," he said mildly. "Your job is to provide your client with the best defense you're capable of presenting. It's not up to you to determine guilt or innocence, and even if it was, even the guilty have the right to a fair trial."

She fixed her gaze on him. "Why did you bring this to me?"

"Because you're one of the best lawyers in the state. Because you represented Sarah when she couldn't afford anyone's help. Because you're the only lawyer I know in the city." He broke off then and grinned as he gave her the last reason. "And because I wanted to see you again."

For a moment her gaze remained locked with his. He saw faint surprise at his last remark, and an even fainter hint of feminine interest that was overshadowed by caution. Then she looked away, pushed her chair back from the table and rose gracefully to her feet. "I need time to think about this," she said, her manner thoroughly professional. "I'll let you know by this evening."

He stood up, too, dropping his napkin on his chair. "And if the answer is no?"

"I know all the criminal lawyers in town. I'll help you find someone else."

It was the best she could give him, he thought as he followed her out, so he might as well accept it gracefully. He couldn't blame her for being reluctant. There was a lot to consider here. The cost of a murder defense could easily exceed two hundred thousand dollars. She had to consult her partners; that was one of the responsibilities she'd taken on when she had accepted the partnership. And even though she didn't have to believe in a client's innocence to present a good defense, it would certainly help, especially in a case like this one.

They stopped on the sidewalk outside the restaurant. It was a few blocks in one direction to Beth's office, a few blocks in another to his truck.

"Are you going back to Sweetwater today?"

He shoved his hands into his pockets. "I'm meeting Carrie's parents when they come to pick up her kids, then I'm going home."

"I'll call you around seven." She hesitated a moment longer, simply looking at him, then turned and walked away.

Zachary watched until she was out of sight. Then, slowly becoming aware of the chill and the passage of time, he spun around and headed for his truck. It was time to meet the Morrises and their grandchildren.

The Lewis children were four of the most somber kids Zachary had ever seen. There was a brief flash of pleasure in the little ones' eyes when they recognized their grandmother, but it quickly faded. The three-year-old clung to his older sister while his brother clutched a handful of her sweater, and they were all fiercely guarded by fourteen-year-old Tyler.

The younger three were mostly afraid, and Zachary figured they would come out of it once they realized they were safe at their grandparents' house. Tyler was afraid, too, but he was also filled with anger, the cold, destructive kind that could last forever. He was a good-looking kid, in spite of his painful thinness and the bruises that shadowed his cheek and jaw. A recent gift from his father, Zachary thought grimly. He must have tried to help his mother or to protect his brothers and sister. What an overwhelming responsibility for a fourteen-year-old boy.

Crying softly, Ruth hugged each of the children, including Tyler. He didn't shy away, but he remained stiff and unyielding in her arms, and his eyes were empty of all emotion but bitterness—and rage.

"Look at his face," Dutch said, moving close to Zachary so he could speak softly. "Look what that bastard did to him. I always figured there must be a special place in hell for people who hurt their kids. I hope Del's burning there now."

Zachary murmured his agreement.

"Have you found a lawyer for Carrie yet?"

"I'm working on it. I should have an answer tonight."

Dutch's voice was uncharacteristically emotional when he asked, "How is my girl?"

"She's still pretty shaken by what happened, but she'll be all right." He picked up his coat from the chair behind him, then looked at the older man once again. "Why don't you take the kids home and get them settled in? I'll get in touch with you as soon as I hear anything."

Dutch took his hand in a bruising grip. "Thanks, Zachary. Thanks so much."

The sky was dark, and the few stars that shone were no match for the brilliance of the city lights. It wasn't like that out in Sweetwater, Beth thought somberly. If Zachary was looking out right now, he was seeing the same black sky dotted with hundreds of distant stars, each separate and distinct from its neighbors.

Zachary. She had promised to call him with her decision around seven o'clock. It was ten after now, and she still didn't have an answer. It rarely took her more than a few minutes to make up her mind about a case. Her choices were usually clear-cut: yes, she could defend this client, or no, she couldn't.

But there was nothing clear-cut about Carrie Lewis's case. The very definition of self defense ruled it out as a defense in this case. How could Carrie have been in fear for her life at that time when the man who so terrified her was sound asleep? What harm could he have done her then?

And so Beth had spent the afternoon in the firm's library, combing the law books for precedents, reading about similar cases in California, Texas, Colorado, North Dakota—the list went on. She had gained a more in-depth understanding of battered woman syndrome and had begun to understand the reasoning that had led courts to accept the syndrome as a defense, to place the victim in the role of villain, responsible for his own death.

But she still wasn't convinced that what Carrie had done was right. She wasn't convinced that it was self-defense. She wasn't convinced that it was justified.

Sighing, she reached for the phone on her desk, punching in Zachary's home phone number. She knew as the first ring sounded in her ear what her answer would be. In the end it was simple enough. As Zachary had reminded her, it wasn't her job to judge Carrie's guilt or innocence. All an attorney was obligated to do was provide the best defense possible, and she, better than any other lawyer in town, could do that.

When he answered on the third ring, she didn't bother to identify herself. "The next time you want to see me, just pick up the phone and call. Don't go looking for some impossible case for me to take on."

"I take it that means you're going to represent Carrie." He sounded amused and more than a little relieved. That was another reason she'd said yes, she silently acknowledged. She hadn't wanted him to think that she chose her clients on the basis of their bank accounts rather than their needs. She hadn't wanted him to believe that her sense of justice and fair play had been warped by the money.

"Yes, I'm going to represent her," she replied, her ambivalence audible in her voice. "Even though I have a full schedule of paying clients. Even though the partners abhor anything sensational or controversial, and this case is going to be both. Even though they'll probably want to buy out

my partnership when I tell them that I'm going to tie up
most of my staff for God knows how long on research and
interviews on a case I'm handling for free.''

"Let me help," Zachary offered.

Beth saw her hand tremble slightly at his suggestion,
matching the fluttery feelings in the pit of her stomach.
Hunger, she told herself as she slowly, deliberately folded
her fingers into a tight ball. It had been a long time since
lunch. "Help in what way?" she asked cautiously.

"I told you that I'm willing to learn. Research isn't one
of my favorite jobs, but I can do it, and I know I can con-
duct interviews as well as any junior attorney in your firm."

She forced herself to consider his offer. It would certainly make the partners happier if she could tell them that
a major portion of the work was being handled at no cost to
the firm. But did she want to work that closely with Zachary?

No. She'd had no problem deciding after Sarah's wedding that she couldn't go out with him because he was so
different from the men she normally dated. Wouldn't
working with him for weeks at a time be almost as bad as
dating him? Their differences still stood between them, and
so did their attraction. She had been pleased to see him this
morning, disappointed to discover that it was business that
had brought him to her office. She had been all too aware
of how handsome he was, how charmingly he smiled, and
how sincere and *real* he seemed.

Considering all that, how could she let herself even think
about working with him?

"I thought you offered this case to me because you
couldn't afford it?" she asked, keeping her voice coolly
neutral.

"I can't. But I *can* afford to spend a few days a week in
the city. I can help cut your costs by doing some of the work
myself. You won't be saving a lot, maybe it will be
enough to satisfy your partners."

"Have you ever worked for a woman?" Was she actually considering his offer? she silently moaned. Wasn't it

enough that she'd taken this case, that she was giving up the next few months of her life to help out his friends' daughter? Did she have to take *him* on, too?

"I've followed orders from my mother and my grandmother all my life," he replied with a chuckle. "I don't have any problems with that, Beth. If it's my ability as a lawyer that concerns you—"

Pressing her fingertips to her temples, she interrupted him. "No, not at all." Her dealings with him on Sarah's behalf had been extensive enough that she knew he was more than competent. Some people might be fooled because he practiced small-town law, but she knew that was his choice. If he'd wanted to work in the city, he could have.

He *had* brought the case to her attention. He *was* largely responsible for her taking it. And any help that would minimize the firm's losses would be greatly appreciated by the partners. And he was a good attorney, willing to work hard for nothing more than the learning experience.

They were both professionals. Working with him didn't mean getting involved with him. She worked with male attorneys all the time without ever getting personal... though none as handsome as Zachary. None who tempted her to forget everything she'd ever learned, everything she'd ever promised herself, everything she'd sworn she would never do.

She heard her voice, heard the faint echo of the words as they passed through the telephone lines, and wondered dimly how her mouth could form words without the knowledge of her brain. Surely she wasn't agreeing to this. Even if it was sensible. Even if it was the most prudent course of action.

But she *had* agreed. She'd heard the words clearly.

"All right. When can you come back to Nashville?"

Zachary compressed the rest of the week's work into one morning, then headed back to Nashville Wednesday afternoon. He had a suitcase in the back of his Jeep Cherokee, packed with his usual attire—jeans and comfortable shirts—

plus the one suit he owned. He might not need it, but, on the other hand, it never hurt to be prepared.

Beth hadn't been too happy about accepting his help on this case, and on the return trip he allowed himself to wonder why. Because she knew his education and previous track record didn't begin to measure up to her own? Because she didn't want the added complication of teaching a relatively inexperienced lawyer? Because she didn't want anyone's input but her own?

Or maybe it was something personal. Maybe she disliked him and didn't look forward to spending time with him, not even working. Or maybe, as he'd once told Sarah Ryan, Beth disliked men in general. Sarah had suggested that perhaps it was because Beth handled a lot of divorces; too often she saw the darker side of men. And now she was going to be spending her days thoroughly examining Carrie's relationship with one of the most brutal and vicious men Zachary had ever come across.

Well, if nothing came of this but a better understanding of how a brilliant lawyer operated, he would be satisfied. If he gained Beth's friendship, he would be lucky. And if he somehow managed to earn her trust . . .

Laughing aloud at his optimism, he left the freeway and pulled into the parking lot of a popular budget motel. It took him less than five minutes to fill out the registration card and get his key, and another five minutes to hang his clothing on the bar beside the sink. Then it was back to his truck, back onto the freeway and downtown to Beth's firm.

The stern-faced secretary escorted him to Beth's office, announcing him in a formal manner that made him uncomfortable. The only secretary he'd ever had was his younger sister, and she'd been more likely to announce a client with a yell through the open door. She'd made mistakes in her typing and hadn't been particularly picky about her filing system, but he'd been comfortable with her. The ever-efficient Mrs. Taylor would intimidate him right out of business.

Beth was on the phone, but she gestured toward one of the chairs. Instead, he took advantage of her busyness to look around her office.

Yesterday he'd been—all right, admit it, he teased himself—*awed* by the books that lined the shelves. He could practice law the rest of his life and never need anything that wasn't contained in those rows of law books and reviews and codes. She had a not-so-small fortune tied up in those alone, to say nothing of the furnishings.

The desk, credenza, file cabinets and tables were all teak, gleaming and sleek, with graceful curves and clean lines. The chairs and the sofa in the corner were also sleek and graceful, and the desk chair was undoubtedly fine-grain leather. A blown-glass decanter filled with what he assumed was some expensive brand of aged whiskey sat on one table, along with a half-dozen fragile matching glasses.

Above the table was a portrait of a woman, undoubtedly one of Beth's relatives. The resemblance between them was strong—the fiery red hair, the green eyes, the porcelain skin, the stubborn jaw. But what added up merely to character for the woman in the portrait had become beauty in Beth. The woman's strength was in Beth, but toned down, gentler. Beth had inherited the passion, too, but it was harnessed, under tight control. He wondered idly if she ever released it, if it was reserved solely for her work rather than her personal life, if he could ever coax a bit of it out of her for himself.

"That's my great-grandmother, Althea Townsend."

He turned and saw that she had finished her phone call and was watching him from across the room. "Townsend, huh? As in the Townsends who once owned most of Nashville, half of Tennessee and about a third of the South?"

"That's us."

He finally accepted her offer of a seat. "Then that means you're also part of the Gibsons who owned everything the Townsends didn't."

She nodded.

He had known from the first time he'd seen her that she came from money. A person had to be born to the kind of sophistication, elegance and class that came so naturally to her. But he hadn't suspected she came from *that* kind of money. From Townsend money. From *those* Gibsons. No wonder she'd been the youngest partner in the history of this old and prestigious firm. Even if she were totally inept as a lawyer, her family name and money could have bought her any position she wanted.

"Does that make a difference?" she asked, sounding more than a little cautious.

Did it? he wondered. Now that he knew her family could buy and sell small nations if they wanted, did it change his opinion of her? Did it make him think less of her skills as a lawyer? Did it make him more reluctant to think about her in terms of a relationship, desire, sex?

"I don't know why it should," he remarked with a shrug. "You're the same person I thought you were yesterday, only richer."

"The family's got the money. I manage on my income."

"Does it make a difference to most people?"

She laced her fingers loosely. "Of course. I spent my first five years here at the firm trying to prove to everyone that I was getting by on ability and not the family name. I've spent most of my life trying to judge people's motives for wanting to be friends with me. Do they like me for myself, or for my name or my money?"

"That's an easy way to become cynical."

Beth smiled dryly. She'd been cynical about most things for longer than she could remember. Her grandparents had made her cynical of marriage, her parents, of love. Her friends had made her question loyalty, her one and only great love had taught her to doubt trust, and her clients had given her a pessimistic view of honesty.

What could Zachary teach her?

She'd thought about him too much after their phone conversation last night. When she should have been concentrating on briefs and opening statements and giving her clients their money's worth, instead her mind had been on him. She had agonized over whether letting him in on this case had been a mistake. She had drawn on every ounce of professionalism she possessed to prepare herself to deal with him today.

And she had wondered almost wistfully why he had never called her after Sarah's wedding, why he had never made an effort to see her.

Wistfully. She hadn't been wistful about anything since she was eight years old and had cowered in her closet, hands over her ears to shut out the screams and crashes coming from her parents' bedroom during yet another of their spectacular disagreements. She had longed for parents who didn't despise each other, for a home that wasn't rocked by anger, jealousy and rage, for the nighttime peace that she imagined other children enjoyed, that she all too often hadn't found in her own home.

But she had been wistful about Zachary, and that had answered her earlier question. Yes, working with him was a mistake, one she might regret for a long time. But she was stuck. The partners had agreed to this case with the stipulation that Zachary contribute as much as possible. He had already rearranged his own schedule to accommodate this, and he was clearly looking forward to the work.

And, even knowing that it was a mistake, even knowing that she might have to pay for it in ways she hadn't experienced in more than ten years, she couldn't find the desire within herself to send him away. She hadn't been able to turn down his offer of help yesterday, and she didn't *want* to turn it down today.

"So... tell me about Carrie's children," she said, deliberately turning the conversation to business.

"They're with her parents. I met Dutch and Ruth yesterday afternoon, and they picked them up from Social Services. Del's family moved to Texas a few years ago. They're supposedly on their way to Nashville now to claim the body. I don't know if they'll want the kids, but to be on the safe side, the Morrises are applying for legal guardianship. I think it's best if the children stay here with the grandparents they know rather than go off to Texas with people they've met only a few times in their lives.''

"I hope that won't be a problem. I don't think it would do Carrie much good if the Lewises got custody.'' She flipped open the legal pad on her desk. "I've got calls in to several psychiatrists who specialize in the treatment and study of abused women. One in particular has testified in several of these trials. His credentials are very impressive, and he's good on the stand. I'm hoping we can get him down here for Carrie."

"So what's first?"

"We've got to get copies of the police and autopsy reports. I want to talk to the prosecutor before the arraignment, and afterward we'll interview the Lewises' families, neighbors, Del's co-workers and former employers, his drinking buddies—anyone and everyone who knew them. First, though, I want to talk to Carrie again."

She removed her coat from the tiny closet behind the door, then returned to her desk for her briefcase. Zachary wasn't carrying one today, and she asked him about it as they walked to the elevator.

"Yesterday's the first time I've used a briefcase in months," he replied with a grin. "There's not much need for one at home. No one's impressed by it, and my office, with everything I need, is only a few minutes from every place in town. But just in case, I keep a notebook and pen in my pocket."

She never went anywhere without *her* briefcase. It was her lifeline. Sometimes—like today—it was so stuffed with work that simply carrying it was a chore. The strain on her muscles made Zachary's way of doing business sound more appealing than it should.

Lately, she thought with dismay as they walked along the sidewalk together, too many inappropriate things appealed to her. Like throwing away everything she had accomplished and dumping all the possessions she had accumulated and starting over again. Like making that new start someplace where no one had ever heard of the Townsends or the Gibsons.

Like making that new start with Zachary.

She scowled at the idea and continued scowling until they were seated across from Carrie in the interview room. There the scowl faded as she gave her client a critical once-over. The bruises were vivid and ugly, and the swelling made her face look heavier than it actually was. What kind of force had it taken to do such damage? Beth wondered with revulsion. What kind of man could do that to his own wife?

She knew the popular excuses for such behavior—insecurity, immaturity, jealousy, inadequacy—but she didn't understand any of them. Plenty of insecure, inadequate men managed to marry and have normal relationships without ever resorting to physical violence.

She knew, too, that alcohol was often a contributing factor. Del Lewis had been drunk when he'd beaten Carrie Sunday night. He'd been sleeping off the effects of a full day's drinking when she killed him. Had he merely been a mean drunk? Was it the liquor that had caused him to batter his wife, or had that been just an excuse? Had he gotten drunk simply to make his behavior more acceptable? After all, society routinely forgave behavior in an intoxicated man that would be strictly prohibited in a sober one.

"Zachary and I are going to handle your case together, Carrie," Beth announced. "Your arraignment is tomorrow afternoon. That's when you'll be formally charged with Del's death. I'll ask the judge to release you without bail, but I don't believe he will. If he refuses, you'll have to stay in jail until the trial, which might be only a few weeks or as long as several months."

"Will I ever get to see my kids?" Carrie's voice sounded distant and detached.

"We'll see about arranging a visit sometime next week."

"Are they all right?" she whispered mournfully.

"I saw them yesterday," Zachary replied. "They'll be fine. They're with your folks now. You know they'll take good care of them."

Beth pulled a small tape recorder from her briefcase, checked the tape, then set it on the table. "We need to know about your marriage, Carrie. Tell us everything you can, good or bad, about living with Del."

The silence lengthened from one minute to two, three. It was broken only by the soft whir of the recorder, then suddenly by the scrape of Zachary's chair as he shifted positions. "How long were you and Del married, Carrie?" he asked softly.

Beth quickly tamped down the annoyance that flared inside her. She had agreed to Zachary's help on this case, even if she wasn't accustomed to working with someone. That meant cooperating, sharing, relinquishing some of the control that she always enjoyed in her work.

"Nearly fifteen years."

"And you have four kids, plus this little one on the way."

"Yes. Tyler's fourteen, my girl is nine, and the youngest two are six and three."

"When is the baby due?"

Carrie laid her hand on her stomach, then shyly looked up. The slight curve of her mouth qualified as a smile, Beth thought, but just barely. Even so, in spite of its hesitance, in spite of the bruises and cuts, it made her look five years younger and ten times prettier. It made her look alive. "In the spring. March."

Zachary leaned back in the chair. "Right after you and Del got married, you moved to Nashville. Were you happy here?"

Her smile faded. "No. It's such a big place, and I couldn't find my way around. I used to get lost going home from the grocery store. And I couldn't see my family very often. They couldn't take time away from the farm to come here, and Del . . . Del didn't much like going to Sweetwater. He said it was nothing but a hick town full of people who would never amount to anything."

"Do you remember the first time he hit you?"

Dropping her gaze again, she nodded.

"Tell us about it."

"I was pregnant with Tyler. I was tired, and my back was hurting, so I lay down, just for a little while. I didn't mean to fall asleep, but I did. When Del got home, the housework wasn't done and dinner wasn't ready. He pulled me off the sofa, and he slapped me twice." She looked up, first at Zachary, then Beth. "He didn't mean to do it. He just lost his temper, and he was so sorry later. He swore it would never happen again."

And she had believed him, Beth thought. She still believed, even after killing him, that he had never meant to hurt her. That he was sorry. That each time was the last.

"But it did happen again," Zachary said quietly. "When?"

"It was about six months later. He'd lost his job, and he came home drunk. He cut my lip and left bruises around my throat. After that, it was about three months until the next time."

From the articles she'd read, Beth knew that was typical. Most abused women and their husbands fell into a vicious cycle: the buildup of tension, the release of that tension with physical violence, followed by contrition. Regrets. Promises. If the pattern wasn't broken early, it altered: it took less stress to set the man off, the beatings became more brutal, the contrition was perfunctory at best, and the safe time between cycles diminished. Six months had lapsed between Carrie's first and second beatings, but only three months between the second and third. By the end of their marriage, the abuse had been a weekly, sometimes daily, occurrence.

"Why didn't you leave him then, Carrie?"

The look she gave Zachary was bewildered, as if the idea had never occurred to her at the time. "I loved him," she said simply. "He was my husband."

"But he was hurting you."

"He was always sorry for it afterward. Besides, it was just mostly bruises and cuts. They went away. And he was always promising to be better, and..." She broke off, wet her lips, then swallowed hard. "And it was my fault, too. I wasn't doing the things a wife was supposed to do—keeping the house clean enough, taking care of the kids, having dinner ready on time. A wife's supposed to do those things the way her husband wants, and I—sometimes I didn't.''

"A woman has responsibilities in a marriage just as a man does," Zachary disagreed. "But getting beaten because she doesn't fulfill them…that's wrong, Carrie. Del was wrong. It wasn't your fault."

Rising from his chair, he paced the length of the small room, then leaned against the wall where he could see both women. "Go on, Carrie. Tell us whatever you want. Tell us what happened."

She spoke haltingly, sometimes beseechingly, as if pleading with them to understand. She talked about the children, about how Del had initially been thrilled with his baby son, but his pleasure had quickly given way to irritation over the baby's crying and the needs that had to take precedence over his own, how he had objected to the expense of formula, diapers and doctors' visits for the child. The pattern had been repeated with Becky's birth five years later—excitement, pleasure, then annoyance—but with the younger two boys, Del's only emotion had been indifference. And when she'd told him she was pregnant a fifth time, he had reacted angrily, violently.

Zachary looked at Beth while Carrie spoke. She hadn't said anything since she'd started the tape recorder. He wondered if she resented his interference in this interview, if that was why she was holding her hands laced so tightly together in her lap that her knuckles had turned white. Or was it outrage over the story they were hearing, anger toward Del Lewis for being a bastard, or toward Carrie for allowing herself to become a victim? Or was it sympathy for the children, who'd lived all their lives unloved by their father, frightened by his temper and terrified that his rages would one day take their mother from them?

He suspected it was the latter. Beth was a tough woman. In her job she had to be. She knew what people could do to each other, knew what pain they could inflict, what damage they could cause. But anyone, no matter how tough, had to be touched by tales about children. She had to wonder, as Zachary did, how any man could subject his kids, his own helpless, innocent kids, to the kind of life Del had given his. She had to despise the man if not for what he'd done to his wife, then for the misery he'd brought his children.

"Why didn't you leave him?" he asked when Carrie finally fell silent. "Why didn't you take the kids and go away?"

"I couldn't," she said with a helpless shrug.

"Of course you could. You could have waited until he left for work one morning, then packed and been out of there before he got home that evening."

For a long moment she slowly shook her head back and forth. "I told him once that I was going to leave. He said that he would find me. He said he would take the kids away from me, that he would tell the judge what kind of wife I was, what kind of mother I was, and the judge would give the kids to him. He said I would never get to see them again." She anchored her hair behind her ears. It made her look more vulnerable. "I'm not real smart, I know that. The only work I know is housework and farmwork, and I can't support five kids at either one. I don't know how to get along with people anymore. I don't have any money. I don't have a car. I don't even have a place to live. What judge in his right mind would let me keep the kids when their daddy, with his house and his job, wanted them?"

Of course the issue wouldn't have been decided that simply, Zachary thought, but there was no use in pointing it out now. Instead, he pushed his hands into the pockets of his jeans and asked, "Did you ever call the police when he was beating you?"

"No."

"Did you ever ask for help from anyone?"

"Only twice. Once I had to go to Tyler's school—he'd been in trouble—and the counselor saw that something was wrong. She kept asking, but I didn't tell her anything. I couldn't. Finally she gave me a number to call. She said it was a shelter for abused women and that they could help me and the kids.'' She sat silently for a moment, then took a deep breath. "Del found the number in my purse, and he called to see whose it was. When he found out, he—he almost killed me. I thought he surely would.''

"And the second time?''

"His folks had come up from Texas for a visit, and I asked his mama to talk to him, to see if she could make him stop.'' Carrie fell silent again, her head lowered, her shoulders rounded. When she continued, her voice wasn't quite steady. "I had bruises all over, and my eye was swollen shut, and his mama looked me over and said, 'It's not like he really hurt you. Nothing's broken.'''

Nothing's broken. Zachary gave a disgusted shake of his head. Del was dead, Carrie in jail, the children's lives shattered. Was there enough damage, enough hurt, to satisfy Mrs. Lewis now?

Chapter 3

Beth sat in the corner booth of a quiet bar, her hands folded loosely on the table. It wasn't even five o'clock yet, but she was tired. She wanted nothing more than to go home, take a long, warm bath, curl up in bed and sleep for the next few months.

Few of the cases she'd handled had had that effect on her, making her want to hide away from the world until the case was somehow miraculously resolved without her. Sarah Ryan's divorce had been one. It had been impossible to remain cool and detached because of her friendship with Sarah. Because Sarah's husband Brent had been a first-class bastard. Because there had been a child involved, a tiny little boy named Tony who was dying, a sweet loving child whose father wanted nothing to do with him. Did Brent know his son had died one warm June day? she wondered. Did he even care?

"You look grim." Zachary slid onto the leather bench across from her, folding his coat into the corner.

"I was thinking about Sarah and Tony."

He acknowledged that with a simple nod. He knew all the details, knew that Sarah's first marriage and divorce had, indeed, been grim.

"So..." She smiled politely as the waitress set their drinks before them. Apparently Zachary was no more of a drinker than she was. He'd ordered a soda to her sparkling water. She liked that. "What do you think?"

His grin came quickly. It was wide and even and crinkled the corners of his too-blue eyes. "That's a broad question. Am I supposed to read your mind to narrow it down, or can I choose any subject that comes to my mind?"

"About Carrie. About this case. About strategy. Pleas. Deals."

"What kind of deal would the district attorney offer?"

"On a murder case this controversial?" Beth shook her head. "Probably a lousy one. The DA himself will probably handle this case. He'll want to make an example of Carrie. He'll want all battered women in Tennessee to understand that they can't take the law into their own hands. He'll go for the toughest sentence he can get."

"So if we have a hard-line prosecutor, what are our chances?"

She sipped her water, savoring the faint tang of lime, and listened to the silent echoes of his question. *We. Our.* She had worked cases with other lawyers before, but she had always been one-hundred percent in control; the others were there only for assistance, and they had understood perfectly that the case was *hers*. She wasn't sure if she liked this new sharing. It meant she wasn't totally in charge anymore ... but it also meant she wasn't totally responsible, either. If they lost, she would have someone to share the defeat. If they won, she would have someone to share in the victory celebration.

And what a celebration *that* could be, she thought, stealing a look at Zachary.

Folding her hands together again, she slowly answered his question. "I guess our chances depend on the jury. Too many people still believe that it's all right for a man to hit his

wife to keep her in line. Too many others believe that a
woman who is beaten must have done something to deserve
it, or even that she enjoyed it. Others won't be able to understand why Carrie didn't just leave. That's where our defense might run into trouble. Our expert witnesses are going
to get up there on the stand and tell the jurors that all the
years of being physically and emotionally abused left Carrie helpless and hopeless, so demoralized that she couldn't
take any action to improve the situation, such as leaving Del.
And the prosecutor's going to point out that this helpless,
hopeless woman who couldn't do anything somehow managed to put a knife through her husband's heart.''

"I'm glad that's your problem and not mine."

She smiled faintly. "Depending on the jury, we might
make it your problem. A man's opinion still holds more
weight at times than a woman's. Seeing a man who is clearly
sympathetic to Carrie might influence some jurors. At the
very least, it should balance the male prosecutor who wants
to hang her." With a shrug she finished the water in front of
her. "If we get a decent jury we should do all right."

But "all right" in this case, she silently admitted, wasn't
likely to be an acquittal. She would be satisfied with a conviction on the lesser charge of manslaughter, which might
include a suspended sentence or only a few years in prison.
It wouldn't be the freedom Carrie—and Zachary—wanted,
but it would be better than spending the rest of her life in
prison.

"How are you going to handle this?" she asked. "Will
you be staying in town or driving back and forth?"

"Right now I'm planning to stay here a couple of nights
a week. Later, who knows?"

By "later," he meant when his money ran out, Beth knew.
She thought briefly, guiltily, that she should offer
him…what? A salary? An expense account? Either of those
would be difficult to get past the partners, especially when
the whole purpose of his helping was to cut back on the
firm's losses on this case. Maybe a place to stay? One of the
numerous empty bedrooms in her condo? Not likely. If she

had already figured out that working with Zachary was a mistake, how badly would she compound it by inviting him to move into her home?

She wasn't responsible for him. He had volunteered his help, had been willing to pay his own expenses in exchange for the opportunity to work with and learn from her. If the cost became more than he could afford, he could back out, and she would finish alone. At the very least, he would get a break on his taxes, once he deducted his contribution to Carrie's defense.

"I have to get back to the office," she said as she slid out of the booth and reached for her coat. "I have an appointment with the DA's office at eight tomorrow, so why don't we meet at my office at ten? We'll go out and start talking to some of Carrie's neighbors." She looked at him, waiting for him to agree. His expression was solemn, with just a hint of disappointment in his eyes, just a bit of resignation in the set of his mouth. Had he wanted to spend more time together this evening, maybe even have dinner with her? If so, she wished he would ask... even though she would have to turn him down. Even though she would have to explain to him that she didn't, forgive the cliché, mix business with pleasure.

But he didn't ask. He simply smiled, a friendly but impersonal sort of smile, the kind he might give a stranger on the street, and nodded. "Tomorrow at ten. I'll see you then."

"How did the meeting go?"

Beth stepped off the elevator into the top level of the parking garage and gestured toward the space marked with her name. She had been late returning from her meeting this morning and had hustled Zachary out of the office after little more than hellos had been exchanged. But they would have time to talk now on the way to Carrie's house. "About as well as I expected. The DA's office wants to make an example of Carrie. He sees this as a chance to boost his tough-on-crime image."

"Yeah, let's lock up this woman who's been someone's victim half her life while the repeat offenders are going free." Zachary looked and sounded disgusted, and even though more than a few of her own clients were repeat offenders, Beth shared his disgust.

"Remind me when we get back, and I'll have my secretary get you a parking pass. It will allow you to use any of those spaces on the end there," she said as she unlocked her car door. It was a German import, typical of the kind of car her associates drove: a status symbol, suitably expensive but not obscenely so, impressive but not flashy. She had bought it because it was expected of her, even though secretly she had longed for a fast little fire-engine-red Corvette.

"Spending so much time in the city, how are you going to manage your own clients?" she asked as she headed for the neighborhood where the Lewises had lived.

"In an average week I spend fifteen, maybe twenty, hours in the office. It won't be any problem fitting them in with this."

"What do you do with the rest of your time?"

"I go fishing every Tuesday morning with the sheriff and the mayor. In the spring and summer I coach the church Little League baseball team, and in the fall it's soccer." He grinned disparagingly. "A real thrilling life, isn't it?"

She wasn't surprised to find a bit of envy in her sigh. "I haven't had a Tuesday morning off in longer than I can remember. The last time I set foot in church, besides Sarah and Daniel's wedding, was for my own christening. I haven't seen a baseball game since college, and I've never had time to learn anything about soccer."

"And you haven't missed any of it," he retorted, confident that he was right. "You thrive on your schedule. Who needs Tuesday mornings off, or baseball or soccer?"

Would he be disappointed if she told him that he was only partially right? she wondered. That she *had* thrived on her schedule until recently, but now she was looking for something more? Not Tuesday mornings fishing, of course, or baseball or soccer, but *something*.

Refusing to even think about the dissatisfaction that was plaguing her all too often these days, she turned the conversation back to him. "That takes care of spring, summer and fall. What do you do in the winter?"

"Most of my time right now is taken up with the house. My grandfather left me a piece of land up on Laurel Mountain, and I'm building a house there."

"By yourself?"

"More or less. Daniel helps out with some of the more complicated stuff, and a few people I've done work for have paid their bills with electrical and plumbing services, but the majority of the work is my own. It should be finished by spring."

The conversation faltered then as they reached Carrie's neighborhood. Beth automatically slowed down to scan the house numbers. When Zachary spotted the correct address, she parked across the street and shut off the engine, then for a moment simply looked around.

Zachary didn't need to look; he knew what he would see. He knew how poor people lived. So instead he watched Beth, seeing the stunned disbelief slip into her eyes. Logically, of course, she'd known that Nashville had its share of low-income families, but he would bet she'd never been in a neighborhood like this. She had never seen such poverty.

Finally he released his seat belt and got out of the car, glancing around as he circled to open Beth's door. The neighborhood was what he'd expected. The houses were set uncomfortably close together, often no more than the width of a driveway separating them. Every house on the block needed painting, repairs and a general cleaning. Trash drifted unimpeded by fences from one grassless yard to the next, and toys, broken and worn, were scattered everywhere. He counted a half-dozen cars in varying stages of disrepair and spotted a pile of rusting junk beside one house that reached almost to the roof.

What a depressing place to live, especially compared to the farm where Carrie had grown up. The Morrises had had no more money than these people, but their place had been clean and cheerful, surrounded by fields, meadows and mountain forests. No wonder Carrie had grown so hopeless here. There was a sense of decay in the air, of despair and failure and giving in. Giving up.

"Welcome to the poor side of town," he murmured as Beth stepped out.

"Why don't we try over there first?"

He glanced at the house she was pointing to and nodded, crossing the street at her side. It was narrow and in need of repair, and it had no gutters, no curbs, no sidewalks. He supposed it was a miracle that the city had even bothered to pave it. The neighborhood obviously didn't rank high on their list of priorities—on *anyone's* list of priorities.

A mangy, scrawny dog tied to a tree in the yard raised his head and gave them a long, disinterested look before settling down again. He didn't make a sound, but he didn't need to. His owner was already standing in the doorway, watching their approach.

The screen door was latched, but there were torn places big enough for him to slip his hand inside and free the latch, Zachary observed. It provided minimal security for the stout, scowling woman on the other side.

Beth smiled at the woman but received no response. It didn't stop her. "Hello. I'm Beth Gibson, and this is Zachary Adams. We're representing Carrie Lewis." She drew a business card from her pocket and offered it to the woman, who accepted it through a tear in the screen. "We'd like to talk to you about Carrie and her husband."

"I already talked to the police." The woman handed the card back after studying it for a moment, but Beth shook her head.

"Keep it, please. I understand that the police questioned you about the night Mr. Lewis died. I'd like to talk to you about other things—what kind of neighbors they were, how often you saw Carrie, if you ever heard them fighting. Could we come in?"

She gave them each a long, critical look; then she said to Zachary, "You don't look like an attorney."

"No, ma'am," he agreed with a grin. "I try not to."

That brought the beginnings of a smile to her face. She unlatched the screen door and stepped back so they could enter. She showed them into a small kitchen, where a tiny square table filled the center, asked them to sit down and offered them coffee. Beth accepted the chair but refused the coffee, while Zachary took both.

"I'm Marva Janssen," the woman said, setting a mug of fragrant, steaming coffee in front of him, then sitting in the third chair at the table. "I've lived here with my family since before the Lewises moved in. It used to be a nice-enough place to live, but lately folks around here have been having some hard times."

That was an understatement, Beth thought, her first view of the neighborhood flashing into her mind once again. "Do you know Carrie, Mrs. Janssen?" she asked before the woman could say anything more.

"Only to say hello to. I don't think she ever spoke to anyone. She was kind of the shy type, you know?"

"Were you aware that her husband was beating her?"

"I live right next door to her. How could I *not* be aware of it? All the screaming and the shouting and the crying." Mrs. Janssen shook her head. "Those poor kids never knew a moment's peace. They never knew when their daddy was going to start in on their mama again—never knew when one day he was going to go too far and kill the poor woman right in front of them. Odd that she killed him instead."

Beth had flinched at the mention of the children, but her feelings didn't show in her voice. "Did anyone ever call the police when this was going on?"

"I did a few times, and I know that Alice Mitchell, on the other side of them, did, too. But Carrie never would do anything. She claimed she got all those bruises and black eyes and broken bones because she was clumsy, because she was always slipping and falling." She snorted. "Nobody could be *that* clumsy."

"So when she refused to take any action against her husband, you quit reporting it."

"Del Lewis didn't take kindly to us calling the law on him. It made things hard around here for a while. We have to live here, you know? And if she wasn't willing to help herself, why should we stick our necks out for her?"

The woman sounded defensive, and Beth hastened to reassure her. "I understand completely, Mrs. Janssen. You did what you could. Now . . . you mentioned broken bones earlier."

"He broke her arm twice. And she had to have stitches in her face once. Heavens, I can hardly remember a time when she didn't have one injury or another. Everybody on the whole block used to talk about it."

Broken bones and stitches. Why hadn't Carrie mentioned that during yesterday's interview? Beth wondered grimly. Before the arraignment this afternoon, they would have to find out why Carrie had withheld the information, get the names of the doctors who'd treated her and get her signature on a release for her medical records. Then Zachary could pick them up while she and Carrie were in court.

After a few minutes more, they left the Janssen home and walked down the block to Alice Mitchell's house. She told them virtually the same story: about fights, threats and Carrie's tearful pleas not to be hurt again. "My son went over there once a few months back," the gray-haired woman recalled, "and told him to knock it off before someone called the cops. I thought Lewis was going to come after him, and he was a big man—more than twice my boy's size. We all expected him to kill his wife in one of his rages. It sure would have been easy for him to do."

"Were you surprised to hear that she had killed him?" Zachary asked.

Mrs. Mitchell considered the question thoughtfully. "Surprised that she found the gumption to do anything at all," she replied. "But nobody's sorry he's dead. If ever any man deserved to die, it was him. Why, do you know those kids didn't cry or make a sound when the coroner's people took their daddy's body away, but they sure let loose when the police took their mama. Except for the boy,'' she added thoughtfully. ''That Tyler...he's one angry boy.''

''One last question, Mrs. Mitchell,'' Beth said as she got to her feet. ''Did you or anyone you know actually *see* Del Lewis hit his wife?''

She shook her head. ''But it doesn't take much to figure out what's happening when she's screaming, 'Please don't hurt me again,' does it?''

''No. It doesn't. Thank you, Mrs. Mitchell.'' She followed Zachary outside and back into the street, stopping in front of the Lewis house. It didn't stand out from its neighbors. It was small, square, a little shabbier than the other houses, but nothing special, nothing out of the ordinary. There was nothing that gave any indication of the violence that had been played out inside this house for the past fourteen years. Nothing that said a man had been murdered here. Nothing that hinted at the seven lives that had been destroyed here.

Zachary stepped in front of her, deliberately blocking her view. She blinked, then focused on him. ''Now what?'' he asked. ''More neighbors? Lunch? The jail?''

She gave it a moment's thought. ''Lunch, then the jail.''

They walked back to the car and settled in, loosening coats, fastening seat belts. They were out of Carrie's neighborhood and back on the interstate when Beth spoke again. ''Tell me again why you're doing this. Why are you spending your time and your own money on a case that isn't going to benefit you?''

''It *will* benefit me,'' he replied. ''With any luck, it will make me into a better lawyer. Don't be modest, Beth. You know what kind of reputation you have.''

''Yes, bitchy, pushy, abrasive—''

''And tough, talented, smart and shrewd,'' he interrupted her. ''Do you know how often a chance like this comes along for a country lawyer like me?''

Of course, he thought privately, the opportunity to learn from one of the best in the business hadn't been his only motivation for volunteering to help. There was the chance to spend time with Beth, not only to see her in action, but out of action, too. One on one. Up close and personal.

And there was the opportunity to get to know her better, to get inside her head and find out what Beth Gibson the woman was like. And there was the possibility—or so he hoped—of developing a relationship with her. Nothing permanent—he wouldn't kid himself about that. Nothing lasting. But something worth having.

Her voice, soft and elegant, interrupted his thoughts. "What made you decide to be a lawyer?"

"My grandfather was one."

"The same grandfather who left you the mountain?"

"Yes. He practiced in Sweetwater, too, in the same office I'm in. He was a very bright, very gentle and very just man. I always wanted to be exactly like him when I grew up."

"Sounds as if he had quite an influence on you."

He caught a hint of—was it envy? wistfulness?—in her voice, and he wondered what kind of relationship she'd had with her own grandfather, with any member of the rich and powerful Gibson-Townsend clan. Was she close to her mother? Spoiled by her father? "Granddad and I were going to be partners," he replied with a regretful smile, "but he died just a few weeks after I graduated from law school. He was sixty-nine years old, and he died at home with my grandmother at his side." Briefly he remembered his sadness at losing his grandfather, and his gratefulness that the old man had gone the way he wanted: peacefully, quietly, holding hands with his wife of forty-nine years.

Then he shook off the memories and looked at Beth. "What about you? Who led you into law as a career?"

"My father."

"Is he a lawyer?"

"No," she replied dryly. "He runs the family empire, and he fully intended for me to follow in his footsteps. I became a lawyer to spite him."

Uncomfortable, Zachary looked away. Just as he'd always been extraordinarily close to his grandfather, he couldn't imagine having a less-than-loving relationship with his father. Josiah had never put any pressure on him to do anything but his best, and he'd always been proud of whatever Zachary had accomplished. They had shared a mutual love and respect even when their interests were at odds.

At least that answered one of his questions. She wasn't spoiled by her father, not if she'd planned her entire career around what he *didn't* want her to do. Why? he wondered. What caused a daughter's natural love for her father to turn sour?

And it made him wonder more about her mother. Did Beth get along with her, or had she also planned certain aspects of her life—such as being single and childless at the age of thirty-six—to spite *her?*

But he didn't ask his questions, didn't probe or pry. Maybe someday—someday soon—he would feel comfortable enough to delve into her personal life. But not now.

Not yet.

After a hurried lunch and a brief meeting with Carrie, Zachary spent the rest of the afternoon on his own. He'd gotten the names of the hospital emergency rooms where Carrie's more serious injuries had been treated—a different one each time—and he'd gone to the closest two, each time identifying himself, presenting the release form Carrie had signed and, after much delay and verification, receiving copies of her records. Tomorrow morning he would repeat the process at the third hospital on his list.

Now it was after five o'clock, and he was miles away from Beth's downtown office and not far at all from his motel. He could get out of the heavy rush-hour traffic, stretch out on the bed, read the hospital reports, think about dinner and see Beth in the morning.

Or he could fight traffic and catch Beth in her office—he had no doubt she would be working late—and . . . Ask her to dinner? Maybe, but he didn't think she would go. She would probably give him some excuse about how she didn't go out with the people she worked with.

He could turn over the reports and find out how the arraignment had gone, if there had been any surprises. Those were both valid reasons for going so far out of his way in this traffic.

But the real reason was simpler and just as valid. He wanted to see her again. Even for just a few moments. Even just as one lawyer to another.

He drove past the exit for his motel and continued downtown. Construction on the interstate slowed the already-congested traffic even more. It took him another half hour to reach Beth's building. He inserted the card her secretary had given him at the gate to the parking garage, and it lifted, allowing him access to the nearly empty garage.

He parked on the fifth level and started toward the elevator. Besides his Jeep Cherokee and Beth's Mercedes, there were only four other cars on this level. Like Beth's, they were all imports, all expensive, all impressive. Apparently all of the lawyers here were well paid—people whose education and training were little different from his own—but he wasn't even slightly envious. He might appreciate the sleek lines of the Jaguar parked beside Beth's car or the flashiness of the BMW convertible next to the elevator, but he would never want such a car for himself. The winter snow and mountain roads around Sweetwater made anything but a sturdy, four-wheel-drive vehicle impractical for him.

Beth's office was on the next-to-the top floor, and the elevator took him there swiftly, settling with a soft thump as the doors slid open. A few lights burned, illuminating long hallways and empty work spaces. Down one hallway he heard the clack of a printer, down another came one side of a heated phone conversation—*Do you think I put in fourteen-hour days because I like it?* The hall that led to Beth's office was silent, lit every ten feet by twin brass sconces high on the walls.

He passed the empty desk where Beth's secretary, Loretta, guarded the inner office during regular hours. Beth's door was open a few inches, and when he gave it a slight push, it swung silently in.

She sat leaning over her desk, one hand supporting her cheek while she scribbled notes on a yellow pad with the other. Her jacket was discarded on the credenza behind her desk, and he saw a pair of heels nearby, one standing perfectly balanced on the thick carpet, the other lying on its side. Her hair tumbled over her arm, the gleaming red a stark contrast to the blue silk of her blouse and the polished teak of the desk, and a pair of designer-framed glasses were slipping down her nose. She was mumbling to herself as she wrote. "We will prove... Uh-uh. We will show proof..."

He had never seen her looking less than perfect, not even at Sarah and Daniel's wedding, when their little girl Katie had accidentally smeared chocolate frosting all over Beth's ivory wool dress. He had never seen her looking remotely touchable, not even all those times when touching her was the only thing he could think of.

He had never seen her looking quite so real.

Quite so lovely.

For a long time he simply stood there, watching her. Wanting her. Then she became aware of him, and he left his vantage point, moving closer, finally taking a seat in one of the chairs near her desk.

She slowly straightened, combing her hair back into its usual sleek style, removing the glasses that had reached the tip of her nose, scooting her chair closer to the desk and tucking her bare feet safely out of sight underneath. "I wasn't expecting you."

He held up the folders he was carrying. "I made it to two of the hospitals this afternoon. I'll go to the third one tomorrow."

She accepted the folders but didn't look inside them. Instead she added them to the stack of work that already filled one corner of her desk.

"How did the arraignment go?"

"As we expected. The judge set her bail at a hundred thousand dollars. The preliminary hearing is set for Wednesday the eighteenth, less than two weeks away."

"And the charge?"

"First-degree murder."

He nodded grimly. He had hoped for the lesser charge of second-degree murder or even manslaughter, but apparently the prosecution thought they could prove that Carrie had calmly and cold-bloodedly planned and carried out her husband's murder. And if they believed that, the jury might. Carrie might have been better off it she *had* simply sat back and waited for Del to kill her.

"After you go by the hospital in the morning, why don't you go back out to Carrie's house? Talk to the rest of her neighbors and see if you can find out what school the oldest boy went to. We'll need to get in touch with the counselor Carrie told us about."

"Okay. What about you?"

"I've got to be in court tomorrow morning." She gestured to the pad with her notes. "In the afternoon I have an appointment with a psychologist here in town who's going to tell me more about battered woman syndrome. If you'll be done with the interviews by one o'clock, let me know. You might be interested in what the doctor has to say."

"What about this evening?"

She looked blankly at him.

"You have to eat sometime."

Her face remained expressionless.

"Dinner?" he prodded, then shook his head. Hadn't he decided on the way over that he wouldn't invite her to dinner? Hadn't he already known what her answer would be? So how had it slipped out, anyway?

"The restaurant down the street delivers. I'll call them when I'm ready."

"No one would mind if you took an hour off and went out for dinner. It's already past quitting time."

"This client would mind," she disagreed, tapping her finger on her notes. "I would already have been prepared for this case if I hadn't spent most of the last two days working on Carrie's case instead."

He considered trying to change her mind, but only for a moment. It would be a wasted effort. Hadn't she just not-so-subtly reminded him that in taking on Carrie's defense she'd already given him more than he'd had any right to expect? She was a busy woman, and he'd brought her more work. He couldn't reasonably ask her now to make time in her schedule for him, could he?

At least work was an excuse his ego could more easily accept. It was better than, "Sorry, Zach, but you're just not my type. You're not rich. You're not successful. You're not a hot-shot lawyer/banker/business tycoon." It was better than, "I'm doing you one favor already. Don't ask me for another."

It was better than, "I'm just not interested in you."

It was better than all the excuses, all the answers, she could have given . . . but it still hurt.

Smiling even though he didn't feel like it, he got to his feet and pushed his hands into his pockets. "Then I'll see you sometime tomorrow."

It was an abrupt goodbye, Beth thought, watching him go. Almost as if he were angry. Annoyed. *Disappointed*.

Maybe she should have accepted his invitation, she thought morosely, swiveling her chair around to face the window. She didn't want him to be disappointed or angry with her, and after all, he was a stranger in town. He could probably use some help in finding his way around and locating good restaurants. He could probably use a little conversation that had nothing to do with death or violence or despair.

Besides, there had to be more to life than take-out meals and long evenings in the office. What about pleasure? Fun, relaxation, relationships? When was the last time she'd partaken of any of those things?

The answer came to mind more easily than she would have liked. Philip. After ten years, she would have liked to have forgotten something—his name, his face, his game—but all the details remained clear in her mind. How handsome he had been. How sexy and charming. How his French accent had captivated her the first time she'd heard his voice.

And how he had fooled her. Used her. Betrayed her. How *she* had believed that their relationship was leading to a declaration of love and a proposal of marriage. How *he* had explained that it was merely a quest for money, huge sums of it, in exchange for his companionship.

Beth pressed her fingertips to her temples, massaging the ache there. Her mother had meekly suggested that it might not be such a bad arrangement, and her father had gloated over her glaring lack of good judgment. Neither of them had guessed that, for the first time since Great-Grandmother Althea, Beth had dared to love someone. Neither had suspected that he'd broken her heart, and, almost worse, he had destroyed her trust.

Neither of them had cared.

There had been other men after Philip—casual acquaintances, for the most part—and there had been a few more intimate liaisons along the way, but not another relationship. No giving and sharing and caring. No loving. There never would be.

And *that*, she thought with a twinge of sadness, was why she'd turned down Zachary's dinner invitation. *That* was why, even if all he wanted was an hour of her time to assuage his own loneliness, she couldn't give it.

Picking out a dim star in the night sky, she whimsically recalled the nursery rhyme Althea had taught her more than thirty years ago. *Star light, star bright* . . . If she could have any wish she wished tonight, what would it be?

Zachary.

Then quickly, before the fleeting thought could turn into longing, she changed that. She would wish to be someone, anyone, but who she was. She would keep her best qualities, whatever they might be, and discard the rest—the fears, the defenses, the insecurities, the doubts—and she would become a new woman. A better woman.

A woman who might deserve Zachary.

Slowly, reluctantly, she turned away from the window and the wishes and back to her desk. Back to the files and notes and reports. Maybe for other people there *was* more to life than take-out dinners and lonely evenings in the office, but not for her. This was the life she had chosen.

This was the life she lived.

Chapter 4

It was only his second night in the city, and Zachary was already homesick. He wasn't used to eating alone in restaurants or lying in a strange bed or watching television with more than two channels available. He felt about a million miles from home, and he didn't like it. Not one bit.

No wonder Carrie had been so miserable here. They were both country people at heart, not meant to wander far from the place where they were born. He didn't know how anyone could stand living in the city—although the half million residents of Nashville seemed to manage just fine.

Beth managed just fine.

He smiled wryly as he propped an extra pillow beneath his head. If he'd been spending the evening with her, he wouldn't even have noticed that he was so far from home. In fact, he suspected that it wasn't homesickness so much as loneliness that was eating at him—and not just the garden-variety type of loneliness, either. He could have solved that with the friendly little blonde who'd waited on him at the restaurant and coyly informed him that she got off at eight. He didn't want to spend this evening with just anyone, but with Beth. He would have liked to have dinner with her. He would have enjoyed sitting across from her and discussing futures and pasts and life in general. He would have been satisfied with just looking at her.

But obviously she didn't share his desire. She seemed to have no interest in him other than business. She didn't care for his company, and apparently physical desire hadn't even entered her mind.

Maybe it would be best for him to pull out now, to tell her that he was sorry, but he'd already had his fill of big-city legal work, that he was going back to Sweetwater where he belonged. Back to minor cases and part-time hours and working on his house. Because as much as he relished the experience of assisting her on this case, he wasn't foolish enough to go looking for a broken heart. He'd made it to the age of thirty-four without suffering one yet, and he would like to extend that luck a while longer.

Yet he could see no other outcome for this situation. His attraction to her was already stronger than anything he'd ever experienced. He admired her. He respected her. He lusted after her. He wanted to touch her, to stroke that fiery red hair, to feel its softness give way beneath his fingers, to caress the porcelain beauty of her skin. He wanted to find the passion he was positive burned within her, wanted to unleash it and let it consume them both. He wanted...

His expression turned grim. He wanted more than she would ever give him. He wasn't sure exactly how she thought of him—as Sarah and Daniel's friend; as a fellow, though less-competent, lawyer; as a tool to quiet her partners' grumbles while she dealt with this case—but he *was* sure of one thing. She didn't think of him as a man. She certainly didn't think of him as a prospective lover. What could he offer her? Certainly nothing she needed. Apparently nothing she wanted.

He'd had relationships in the past—not so many that he couldn't remember the pertinent details of each and every one, but enough to recognize danger. And that was what Beth Gibson represented: danger. The danger of experiencing, for the first time in his life, the love of a man for a woman. The danger of getting hurt. The danger of heartache.

If he had any sense at all, he would pack his bags right now and go home. He would call her office in the morning and give the terribly efficient Mrs. Taylor the message that he wouldn't be back. He would somehow erase Beth from his mind, from his system, from his longing.

His father would say that was probably the wise thing to do. His grandfather, he thought with a sudden grin, would call it cowardly. If a man couldn't face up to the woman he wanted, then he didn't deserve to have her. If he wasn't willing to expend a little effort to win her, if he gave up without even trying, then he got what he'd earned: nothing. If he couldn't accept the risk, then he didn't merit the reward.

And his grandfather would be exactly right. Few things worth having came easily. Even as a small child he'd learned that working for something made it more valuable.

Of course, he would take Beth any way he could get her, but if it meant working, if it meant earning her trust and overcoming her reservations and risking failure, then that was what he would do. As long as there was a chance, as long as even a slight hope remained, he would reach for it. After all, sooner or later she had to trust *someone*.

Why shouldn't it be him?

Beth was sitting at her desk on Friday, reading glasses on again, two manila folders open in front of her, when Loretta announced Zachary's arrival. She barely responded to her secretary, but the moment Zachary walked in, she motioned for him to circle the desk and read over her shoulder.

"These are Carrie's medical records," she explained. "Did you read them yesterday?"

"I didn't have time. Anything interesting in there?"

"This one says she went to the emergency room complaining of pain in her left arm. The doctor noticed that she

was having trouble breathing, so he ordered chest X rays.
They revealed—'' she flipped through the pages to the radiology report and read from it ''—'evidence of healed
fractures of the fifth, sixth and seventh ribs,' as well as a
recent hairline fracture. The X rays of her arm also showed
an old, healed fracture plus the new one, right here.'' She
indicated on her own forearm.

"As if she had raised her arm to ward off a blow," Zachary suggested.

She tested his theory, lifting her arm, bent to protect her
face, then nodded. "That must have been it. But look here."
Flipping back to the doctor's narrative, she read aloud,
"'Although patient states injuries were suffered in a fall,
they appear to be consistent with an assault.' The bastard
had just broken her arm and one rib, and she lied for him."

Zachary rested one hand on her desk, the other on the
back of her chair, and she tensed. It was a perfectly natural
position for someone reading along with her. Other men in
the office had done it before, and she had never minded. She
had never felt threatened.

But she did now.

He was so close that she could smell the rich scent of his
suede jacket. So close that she could tell he wasn't wearing
after-shave. So close that she could feel the heat escaping his
body where his coat fell open. So close that touching him
would be as simple as shifting an inch to the right, that a kiss
would be as easy as tilting her head back.

So close . . . and he hardly seemed aware of her.

"Protecting him isn't inconsistent for someone in her situation," he pointed out, his attention still on the report.
"Remember, she had to go home with him. She had to live
with him. Broken bones might have been nothing compared to what he would have done to her if she'd told the
doctor the truth."

Beth took a deep breath, taking in the enticing scent of
Zachary, then subtly leaned to the left, away from him. "I
know. I try to keep an open mind, to put myself in Carrie's
place, to think and react the way she would. But sometimes

I get in my own way. I'd like to find just a hint that at one time in all those years she stood up for herself.''

Leaning closer, Zachary fished one report free of the others and tossed it on top of the file she held. It was Del Lewis's autopsy report. "There. One time she stood up for herself."

She fingered the report. "What was it Mrs. Mitchell said? That if anyone ever deserved to die, it was Del Lewis?" She sighed softly, bleakly.

"What's wrong?" Zachary asked, shifting to lean against the edge of her desk so he could see her face. He immediately thought, as he always did on first seeing her, that she was beautiful. Then he noticed the faint shadows beneath her eyes and the lines of stress around her mouth that her smile couldn't quite hide.

"It's a sad case," she replied softly. "With sad people and sad lives and sad endings. We're probably not going to get her off. You realize that, don't you?"

He simply nodded.

"I suppose it's possible that the jury might be so sympathetic, so swayed by the pathetic figure they have to pass judgment on, that they might acquit her," Beth continued. "But I doubt it. A victory in this case will be a conviction on any charge less than first-degree murder or a sentence of anything less than life."

So Carrie would almost surely go to prison. How would she ever survive that? he wondered, then immediately answered the question. She simply *would*. The same way she had survived fourteen years of hell with her husband. She would endure.

"We're going to have to prove that Lewis abused her. We have statements here from the doctors who treated her, who suspected abuse—although she denied it. We can get statements from the police officers who answered complaint calls, who also suspected abuse—although she denied it to them, too. We have statements from the neighbors who heard the fights and saw her injuries, but she also denied it to them."

"Proving it won't be difficult. We have the photographs the police took of her the night she was arrested. We have the school counselor. We have the neighbors who heard her screams."

There was a long silence, then Beth slowly looked up at him. "And we have the children."

Zachary shook his head before finding his voice. "No. Not the kids, Beth. Leave them out of this."

"There are only five people who knew what went on in that house," she continued, ticking them off on her fingers. "Lewis, of course, who's dead. Carrie. And their children. The little boy is too young, but the three older ones are six, nine and fourteen. They're old enough to tell us what happened." She paused for a moment before finishing. "They're old enough to testify."

He held her gaze for a long time, thinking of the kids he'd met Tuesday. The three boys and the girl, thin, raggedy, weary and solemn beyond their years. What had they already been through during their short lives? How much more would they, like their mother, have to endure?

"I know you don't like the idea," Beth said, touching her fingertips to the back of his hand where it rested on the desk. "No one likes to see children in court, especially in cases like this. But if that's what it takes to help their mother..."

Then that was what they would do, Zachary thought grimly. That was what any good attorney would do—provide the best defense possible for the client. Even if it meant putting three innocent, frightened, helpless kids on the witness stand. Even if it meant prolonging the nightmare their father had created for them.

He didn't want to think about it, not now. For the next hour or two, until their appointment with the psychologist, he didn't want to think about anything at all that even vaguely resembled work. Turning his hand over, he captured her fingers, then stood up and pulled her to her feet. "We're going to lunch," he said when she made a sound of protest. "And from the minute we walk out this door until the minute we come back through it, we're not going to discuss business.''

She looked as if she were going to argue, to snatch her hand free and command him never to do such a thing again, and when she opened her mouth, he waited for her anger. But it didn't come. Instead, in a cool, subdued voice, she suggested a restaurant a few miles away, a place with good food and excellent service, with quiet surroundings and patient waiters.

Once they were seated in a small, quiet dining room and had placed their order with her usual waiter, Beth folded her hands together in her lap, looked across the table at Zachary and couldn't think of a thing to say. She felt entirely empty except for the warm feeling that simply being with him brought. It was a warning sign, she tried to remind herself. Hadn't she felt the same low-grade fever with Philip in the beginning? And wasn't he the first—and, thank God, the only—man she'd ever made a fool of herself over?

She didn't need this, particularly now. Of course, any time was a bad time for a man in her life. It was against the rules, rules that she had designed and implemented for her own safety. After seeing what her grandfather had done to her grandmother, after witnessing for years what her parents could do to each other, she had sworn she would never marry, would never have even a serious relationship with any man. Casual friendship, casual sex and casual satisfaction—that was all she'd wanted.

She had broken all the rules with Philip, and look how badly that had turned out. Her affair with him was proof that, contrary to old clichés, rules *weren't* meant to be broken. Broken rules had led to a broken heart, and she would never risk that again.

Not even if Zachary was probably the best-looking man in the galaxy. Not even if he did have the most charmingly sweet smile she had ever seen. Not even if he was absolutely nothing like Philip...or her father...or her grandfather...or any of the other men she had ever known.

He was still off limits. This was a professional relationship, even if she wasn't allowed to discuss work right now. There was nothing personal between them. *Nothing.*

No matter how badly some rebellious part of her might want it.

The silence extended for another minute, then another. He was as much at a loss for words as she was, Beth thought with a thin smile. That was just further proof of their total unsuitability. Take away their jobs and they had nothing in common, not even small talk.

Almost as if he'd read her mind, he grinned sheepishly and said, "All right. At least we both know Daniel and Sarah. Let's talk about them."

"What about them?"

"How did you get to be friends with Sarah? You two seem to be even more different than you and I are."

"We both went to Tennessee State. That was my first time in a public school. From kindergarten through high school I'd gone to a series of private, very snooty, all-girls schools. I was supposed to go to a private women's college, too, but I won that argument. Sarah and I were taking the same history class. Somehow our instructor made the connection between the Townsends and the Gibsons and me, and when we covered the portion of history that dealt with them, he made a big deal of it. Sarah was the only person in the class who wasn't impressed or resentful."

"So you became friends because she didn't mind being seen with one of *those* Gibsons," he gently teased. "Then you must have known her ex-husband."

"Unfortunately. Brent Lawson was a self-centered, smug, arrogant, mean little man. I was more than happy to handle the divorce for Sarah. I just wish we could have gotten her a better deal." She didn't go into detail. Zachary already knew how Sarah's ex-husband had left the state to avoid paying the court-ordered child support to his son, who died before his third birthday. She suspected he also knew how angry and frustrated and impotent she had felt because she couldn't do anything about it. If Sarah had been his client, he would have felt the same way. "Daniel's been good for Sarah."

"I had the distinct impression that you didn't approve of him."

"The first time I met him was when I approached him about taking custody of Katie. He scared me," she admitted.

That made Zachary scowl. He thought she had judged his friend on physical appearance alone and found him unacceptable, Beth realized, but that wasn't the case.

"So he isn't what you would call handsome," he started to protest.

"No, he isn't," she said before he could continue. "And he is absolutely the biggest man I have ever seen. And let's face it, Zachary, living up there in those mountains all those years by himself didn't do wonders for his personality. He was rude, unfriendly, unwelcoming and intimidating."

"Until he found out that he was a father and you could give him his daughter."

Beth nodded. "Even if I did have trouble understanding what had attracted Sarah to him, I had to admire him for the way he took Katie in. Every child should be so lucky as to have a father like him."

"We agree on that," Zachary said with one of his most charming smiles. "Daniel's a good man. He'll devote the rest of his life to Sarah and Katie and any children they have in the future."

Why hadn't Zachary devoted *his* life to some lucky woman? Beth wondered. Granted, Sweetwater wasn't exactly a singles' paradise, but there had to be at least a few unattached women there. Plus, he had clients in other towns, met other lawyers in court and made occasional trips such as this one into the city. Why hadn't he found someone to settle down and raise children with?

The question slipped out before she realized it, before she had a chance to call it back. She blushed faintly, but Zachary didn't seem to notice her discomfort. Instead, he was toying with the silverware neatly lined up beside his empty wineglass. When he finally looked up, there was a slight edge to his smile. "You sound like my mother and my grandmother. They're tired of waiting for Alicia and me to do something."

A slow chill crept over her, stiffening her spine and making her hands trembling cold in her lap. "Is Alicia your...?" What was the proper way of phrasing it these days? she wondered. Friend? Girlfriend? *Lover?*

"Yeah, she's my..." He mimicked the way she had let the question trail away, then chuckled. "She's my kid sister. You must have seen her at least once or twice when you came to my office. Blond hair, pretty, a little bit flaky?"

"That's a wonderful description," she said dryly, more relieved than she wanted to be. "And how does she describe you? Blond, pretty, a pain in the—"

He interrupted her with a wagging finger. "Ladies don't use such language."

"I'm a lawyer, not a lady."

"Of course you are. You can be more than one thing, Beth. You're a lawyer, a partner, a woman, a daughter, a friend. You must be a lady for somebody."

The images that conjured up, to be somebody's lady... She shook them away before they could take root in her dissatisfaction and grow out of control. "We were talking about you, not me," she coolly reminded him. "And why you're not married and raising your own little baseball team."

"I would like to be in love with a woman before I ask her to marry me," he replied, sounding entirely too cheerful about a subject that *she* avoided as much as possible. "While I've met numerous women that I like and admire and even feel a great deal of fondness for, I haven't yet met one that I love. So I'm still waiting."

"Why don't you settle for 'a great deal of fondness' and get on with it?" she asked. "Maybe that's all you'll ever find."

Zachary simply looked at her for a long moment before scoffing, "Oh, please, Beth, don't tell me you're *that* cynical. You don't *believe* in love?"

"Carrie Lewis loved her husband, and he promised to love her, too. Look at what she endured from him . . . and what she did to him."

He repeated his earlier demand. "No talk of business, remember? Besides, Carrie and Del are hardly typical of most married couples."

"What *is* typical, Zachary?" she challenged. "Is there even such a thing? I can guarantee you that typical for you doesn't have anything in common with typical for me."

Accepting her challenge, he leaned forward, his arms resting on the tablecloth. "Are your parents still married?"

"Yes. They celebrated their thirty-eighth anniversary last month."

"Well?"

"They're still married to each other because no one else would have them. No one else would tolerate them. No other man would let my mother torment him the way she torments my father, and no other woman would let my father degrade her the way he degrades my mother. Oh, yes," she added sarcastically. "And they still *love* each other...or so they say."

Well, that helped explain why Beth was still single, Zachary thought silently. It also made yesterday's comment about becoming a lawyer to spite her father a bit easier to understand. It must have been hard on the little girl she'd been to live with parents who were constantly fighting, who couldn't stand to be together and couldn't stand to be apart.

"What about your grandparents?" he asked quietly.

"My father's parents died before I was born. My mother's father is dead now, too, but for fifty years he flaunted his mistresses and girlfriends and one-night stands in front of my grandmother and the whole city, all the while proclaiming himself a good family man who loved his wife dearly. And she put up with it because she loved him." She smiled elegantly, coolly, certain that she had proved her point, Zachary thought. But she hadn't.

"That's not love," he informed her. "That's pride. Obsession. Fear of being alone. Love is what Sarah and Daniel have, what my parents have. It's what my grandparents had. Anyone who would settle for less doesn't deserve it."

She shrugged carelessly, unconvinced. "So we don't agree on that. What other subjects do we see from different sides?"

What else could they talk about? he wondered. They hadn't gone to the same schools, didn't know any of the same people beyond the Ryans and didn't share any of the same interests as far as he could tell. "Have you always lived in Nashville?"

"That's really reaching."

She knew he was as stumped for conversational topics as she'd been when they first sat down, he realized. What she didn't know yet was that he was persistent. Given enough time, he would find common ground. If he didn't, he would create it. "That's called getting to know you," he said. "It's hard to know what we can talk about when I really don't know you very well."

"You really don't want to," she warned him conversationally.

He gave her a long look, from her sleek, red hair to her unfreckled ivory skin, from the eyes that were too green to be natural—but were—to the sensual bow of her mouth, from the long line of her throat to the soft curves underneath her navy jacket. Then he smiled and murmured, "Oh, I do, Beth. I really do."

She held his gaze, and for just a moment he knew that what he felt wasn't totally one-sided. There was a softening—nothing specific, nothing he could point to, but for just that moment she seemed warmer, more touchable, less tough—and the look in her eyes was tinged with awareness. With the slightest longing. With insubstantial, slipping-away-even-as-he-watched desire.

Then she broke the contact and reached for her water glass. After a sip, she folded her arms loosely—protectively, he thought—and answered the question he'd forgotten asking in a perfectly normal, perfectly businesslike voice. "Yes, I've always lived in Nashville, except for a brief time away at school. Next question?"

"Are you an only child?"

"Yes. God saw fit not to subject more than one of us to my parents."

He ignored the bitterness underlying those words. "You're thirty...what?"

"It's impolite to ask a *lady* her age, but since I'm not vain, I don't mind answering. I'm thirty-six."

He ignored her emphasis on lady, too. No matter how she might deny it, there was no doubt that she embodied all the qualities required of a lady in his book. She was bright and sensitive, inherently good and honest. She cared about people—about Sarah and Katie, about Carrie and all her other clients—even though she did have problems with the people in her personal life. She hated injustice. She was passionate about things that mattered to her. She used her talents and her strengths to help those who were weaker than she was.

Too bad she was too stubborn to help herself. In spite of the examples set by her parents and grandparents, in spite of working in a job that required her to deal with failed marriages on an all-too-regular basis, she was far too good a lawyer to condemn the entire institution of marriage. She had too much to offer never to share her life with someone else. She was too special to turn her back on the opportunity for that kind of happiness, satisfaction and joy.

"What do you do when you're not working?" he asked, anticipating her answer even as he spoke.

"I'm always working."

"No social life, huh?"

"I do occasionally date."

"But you make a point of not enjoying it, don't you?" he gently teased.

"I enjoy it a great deal," she disagreed. "I enjoy it for exactly what it is—a diversion. Nothing serious or permanent or passionate, but a nice break from work."

"And of course the men you date are simply looking for a diversion, too."

"That, or the somewhat questionable prestige of being seen in the right places with Walter Gibson's daughter."

He silently considered her frank admission. Yesterday she had told him that she'd grown up judging people's motives for wanting to befriend her, and he had called her cynical. He hadn't even considered the possibility that she had good reason to be cynical. Of course, he had a defense: it was incomprehensible to him that anyone could need a reason other than Beth herself for wanting her. That was enough for him. He didn't care about her family, her background or her money. He simply wanted *her*.

"Isn't there somebody whose motives you trust?"

She gave him one of her cool, not quite pleasant smiles. "I trust my partners. They're driven by greed, by profit and the need to succeed. That's the motivation behind everything they do. And I trust the men I date. They're very clear about what they want, and they don't expect anything else from me. To them I'm an ornament, something to impress others. For me, they're a few hours' pleasure with no entanglements."

That was cold, Zachary thought grimly, on the part of both the men and Beth. What kind of man could care more about appearances than about Beth? And how could a passionate, intelligent woman prefer that kind of cold-blooded arrangement over a normal, giving and taking, sweet and satisfying and occasionally painful, relationship?

Unless at some time there had been too much pain. Had she been in love before and lost her heart? Had she been hurt so deeply that she wasn't willing to risk it again? Was that the real reason behind her decision never to marry?

But he didn't ask her. If she'd loved some man, if she still loved him, he didn't want to know.

After a moment's silence, Beth quietly asked, "When are you returning to Sweetwater?"

"This evening. I'll be back next Tuesday."

"Do you work on your house on weekends?"

"Usually." They were awkwardly not looking at each other, and Beth's voice had been subdued. Did she regret the answers she'd given him? Zachary wondered. Had his distaste for her social life been obvious to her? Whatever the cause, there was little easiness between them now.

"What made you decide to build the house yourself?"

At least she wasn't giving in to uncomfortable silence, he acknowledged with a humorless smile. "It's the only way I could afford it. I saved a long time for this. If I'd waited until I could pay a builder to put it up, I would have been dead before the foundation got laid."

"And now you're spending money that could be used on the house on this case."

He shrugged carelessly. "It's costing you more than me."

"It's a little different for me. I'll simply get less profit this year. It's an outright loss for you."

"You're twisting words, counselor. 'Less profit' and 'outright loss' mean the same things."

"If it gets to be a burden..."

She spoke hesitantly, reluctantly, and Zachary smiled, those few moments of discomfort gone. Was she going to offer her help? Fudge a bit on her own expense account to cover *his?* He didn't wait to find out. "Don't worry about it. If it reaches the point that I can't afford it anymore, I'll give you plenty of notice."

And hell would freeze over first, he thought privately. He wanted in on this case—for Carrie's sake, for the sake of his career, for himself and for Beth.

Most definitely for Beth.

Beth sat at her desk on Saturday morning, gazing moodily out the window. Although she was the only one in the office and she would be spending her time here alone, she was dressed in a dove gray suit, heels and makeup. It was

habit that made her dress up and come into the office on
Saturdays, she supposed—habit, and the fact that there was
no one to keep her at home, no one to see her leave, no one
to gently poke fun at her for dressing suitably for court when
absolutely no one but the doorman would see her.

Zachary could have done that.

After their interview with the psychologist yesterday afternoon, he'd left for Sweetwater. He wouldn't be back until Tuesday, but she would see him Monday. She was driving
to the small southeast Tennessee town early that morning to
interview Carrie's children. Zachary had made it clear once
again that he didn't like the idea—no more than *she* did,
she'd pointed out to him—but it was something that had to
be done. He was supposed to arrange it with Carrie's parents this weekend.

She had wanted to make the trip on Sunday, but he had
vetoed that. In a town like Sweetwater, Sunday was still a
day for families, he reminded her. The Morrises and their
grandchildren would spend Sunday morning in church; then
they would get together with their other children for a big
dinner. Afterward, the kids would play and the adults would
talk. There would be no time to discuss business, particularly the sort of business that Beth was interested in.

A year ago, or even six months ago, she would have
scoffed at the idea of setting aside an entire day every week
just for family get-togethers. She was usually forced to see
her family at Christmas, sometimes at Thanksgiving and
always on her grandmother's birthday. Three times a year
were enough for her.

But somewhere deep inside she felt an unfamiliar twinge
that she thought was envy for the Morrises and the Adamses
and everyone else who shared that weekly ritual. She envied people who cared enough about their families that they
voluntarily spent that much time together. She wondered
what it was like to *want* to see your family.

Muttering darkly, she swiveled her chair so that she faced
her desk. She'd been here for an hour already and hadn't
even so much as opened the files she'd removed from her

bottom drawer. Kicking her shoes off, she settled more comfortably and reached for the top folder.

It contained the summaries of the interviews Zachary had conducted yesterday morning. In comparison with her own atrocious writing, his was graceful and fluid, almost too pretty for a man. So was he, she thought. Not just handsome, but pretty. Pretty face, pretty hair, pretty blue eyes. Pretty enough to distract her from her work.

Wasn't distraction just another word for diversion? she reminded herself dryly. And hadn't she told him just yesterday that a diversion was just what she was looking for? Did that mean that *he* was what she was looking for?

He hadn't liked that part of the conversation at all. Oh, he hadn't said anything, hadn't told her that she was shallow, shameless, manipulative and cold. But he'd become awfully quiet, and there had been a look of disapproval in his pretty blue eyes.

Not that it mattered, of course. She *wasn't* going to distract herself with him. She wasn't going to let his feelings, his opinions or his values affect the way she lived. She was simply going to take advantage of his legal skills in order to present the best damn defense possible for Carrie Lewis. Once that had been accomplished, she would probably never see Zachary again except on rare trips to Sweetwater to visit Sarah. Then she would go back to her normal routine.

Her normal, dull, boring, dissatisfying routine.

She sighed, and it seemed to echo around her. This office was big—tangible proof of her value to the firm. Sometimes she felt almost lost in here. Lost and cold, with all the sleek modern lines and cool colors and contemporary art. The only thing in the entire room that belonged to her was the portrait of Great-Grandmother Althea. It was all that she'd brought with her when she came, and it was all that she would take with her when she left.

When she left... She'd never given any thought to leaving the firm. She had joined it straight out of law school and assumed that she would be here until she was too old and her mind too feeble to practice any longer. She had worked hard to make partner, to reach the goal of owning a piece of the firm for herself. She had worked hard for her future.

But what sort of future did she have here? Another thirty years like the last eleven? Giving all her energy, all her concentration, all her passion, to the business of law—and to law practiced in a way that she was coming to dislike more with each passing day?

That was pathetic, Althea would say. Life was meant to be lived, not worked. A person should leave something behind when she died—a family, a home, some accomplishment that would tell those who followed that she had been here. Althea's children, grandchildren and great-grandchildren were the marks that she had left behind.

Sarah Ryan had her family and the lives she'd touched as an elementary school teacher. Daniel Ryan had his family, too, and his rambling ancestral home and the craft of building fine furniture that had become a business for him. Zachary would leave the children that she knew he would one day have, along with the lifelong friendships he'd formed, the legal services he'd performed for no fee other than satisfaction and the house he was building on his mountain.

What would *she* leave behind? Her name on a letterhead? Not even that, because whatever ambitious young lawyer eventually took her place in this office would also take her place in the firm's name. Her condo? It hardly held the same impact as a house built with your own hands. Friends? A family of her own? Anyone whose life was better because she had lived?

No. At the rate she was going, all that would survive her would be her money, because she certainly couldn't spend it all before she died. There wouldn't even be anyone to leave it to.

What a legacy.

Sundays *were* family days, just as Zachary had told Beth, and he was spending this Sunday with his family and the people who were almost like family to him—Daniel, Sarah and Katie Ryan.

Daniel and Sarah had celebrated their engagement with an impromptu party at Zachary's parents' house, and it seemed that they'd been included in the Adams family ever since. Katie substituted for the grandchild that Bonnie and Josiah Adams were still waiting for, and they filled the empty place in her life left by her own lack of grandparents.

They had long since finished dinner, but they still sat at the table, discussing Sweetwater news—gossip, his grandmother called it—over dirty dishes and leftovers. Naturally Carrie Lewis was the prime topic of conversation, and naturally the bulk of the questions were directed at him, but there was little he could say.

"I don't understand why they're even taking her to trial," his mother remarked as she began gathering dishes from those seated closest to her. "The man *should* have been killed for what he did."

"Maybe so," Josiah agreed, playfully slapping her hand away as she tried to take his dessert plate. "I'm not finished with that cake yet, Bonnie. Just hold on, will you?" After a moment in which she ignored his admonition, he continued, "Maybe Delbert Lewis deserved to die, but that didn't give Carrie the right to do it."

"Carrie didn't have any rights," Alicia pointed out. "She's a woman, and women's rights in this country are a joke."

"Don't start spouting that feminist nonsense," Josiah warned his daughter. "Women have rights—"

"Just not as many as they should have," Zachary interjected. "When a marriage breaks up in this country, the woman's income decreases significantly. The quality of her life and the lives of her children decreases significantly. But a man's income generally increases, and so does the quality of his life. Responsibility for the children rests almost solely on the mother. Even when the courts order child support,

too many men won't pay it, and their ex-wives have very little recourse."

"Why didn't Carrie just leave him?" his grandmother
asked.

"Because she had no place to go," Alicia put in. "Because shelters and organizations to assist abused women are
grossly underfunded. Because the legislators both in this
state and in this country are, for the most part, men who
couldn't care less about the problems women face."

Seeing that his father was about to respond, Zachary
quickly took his sister's side. "She's right, Dad. Services for
women don't count for much when budget time rolls
around. If as many men were physically abused as women
and children, it would be treated much more seriously by the
government." Feeling a tug on his shirtsleeve, he looked
down at Katie, sitting in the high chair beside him. "Hey,
sweetheart, you've been so quiet that I almost forgot about
you."

She shyly gestured for him to lean closer. When he did,
she cupped her hand to his ear and whispered, "Shocolate,
please."

Cake crumbs and a messy smear of chocolate frosting
covered the high chair tray, her terry bib, her hands, her face
and now his shirtsleeve. Dabbing at the stain with his napkin, he asked, "Sarah, can Katie have another piece of
cake?"

"Oh, honey, you got Zachary's shirt dirty," Sarah gently admonished.

"Sorry, Sach." Katie made the *s*'s particularly sibilant,
then giggled at the sound. "More shocolate now, please?"

At Sarah's nod of approval, Zachary dished a small piece
of cake onto Katie's plate.

"*Someone* never gave her anything sweet until she was
more than a year old," Sarah said with a teasing glance at
her husband. "Now she's become a perfect little pig for your
cake, Mrs. Adams."

Daniel responded to Sarah's teasing with a dry look of his
own. "And she's getting as fat as a little pig, too."

Zachary watched them for a moment with a sense of yearning. For a long time he had told himself that it was wrong to be jealous of Daniel. But even though he knew no one deserved happiness as much as his friend, how could he *not* envy everything Daniel had—especially his sweet little girl and his loving wife—when he wanted those things for himself and saw no hope of finding them in the near future?

Predictably his thoughts went to Beth. Pretty, intelligent, cynical, didn't-believe-in-love Beth. What had she done in the forty-eight hours since he'd seen her? Work was a given; as she'd said herself, she always worked. But what else? Had she spent last night being lazy for the first time all week, maybe curled up on the sofa in front of the television? Or had she gone out on one of her *pleasant diversions* with some man who only wanted to be seen with one of *those* Gibsons? And did those dates, those few hours of pleasure, also include sex? Did they end in her bed or his? Did she carelessly give to those men she cared nothing about the precious gift of herself that *he* would treasure?

Leaving his questions unanswered, he put her out of his mind, but only for a while. Only until Sarah found him in a quiet moment alone after the table was cleared and the leftovers put away until supper.

"How is Beth?"

"Beautiful. Bright. Efficient. Guarded."

"Hmm. That doesn't sound encouraging."

He gave her a rueful grin. "Beth *isn't* encouraging. But she's a very good lawyer, and I can learn a lot from her, even if I can't get her to agree to dinner or a date." He grew more serious. "She's coming to Sweetwater tomorrow to interview the Lewis kids."

"Tell her to stop by and say hello if she has the time. It's been a long time since I've seen her."

He nodded, then shifted positions, making room for her on the sofa. "Have you ever met her family?"

"Just a few times. Beth looks just like her mother, but that's the extent of the similarities. Francine Gibson is..."

She was thoughtfully quiet for a moment; then she sighed. "Fragile. Easily upset. Weak. She's supposedly very nervous and frail, and that's why she constantly complains and fusses and nags. Personally, I think she's just a terribly unpleasant person."

"And her father?"

Sarah shuddered. "Walter was the man who made me finally realize that maybe growing up without a father wasn't such a bad thing after all. He's aggressive, loud and domineering. He ran Beth's life until she was eighteen, and I imagine he's still trying in one way or another to control her. Apparently he and Francine compete to see who can make life more miserable for the other one."

"And as a kid, Beth got caught in the middle."

"Beth was never a kid," Sarah corrected him with a faint smile. "In your wildest dreams, can you picture her with pigtails and overalls and mud on her face?"

She was right. The image simply wouldn't come. He imagined that Beth as a child must have been a younger, smaller version of the woman she'd become: calm, controlled, well-mannered and wary.

"All in all, she turned out remarkably well, considering her upbringing," Sarah mused. "Her family has financial holdings that would rival the defense budget, and she's always had the best of everything, but she's not the slightest bit snobbish. She was raised in an unstable household where screaming matches and smashing breakables were part of the daily routine, but she's very even-tempered. And although neither her mother nor her aunts or grandmothers ever did a day's work in their lives, she's supported herself ever since law school—which she paid for with student loans, because her father didn't want her to be a lawyer so he refused to pay any of her expenses."

Zachary had been watching Sarah closely while she spoke. When she finished, he quietly asked, "You like her a lot, don't you?" There was a look, a softness, that appeared in her eyes whenever she spoke of someone special to her: Daniel, Katie or Tony. It was there now for Beth.

"She's my best friend," Sarah said simply. "From the time Tony's illness was diagnosed until he died, she was my only friend. I couldn't have gotten through it without her."

From across the room Katie called her mother. Sarah and Zachary both looked up and saw Daniel dressing the wriggly little girl in her coat, hat and mittens. "I guess that means it's time to go," Sarah said, but she didn't rise from the sofa immediately. "Don't be impatient, Zachary. Something worth having is worth waiting and working for. And Beth is definitely worth having."

He walked to the door with her, said goodbye to her and Daniel, and gave Katie a kiss and a hug. Only a few moments after they left, he said his farewells to his parents and grandmother, too, and gave Alicia a big-brotherly hug.

"Why don't you stay for supper, Zachary?" his mother asked. "There's no reason for you to go home so early just to be all by yourself."

"I'm not going home yet. There are a few things I need to take care of at the farm."

"Do you need any help, son?" Josiah offered.

"No thanks, Dad." He needed what his mother had just denied, to be all by himself, but not at home. In his unfinished house.

It was a long drive up Laurel Mountain. Once he moved in, his closest neighbor would be three miles away. To someone used to the bright lights and convenience of the city, this place would probably seem unbearably lonesome, but he loved it here. He was going to love living here.

But he would love it a lot more if someone were living here with him.

He stopped to open the gate that blocked his driveway, then drove through, leaving it open. He wouldn't be here long today. A few hundred feet past the gate he passed the pine he'd cut down yesterday. Next weekend he would start chopping it into firewood. By the time the house was livable, the wood would be well seasoned and would offer many nights of cozy, fragrant fires.

The house itself stood a quarter of a mile up the hill. It was a simple farmhouse, the exterior virtually identical to the house his great-great-grandfather had built down the mountain when he'd first come to this area back in the 1800s. That house was gone now, destroyed by fire before Zachary was born, but photographs of it remained, and he'd used those as a starting point for this one.

Everything was balanced: the double doors exactly centered, the tall windows—three on each side of the doors and seven upstairs—and the twin chimneys, one at each end. The veranda ran the length of the house and, typical of southern homes, was more than ten feet wide, providing shade from the relentless summer sun and shelter from the spring rains. Daniel was making a pair of porch swings, one to hang from each end, to match the two big rockers Zachary had already bought from him.

Zachary walked around to the back of the house. There a tri-level deck with built-in benches took advantage of the best views. In spite of the day's cold, he sat down on one of the benches and stared out across the mountainside.

The little house in town where he'd lived since graduating from law school had never been anything more than a place to sleep and occasionally entertain, but this…this was *home*. Long before he'd had enough money to start the house, he'd come up here as often as he could to hike through the woods. He'd pitched a tent right here where the deck now stood and spent countless nights with nothing but the stars for company. From the time his grandfather had told him that this land would someday be his, he had known that he would live here.

Even if he fell for someone who would find it lonesome.

Even if *he* someday came to consider it lonesome.

Chapter 5

Beth parked in front of the building that housed Zachary's office and shut off the engine, then for a moment simply sat there. She was anticipating this meeting more than she should, and she'd been trying for the last twenty miles to put it into proper perspective—unsuccessfully. Since last seeing Zachary on Friday afternoon, she had discovered that, somewhere deep inside, she'd missed him. She, who hadn't been close to anyone but Sarah in the last ten years, had missed Zachary.

That was not a good sign.

Sighing, she got out of the car and quickly slipped into her coat, belting it at her waist. It was a nice wool coat that fell to mid-calf, the style simple, the color a conservative gray. It was warm and perfectly suitable for business, but she would have preferred the fur that shared its space in the closet at home. She liked its elegance, and she loved its luxuriance.

Taking her briefcase from the car, she locked the doors, then went inside. There were two doors opening off the broad hallway: wide, double glass doors that led into the bank and a single oak door with frosted glass that read Zachary Adams, Attorney. There were no hours listed and no lights shining within, and a twist of the doorknob revealed that it was locked. A glance across the hall showed that the bank was closed, too.

Small towns, she thought. At home she would have been in her office for at least an hour by now, her day well underway. But not Zachary.

She might as well find a cup of coffee, she decided, returning to the sidewalk outside. She had passed a small restaurant a few blocks away. Switching her briefcase to her other hand, she started in that direction.

Rosa's Diner was small, crowded and smelled of bacon and biscuits and rich, dark coffee. Beth was aware that her entrance resulted in a brief silence, but she ignored it and went to the lone empty booth in the back.

The waitress filled her coffee cup without asking, slapped a menu on the table, then walked away.

"My, my, Rosa's hasn't seen the likes of you in a long time."

Beth was searching through her briefcase when the teasing voice interrupted. She looked up to see Zachary leaning against the wall opposite her, a mug of coffee cradled in his hands. He looked less like a lawyer and more like a good ol' country boy than ever. His hiking boots were heavy and caked with mud, his jeans were faded, and his shirt was flannel in a red-and-gold plaid. The sleeves were rolled to his elbows, revealing some sort of long-sleeved thermal shirt underneath. He looked like a logger or a hunter or some other outdoorsy type—anything but a lawyer.

He looked wonderful.

"Mind if I join you for breakfast?"

She gestured toward the empty bench. As he sat down, he called to the waitress to serve his meal over here. When he was settled, she said, "I went by your office."

"I'm not there."

"No kidding," she said dryly. "Do you always sleep late, then eat a leisurely breakfast before showing up at the office?"

"Sleep late?" he echoed. "I've been up since five o'clock, lady, working up at the farm. If you'd told me you would be here at such an indecent hour, I would have been in my office waiting."

Beth pretended not to notice his easy use of the word lady. "Eight o'clock is indecent?"

"It is for business. Nothing gets going around here before nine or nine-thirty except the diner and the feed store." Without a break, he asked, "How was your weekend?"

She blinked, unsure how to answer. Of course she exchanged social niceties with the people in her office and her clients, but that was all they were. Niceties. Questions asked because it was polite. Questions whose answers didn't matter and often weren't even heard. But Zachary was waiting for her reply, and he certainly seemed interested. "It was all right," she said cautiously.

"What does that mean, 'all right'? That there weren't any major disasters? That you rested and relaxed? That you worked all weekend?"

Her patience slipped just a bit. "It means that it was okay. How was yours?"

"Productive. Relaxing." He gazed out the window for a moment before looking at her again. "Lonely."

Her throat was suddenly dry, but she couldn't take a drink because her hands were too unsteady to lift the cup. How could he say so much with only one small word and those pretty blue eyes of his? Because she *knew* he was talking about her, about being lonely for her. She knew it instinctively, in ways she couldn't begin to explain or even understand, ways she didn't *want* to understand.

Another bad sign, she thought uneasily. She could deal with her own errant thoughts. She could control those. But how could she deal with *his?*

"I had dinner with Sarah and Daniel yesterday. Sarah said to stop by if you have time."

It took her a moment to understand what he was saying; then she nodded. "I plan to. Now...about this interview..."

Zachary picked up the menu and offered it to her. "Order breakfast first."

"I never eat breakfast."

"You should. Didn't your teachers in those very expensive, snooty schools ever tell you that breakfast is the most important meal of the day?"

"But I'm not—" She broke off as the waitress set a platter in front of him. Ham, fried potatoes and onions, biscuits and cream gravy. Pure calories and cholesterol, her mind warned her. Heaven, her appetite disagreed.

"Same thing for the lady, Marcy," Zachary requested with a grin.

This time, as the waitress walked away, Beth fixed a cross scowl on him. "Don't call me that."

"I've never met a woman who objected so strenuously to being called a lady. Makes me wonder why."

Because every time he said it, she remembered what he'd said last week: *You must be a lady for somebody.* Because she knew all too well what it meant to be somebody's lady. Because she feared she could learn to want that, to enjoy it.

Because she feared she might want to be *his* lady. Zachary's lady.

"Why should I object to being addressed in such a sexist fashion?" she asked coolly, praying as she looked at him that he saw nothing in her face, no hint of her thoughts in her eyes.

Zachary was quietly thoughtful as he split and buttered a biscuit, then offered her half. She accepted it after a moment's hesitation. "I don't think I'm sexist," he said seriously. "Most of the strongest and most capable people I've ever known are women. I was raised by two independent, strong-willed, opinionated women who taught Alicia and me that every woman has the right to do or be whatever she wants. My grandmother was a schoolteacher and counselor who refused even to consider getting married and raising a family until she became the first female principal in the county. On the other hand, my mother chose to be a full-time wife and mother.''

Then he chuckled softly. ''Just yesterday I was defending my sister's views to my father, who *is* sexist, and now I'm defending my own to you. Sorry, Beth, but I can't see that calling you a lady is any more offensive than me being called a gentleman...except when your secretary does it. She manages to put a generous amount of disdain into that one word. I figure she must be an outstanding secretary, because you certainly didn't hire her for her personality.''

''Actually, I didn't hire her at all. She came with the office. She *is* a little distant, but she's very good at what she does.''

Of course, he thought. Beth was used to having the best. Could she ever settle for someone less than the best, the brightest, the most ambitious, the most successful? Would it count for something that he was trying to be the best *person* he could be? Did her methods of determining quality even remotely resemble his? He wasn't sure. Success for him meant having friends and family, helping people who needed it, managing his career the way he wanted, accepting payment for his services in free electrical work or a tune-up for his truck or a dozen jars of freshly canned preserves. It meant having time to go fishing and coach the Little League team and build his own house.

And success for Beth? It meant respect. Admiration. Outrageous fees. A partnership in an old, established firm. Name recognition. Thumbing her nose at her father.

Their perceptions of success were hardly compatible.

Marcy brought Beth's breakfast, and they remained silent for the first few minutes. When they were almost finished eating, Zachary said, ''I asked the Morrises to bring the kids to my office. They'll be there at nine.''

''How are the children?''

''Frightened. The little one doesn't understand what's happened, of course, but he misses his mother. The others are afraid that they're going to lose her for good.''

"Have they talked to their grandparents about what happened?"

Zachary shook his head. "Ruth has tried, but they just clam up. I imagine they were under orders from Carrie not to talk about their father's temper. She was ashamed of what he did to her, so she wouldn't want them telling anyone."

"Probably. But they're going to have to talk to us. We need their help."

He pushed his plate away, then rested his arms on the table. He didn't like the idea of interviewing the children. This business was ugly enough as it was; did they have to bring three little kids into it?

But the kids had already been brought into it. They had lived all their lives with the violence, the threats and the fear. It was all they knew.

"I know you don't want to do this," Beth said quietly. "If there's any way we can avoid putting them on the stand during the trial, we will. But I need to talk to them. We need to know whatever they can tell us."

"I understand that. I just think children should be protected somehow from adults' problems."

"That's a nice sentiment," she said flatly. "But it doesn't work. People like Lewis, people like—" She stopped suddenly, discomfort and embarrassment shadowing her eyes and her voice when she began again. "People like that don't care about what they're doing to their children. Their only interest is themselves—satisfying *their* needs, expressing *their* anger."

Had she started to include her parents in that statement? he wondered. They had worked at making each other miserable, Sarah had said. Screaming matches and smashing breakables were a daily routine. Beth herself had admitted that her mother and father tormented and degraded each other. And they obviously hadn't cared about what they were doing to their daughter. They hadn't cared that she had witnessed their fights, that she must have been frightened by them, that she must, to this very day, bear the secret scars caused by them.

Considering her own childhood, why had she taken Carrie's case? She had known from the beginning that there were children involved. Surely she had realized that it would stir old memories, old resentments. Why hadn't she told him, "Thanks, but no thanks. I'm not interested"?

He wished he could ask her, but he knew she wouldn't answer. Not only that, but she would probably find his nosiness offensive, and whatever little bit of progress he'd made with her would be undone.

When she finished the last of her coffee, he stood up, pulled some money from his pocket and tossed it on the table. He helped Beth with her coat, then retrieved his fleece-lined jacket from a rack near the door.

"Your town must not get many visitors," she remarked as they started down the street toward his office. "Everyone in there stared when I came in and again when we left."

"Well, you *are* a beautiful woman," Zachary said.

She replied wryly, "Oh, yes, red hair and pale skin are such a lovely combination."

He gave her a long, leisurely look, then softly repeated, "Yes, lovely." Then, his voice normal again, he added, "And, of course, everyone in town knows that Sarah Ryan's big-city, red-haired lawyer friend is defending Carrie, and that she has access to all the juicy secrets they can't find out."

"Ah, gossip. You must be a popular man."

"Not where it counts." He felt her sharp gaze on him, but he didn't look at her, didn't explain what he meant. She was a bright woman. She would figure it out.

At his office, he turned on the lights and the heat, then hung his coat on the tree beside the door. Beth kept hers on, although it didn't take long for the two rooms to warm up. Of course, compared to her office, both rooms were small. It wasn't as if the heating system was even close to over-taxed.

The Morrises were a few minutes early for their appointment. They shepherded the children in, then spent the first few moments unbundling them. Ruth looked tired, Zachary noticed. Caring for four young children at her age couldn't be easy. Maybe once Carrie's trial was over and it was certain that the kids would be with the Morrises for a long time, one of their other three daughters or their son's wife could help out on a regular basis.

He shook hands with Dutch and greeted Ruth, then introduced Beth to everyone.

"Mr. and Mrs. Morris, would you please take the younger children into the next room?" Beth asked. "I'd like to start with Tyler, and I'd like to talk to him alone."

Zachary escorted everyone else into the reception area, where he pulled a box of toys from underneath the empty desk. When he offered them to the children, the nine-year-old held back, but the younger two showed no qualms about digging through the contents.

He returned to his office, closing the door behind him. Beth was seated at his desk, and Tyler remained where he'd been, arms at his sides, head bowed, gaze directed downward. The bruises on his face were no longer vivid and puffy, but they still commanded attention. They were still the first thing he noticed about the boy.

Zachary touched his arm as he passed. "Have a seat here, Tyler," he suggested as he dropped into one of the chairs in front of the desk.

The boy stiffened and drew away from the contact, but accepted the offer of a chair.

"We're your mother's attorneys," Beth said, sounding as professional and businesslike as always, Zachary thought— maybe too much so for a fourteen-year-old boy. "We need to ask you some questions about your parents, starting with the night that your father was killed. What happened that evening, Tyler?"

He didn't speak, didn't look at them, didn't give any sign that he'd even heard her question.

Beth glanced at Zachary, then asked again, "What happened that Sunday night? How were your parents getting along?"

There was still no response.

"We're not asking you to say bad things about your father," Zachary said gently. "We just want the truth. We need to know the truth, Tyler, so we can help your mother."

He looked at Zachary then, his dark eyes cold and filled with anger. "You can't help her. She killed him. She murdered him. The police said so. *She* said so."

Leaning back in her chair, Beth gestured for Zachary to go on.

"Why did she kill him?"

"To make him stop."

"To make him stop what? What was he doing, Tyler?"

"He was hitting her. He was always hitting her. And nothing ever made him stop, not calling the police or threatening to leave, not anything." The anger disappeared from his eyes, leaving an emptiness that was terrible to see in one so young. "So she killed him."

"He hit you, too, didn't he?"

The boy raised his hand to the bruises, touching them, pressing on the worst one in a way that must have been painful. He was reminding himself, Zachary thought, of what his father had done to him. He was remembering the pain and the fear and the utter helplessness he'd felt that night.

"What happened Sunday night, Tyler?"

"He came home drunk, like he usually did. He—" He broke off, and for a moment the only sound in the room was the squeak of his tennis shoe when he twisted it against the wooden floor. Then he continued, his voice lower, more subdued. "He beat her up, like he usually did. Only usually he quit when he hurt her, but this time he just kept hitting her. Her eye was all swollen, and there was blood all over, and every time he hit her, the blood splattered on their clothes and on the wall behind her."

"Where were you when this happened?"

"With the other kids. Watching." He sounded rebellious, defensive.

Guilty? Zachary wondered. Did he feel guilty because he hadn't been able to help his mother? Or because maybe, if his father hadn't hit *him,* he would still be alive? "What happened next?" he asked quietly.

"He finally stopped. He fell asleep on the sofa. Mom went in the bedroom and stayed there."

"And what did you do?"

"I got the kids some supper, then put them to bed. Then I went to bed."

Each time he'd referred to his brothers and sister, Beth noticed, he called them "kids," as if *he* wasn't a child, too. But, age notwithstanding, maybe he *wasn't* a kid. Maybe he'd witnessed too much violence and brutality to retain any of the gentler qualities of childhood.

"What time was it when you went to bed?" Zachary asked.

He gave it a moment's thought. "About eight-thirty."

"Isn't that kind of early?"

The boy's look was tinged with cynicism. "When he was like that," he said flatly, "you didn't want to be around when he woke up."

She understood that in a way Zachary couldn't, Beth thought sadly. All he had ever experienced with his parents was love and respect. He didn't know what it was like to live with anger, rage, hatred and fear on a daily basis. He didn't know that in bed, surrounded by darkness, you could pretend that nothing else existed—only what was there, what you could see, which was nothing. If you tried hard enough, you could will yourself away to someplace safe. You might even fall asleep, in spite of the shouts and the crashes and the screams. You might even dream happy dreams.

And even *she* didn't understand in the way Tyler did. With all the anger and noise and rage of her parents' arguments, there had never been any physical violence. They might have thrown things at each other, but neither had ever raised a hand against the other in anger. What a terrifying thing to watch, knowing that you couldn't stop it.

"What do you remember after that?"

"My mother woke me up about ten and told me to get dressed. She said she had killed my father and that the police were coming to get her and that I needed to get the kids up and dressed."

"How did she act? Was she crying or frightened or distressed?"

Tyler gave Zachary another of those cynical looks. "She acted relieved. We were all relieved."

After the Morrises had taken their grandchildren home, Beth helped Zachary pick up the toys that littered the reception area. "You're the first lawyer I've ever known who kept a toy box in his office," she commented.

"This is a small town. People can't always afford or even find a baby-sitter every time they need to see a lawyer." He added the last stuffed animal, then slid the box under the desk again. "Katie Ryan is the real reason I bought these, although the other kids appreciate them. She was taking my office apart every time Daniel came in on business or to visit. I had to find a way to distract her."

Beth leaned against the desk. "You did a good job with Tyler. Sometimes I think I've forgotten how to deal with children. Other times I'm convinced I never knew."

"What do you think? Do you still want to talk to the younger kids?"

Tyler had blown up when she had suggested that he wait outside with his grandparents while she and Zachary talked to his younger brother and sister. The kids couldn't tell them anything that he hadn't already told them, he'd insisted. If they wanted his cooperation, they had to leave the little ones alone.

"Tyler doesn't strike me as the type to make meaningless threats," she remarked. "If we try to interview the other children, I believe he *will* refuse to cooperate. Since we may need his testimony, that's not something we want to risk."

"I feel sorry for the kid," Zachary said. "For all of them, but especially Tyler. He's too grown up, too responsible, too..."

"Damaged." Beth returned to the inner office to get her coat and briefcase. "He may never get over everything that's happened."

"I don't know. Love can heal almost anything, and even if they can't give him much of anything else, Ruth and Dutch can love him."

Her responding laugh was dry and cynical. "You're a romantic, aren't you, counselor? You really believe in family and commitment and the healing power of love."

He had followed her as far as the doorway. Now, as she approached, her coat on and belted, the handle of her briefcase gripped in both hands, he refused to move aside and allow her to leave. "I guess I am," he agreed quietly. His voice dropping even lower, he asked, "And what are you?"

Before she could answer, he reached out and lifted her hair free of the collar of her coat, his fingers brushing against her neck. Although she knew on one level that they were callused and rough, on another level—one of pure sensation—she thought it was the softest, gentlest touch she'd ever known. The contact fueled the longing she'd been trying so hard to suppress. It filled her with a heat that couldn't be blamed on the room temperature or her heavy coat, a heat that came from inside, a heat that threatened her defenses and her good sense and her self control—all the things that had kept her safe the last ten years.

Then he withdrew his hand, slid it into his hip pocket and waited. For what? she wondered dazedly. Oh, yes, an answer. He had asked her a question, and now he was waiting for an answer. *And what are you?*

"A realist," she replied with just a touch of regret in her voice. "I believe in the law, and I believe in myself. No one else." She took a step closer, pointedly meeting his gaze, letting him see that there was nothing *to* see, and finally he moved aside.

She stopped at the outer door and faced him again. He remained near the other door, both hands in his pockets, his gaze directed at the floor. He looked weary—not physically, but mentally, emotionally. "Will you be in the city tomorrow?"

"Probably in the afternoon. I have a couple of appointments here in the morning."

She nodded, even though he couldn't see. She didn't know what else to say, didn't know if anything else was even necessary, but she couldn't just turn and walk away. "Well . . . be careful."

He looked up then and gave her a bittersweet smile. "You've been careful all your life, Beth. What has it gotten you?"

On that note, she *did* simply turn and walk away. But his question haunted her all the way to her car, all the way up the mountain to Sarah Ryan's house for a brief visit and all the way back to Nashville. What *had* she achieved by being careful? Her heart was intact and guaranteed to stay that way. Her career was on track and could only improve. She was in control of her life.

And she was alone. Unhappy. Dissatisfied. Missing something unknown.

What had she achieved by being careful? she wondered morosely. What indeed?

"How's life in the city?"

"Duck," Zachary instructed Katie, perched on his shoulders, as they walked through a doorway in his new house. With Daniel's help, he was working on the master bedroom this chilly Saturday morning, and together they were baby-sitting Katie until her mother returned from the beauty shop to get her. He didn't mind the distraction of trying to keep up with an inquisitive little girl whose energy level was more than double his own, but work would progress much more quickly once Sarah got back.

In answer to Daniel's question, he shrugged, the action making Katie giggle. "You've been to Nashville. What did you think?"

"Too many people."

"Amen to that," Zachary heartily agreed.

"Amen," Katie echoed, then commanded, "Put me down, Sach." At a look from her father, she amended that. "Put me down *please,* Sach."

"The place is overcrowded, frustrating, confusing, expensive and unfriendly—at least, compared to Sweetwater," Zachary continued as he swung Katie to the floor. "I can't leave the motel without a map, and I still have trouble finding my way around. And the people in Beth's firm—" Breaking off, he shook his head. "They are the snootiest and least helpful bunch of people I've ever come across. Of course, the fact that this case is a freebie and I brought it to Beth's attention doesn't endear me to any of them. Neither does the fact that I'm just a small-time country lawyer."

He pulled his coat off and hung it on the doorknob, then crossed the room to the window on the east wall. Unlike newer windows that consisted of a single sheet of glass and created the illusion of having panes with the use of plastic inserts, this window, filling almost the entire wall, was made of individual panes separated by pine sash bars the color of honey. All the woodwork in the house was the same, and the rockers Daniel had made, as well as the porch swings, matched.

They had positioned the house on the lot so that the best view was here: from his bedroom upstairs and the living room below. There was a wildflower meadow, too many trees to count and, overshadowing it all, the peak of Laurel Mountain, rising a thousand feet above.

Turning his back on the mountain, he studied the bedroom. There were two levels, one comprising about two-thirds of the room, including the big stone fireplace. That was where the bed would go, facing the window. On the upper level was a long narrow space for a couch and chairs, a cozy, comfortable place for reading or watching the sunset.

This house had been designed with a family in mind, he thought with a grim sigh. All of it, like this room, was meant to be shared and lived in and loved in. It wasn't meant for one man alone.

And somehow he was more alone now than he'd been two weeks ago.

Beth had hardly spoken to him all week, other than to give him instructions or directions. The preliminary hearing was scheduled for next Wednesday. He'd told himself that that was why she was so preoccupied and distant. But deep inside he knew it wasn't that at all. He'd made her uncomfortable in his office last Monday, touching her—however innocently—and she hadn't forgiven him for it. She knew that he wanted more from her than a professional relationship, and she wasn't willing to offer it. Although he should have found some comfort in the knowledge that it wasn't anything personal—she wouldn't offer a relationship to *any* man right now—he hadn't.

The work he was doing was the only bright spot. He'd found the case histories Beth had given him to study fascinating. He'd sat in on conference calls with two of their expert witnesses and come away with a much deeper understanding of what Carrie Lewis had been through and why she'd reacted the way she had. He had conducted more interviews, this time with Del Lewis's former employers and co-workers.

His involvement in the case was strictly junior league—on-the-job training that any investigator or fresh-out-of-law-school attorney could have handled just as well. Although he would sit at the defense table with Beth and Carrie for both the preliminary hearing and the trial, he most likely wouldn't speak, wouldn't question any witnesses, wouldn't present any evidence. Still, he was learning. He was gaining a new respect for trial lawyers in general and for Beth in particular.

And along with that growing respect was a growing attraction. A growing need. A growing hunger.

And a growing sense of hopelessness.

Beth stood in front of the full-length mirror in her dressing room and studied her reflection critically, not in a typically feminine fashion to gauge her attractiveness, but rather her professionalism. The judge who was presiding over Carrie's preliminary hearing today was a stickler for appearances. Casually dressed attorneys didn't fare well in his courtroom.

She certainly looked the part of an assured, successful lawyer. Her suit was navy blue, well-made but not flashy. There were no frills, nothing to draw attention to the outfit, and the hem ended demurely at the knee. Her hair was drawn away from her face, twisted and pinned in a loose roll. It was severe enough to project an image of authority, yet soft enough to satisfy her vanity. She wore no jewelry except the gold Rolex she'd treated herself to last Christmas; her makeup was skillfully subdued, and the fragrance she wore was faint and elusive.

A glance at her watch showed that she still had a few minutes before Zachary arrived. They had decided to go straight to the courthouse this morning, so he was meeting her here at the condo instead of the office. Then they would have a few moments with Carrie to explain what would happen today. She'd done that during their meeting yesterday, but it wouldn't hurt to go over it again.

Wouldn't it be a surprise if the judge dismissed the charges? she thought dryly as she moved a few items she needed from her purse into her briefcase. She had proceeded with the case as if it would undoubtedly go to trial. If it was dismissed, what a victory for Carrie. What a waste of all the work she and Zachary had done.

And what a shame, having no excuse to see him again.

Slipping into her heels, she took one last look in the mirror, then left the bedroom and went down the broad stairs. This would be the first time Zachary had been to her home.

She wondered as she reached the entry what he would think of it. He would probably be impressed—everyone who came here was—although not wildly so. Being the practical sort, he would probably wonder how she could stand to live in such a big place all by herself.

He would probably also wonder how she could live in such an unwelcoming place, she added as she walked slowly through the rooms. They were spacious, the ceilings high, the furnishings contemporary, the colors minimal. They weren't the kind of rooms that invited you to snuggle in and get comfortable. There was a formality to them that was daunting, a sterility that was...

Frightening. A home should reflect the people who lived there. Was this place a reflection of her—cold, empty, unwelcoming, sterile? Was that what she had become in the years since Philip had unleashed, then destroyed, her passion, her pride and her love?

Suddenly she wished she had told Zachary to meet her at the office. She didn't want him to see this place, didn't want him to make any connection between her and this emptiness. But the chime of the doorbell warned her that it was too late. He was already here.

She opened the elaborately carved door and invited him inside while she got her coat. As she put it on, she studied his appearance much as she had her own upstairs. His usual jeans and cotton shirt had been replaced by a dark gray suit with a pale blue shirt and a neatly knotted tie. Instead of comfortable boots, he wore black dress shoes, shoes that he'd probably had for years, she guessed, but wore only on special occasions. They would last him forever.

His fleece-lined jacket was gone, too, given up in favor of a plain black overcoat. All he needed was a briefcase and he would blend in perfectly with dozens of other young Nashville lawyers. He would even blend in with the young lawyers in her own office, she thought with some dismay.

She preferred the country lawyer, the jeans and boots, the easy, relaxed, pleasant man whose demeanor invited trust. Who would have believed it of her?

After enduring her scrutiny for several moments, Zachary asked, "Do I look all right?"

She smiled uneasily. "You look fine."

"Like a real lawyer?"

His good-natured grin took the edge off her discomfort. "Like a *city* lawyer. Shall we go?"

They left his Jeep in the parking garage and took her car downtown. When they reached the courthouse, Zachary said, "We have time for a cup of coffee. Do you want one?"

She shook her head. "I never eat or drink anything before a criminal trial."

He gave her a long, surprised look. "Are you nervous?"

"Aren't you?"

"Why should I be? All I have to do is sit back and let you handle everything."

"And that's why I *should* be. There's a lot at stake here."

"There's a lot at stake in most trials."

"Not like this." There was Carrie herself, a sad, helpless person if ever there was one. And her kids—Tyler and his brothers and sister. There was the baby she carried, the baby she would probably deliver in prison. And there were the other women, women in the same situation, women who might be driven to resolve it in the same way. This trial could have an impact on the legal system across the country. If they lost here, it could hurt the cause of battered women everywhere.

"Do you regret taking the case?"

She gave it a moment's thought, even though she knew the answer immediately. "No. I wish I could handle more cases like this. Important cases. Cases where I can really make a difference."

"So why don't you?"

"And spend the rest of my life battling with the partners over expenses and my lack of billable hours?" she asked dryly. "They voted me in, you know. They can vote me right back out."

"Then you could go into business for yourself. You could take only the kinds of cases that you want—important ones," he said, turning her words back on her. "Cases where you make a difference. Cases like this one, where probably no other attorney in Nashville could do for Carrie what you can."

Odd that he should suggest that, she thought as they went into a small, private conference room to wait for Carrie. Just the other day the idea of leaving the firm had entered her mind for the first time ever, and it had stunned her. But Zachary talked as if it were the most logical thing in the world.

Of course, things were different for him. He'd been in practice alone for his entire career. He wouldn't do well in a firm where he was accountable to others, where he had to defend his choice of cases and his expenses, where he was under constant pressure to bring in as much business—meaning income—as possible. He obviously liked being his own boss, setting his own hours, his own agenda, living by his own rules.

She liked to think that she was her own boss, too, that she ran her career and her life herself. She made that claim, but it wasn't true, not really. Her partners had almost as much authority over her as her father had had when she was younger. No matter how much they valued her, she still needed their approval. She still had to take cases that bored her, still had to represent clients who offended her, because it was good for the firm.

But what was good for *her?* she wondered.

Zachary pulled off his overcoat, then sat down at the small table that nearly filled the room. He resisted the temptation to loosen his tie and ran his fingers through his hair instead. "What is there to do in this town at night?" he asked, deliberately changing the subject from business. "I've watched television until my brain is threatening to malfunction; I've read until my eyes are crossed, and there's a limit to how many hours a person can sleep each night."

Beth was standing in the corner, shifting slightly to and fro—a calm, controlled person's version of pacing, he assumed. She gave him a slightly blank look that said her mind was elsewhere, then shook her head slightly as if to clear it. "There are quite a few clubs here, something for every preference," she began. "If you like country music, of course, there's the Grand Ole Opry. Nashville has some excellent restaurants and . . ." She stopped to think.

"You keep so busy that you don't know what night life is, do you?" he asked with a grin.

She responded with a slightly chagrined smile. "I haven't been out in a long time," she admitted.

"That could be changed." He spoke softly, half afraid that raising his voice or using a bolder tone would scare her off. "Tonight."

"I don't mix business and pleasure," she warned.

"I've been waiting for you to say that," he responded with a grin that faded as quickly as it had come. "But at least you admit that it could be pleasurable." It wasn't enough. It wasn't "Yes, Zachary, I'd like to go out with you." It wasn't even any reason to hope.

But he did. He was suddenly very hopeful indeed.

Chapter 6

Before Beth could say anything else, Carrie was brought into the room under guard. She chose the chair farthest away from both of them and sat down, folding her hands over her swollen stomach. The action pulled taut the fabric of the dress they had picked up earlier at her house.

Zachary couldn't imagine anyone who fit the image of a murderer less than Carrie Lewis did. She was such a fragile, harmless-looking little creature. Hopefully, the jury would see her the same way. Her appearance alone might influence them in her favor.

"Carrie, your preliminary hearing starts soon," Beth said, taking a seat nearby. "I explained to you yesterday what would happen. Do you remember?"

She nodded. "The judge is going to decide whether I have to go to trial." She looked from Beth to Zachary, her expression hopeful. "Do you think I will?"

Because her gaze was locked with his, Zachary answered. "Probably. It's not likely that they'll dismiss it at this stage."

The hopefulness faded and was replaced by the same dull, empty look Beth associated with her. "Do I have to stay in jail until then?"

"They won't release you without bail," she replied. "Your family can't afford to pay it, and you certainly can't. Are you having any problems, Carrie? Are the other inmates harassing you?"

"No. Nobody bothers me. It's just..." She trailed off and shrugged helplessly. "I want to see my kids."

That was a reasonable request. He was surprised she'd waited so long to make it. "I'll talk to your parents and see if we can arrange a visit."

"You won't have to testify today, Carrie," Beth said, drawing her attention. "You'll sit at the table with Zachary and me and just listen. The state has to show proof that a crime was committed and reasonable cause to believe that you did it."

"And what are you going to do?"

"Ordinarily, I would try to convince the judge that you didn't do it and that the evidence is insufficient to warrant a trial. But we're not denying that you killed your husband. Instead we're trying to prove that you were driven to it, that you had no other choice."

"Some of the women in the jail say that if I'd killed him when we were fighting, I probably wouldn't even have been arrested," Carrie said softly. "Is that true?"

Beth nodded.

"If I'd tried that, he would have killed me for sure." Her voice dropped to a whisper. "I thought he was going to, anyway."

The effect of her words hovered in the air long after the sound had faded. Her simple statement touched Zachary with its resignation and its utter hopelessness. It made him realize once again the true importance of this case. It wasn't a chance to learn from a better attorney, as he'd told himself, or an opportunity to add a felony defense to his résumé, or even an occasion to get close to Beth.

It was a chance to save Carrie's life.

With a soft sigh, she looked from him to Beth. "So how are you going to convince them that I had no other choice? People are going to think, 'If he was so bad, why didn't she just leave him?'"

"We're going to use the battered woman syndrome as our defense," Beth explained. "In its simplest terms, it means that a woman who has been routinely and brutally beaten isn't truly responsible for her actions, that she's driven by events and forces beyond her control. What she thinks, what she feels and does, is governed by all the trauma, all the fear and stress, that she's lived with over the years. In that state of mind, killing Del seemed to be—to you—the rational solution. He was the source of the fear and the pain. He was the threat to your life and to your children's lives."

"But he was asleep when I killed him. People will think he wasn't much of a threat sound asleep."

Even with her lack of knowledge about the law, Beth thought with a faint smile, Carrie had zeroed in on her biggest concern. "We'll just have to convince them otherwise," she replied as the bailiff tapped on the door. She picked up her briefcase, then reached over and squeezed Carrie's hand. It wasn't an easy gesture for either of them. Carrie wasn't accustomed to receiving casual touches any more than Beth was to giving them. But it was the start of a lesson they both needed to learn. That physical contact didn't always result in pain. That touching could be gentle, tender, friendly, reassuring. That sometimes one person's touch could heal the pain another's had inflicted.

Zachary's touch that morning in his office had been gentle, tender and so many other things. It hadn't caused her pain. Maybe, with time and faith, it could bring healing. Maybe he could make her forget the pain of loving Philip.

But then who, she wondered bleakly, would make her forget Zachary?

Just as the arraignment had been no less than Beth had expected, her predictions about the previous day's preliminary hearing were also borne out. Carrie was held over for trial, the date set nearly a month away. Less than two weeks before Christmas. What a joyous holiday season this was going to be for the Lewis kids, Zachary thought.

He was sprawled on the couch in Beth's office, one heavy law book open on his lap and a half dozen others stacked around him. He'd been reading for the last three hours, and he was considering the benefits of a long nap on the short couch when Beth, across the room at her desk, spoke.

"Thanksgiving."

Marking his place in the book with his finger, he closed it and looked up at her. "What about it?"

She was fiddling with the appointment book in front of her. She looked startled when he spoke, as if she hadn't realized she'd said the word aloud. With a shrug, she closed the book and left her desk, coming to sit at the opposite end of the sofa. "Thanksgiving is next Thursday. Carrie's in jail facing the fight of her life, and her kids are struggling along without her or their father, and I'm moping because I have to spend Thanksgiving at my parents' house."

"At least you'll have something to be thankful for—when it's over." He wondered what the holiday would be like in the Gibson home. He was sure it wouldn't hold a candle to an Adams family celebration. Last year they'd crammed nearly fifty relatives and friends into his parents' house. There had been enough food to feed two hundred and fifty, and enough noise and boisterous play from the young and the young at heart to send any sensitive person running the other way.

"It really won't be quite so bad," she mused, slipping her shoes off and tucking her feet beneath her. "This year we're having company, and my parents are generally well behaved around guests. If I can manage to arrive after most of the guests and leave before them, it should be . . . all right."

"You ought to find yourself a new family. Thanksgivings aren't meant to be 'all right.' They're supposed to be celebrations, days you look forward to, happy times spent with people you love."

''How do you survive in the nineties with an outlook better suited to the fifties?'' she asked dryly. ''I've never met anyone as old-fashioned as you are.''

His eyes narrowing, Zachary considered her remarks. They felt uncomfortably like an insult, but he took no offense. He *was* old-fashioned. And although he hadn't been born until the late fifties, he wouldn't have minded being an adult then. He preferred simpler times and simpler places. That was part of the reason he liked Sweetwater. It was an old-fashioned town, where everyone knew everyone else, where people looked out for one another and offered help to anyone who needed it.

The only place his life got complicated was right here: with Beth. With his taste for simple things, how in the world had he gotten involved with the most complex woman he'd ever met?

''There's something to be said for old-fashioned values,'' he said, opening the book again. ''Look at the problems this country faces—crime, teen pregnancies, poverty, drugs. If people were a bit more old-fashioned, if they took an interest in their communities, if they helped those who need it, if they didn't wash their hands of responsibility even for their own actions, those problems could be brought under control.''

''The Adams solution to the nation's ills,'' she said airily. ''Don't you find that line of reasoning the slightest bit naive, counselor?''

This time he *was* insulted. He gave her a cool, unwavering stare. ''I'd rather be naive than cynical. I'd rather believe in something as old-fashioned as family and as romantic as love than in nothing at all.'' He closed the book, dumped the whole stack on the table and retrieved his jacket. ''If you have no objections, I'll take these books back to the motel with me and finish there.''

Beth felt a panicky flutter in her chest. She truly hadn't meant to insult him. The words had just slipped out without thought. Swiftly she rose to her feet, reaching out but stopping without touching him. ''Zachary, wait. I'm sorry.

I shouldn't have said that. I know you're not naive, and I really didn't mean to make fun of you.''

He stopped in the act of picking up the books, then slowly straightened. "What's the problem here, Beth? Is this your natural superiority coming through? Do you think you're entitled to put me down because of the way you grew up? Because of who you are? Granted, I wasn't raised the way you were, but, hell, how many people in this city were?" Dragging his hand through his hair in frustration, he continued without giving her a chance to respond. "You don't like the way I think or dress. You don't like the things I believe in. You don't like the way I practice law. You don't want to be friends with me or have dinner with me or talk to me about anything except business. Why the hell did you even agree to work with me on this?"

"Do you want to have dinner tonight?" The offer was out before she could think better of it, before she could give herself a hundred and one arguments against it.

For a moment he just looked at her. She half expected him to say no, to refuse her invitation as quickly as she'd refused his in the past. She wouldn't blame him at all if he did. But when he finally spoke, he ignored her offer. "I want an answer," he said quietly, tiredly.

What could she say? That no matter what excuses she'd given herself at the time, she had agreed to his participation in this case partly because of her attraction to him? Not likely. She couldn't tell him the truth, but she couldn't lie to him, either.

So instead she hedged. "I told you last week that I'd forgotten how to relate to children." With a nervous little sigh, she continued. "I guess I've forgotten how to relate to people in general. I can handle clients, associates, partners and family…but I don't have any friends. Sarah is the only one, and I hardly ever see her. I'm not sure I know how to be friends with anyone."

He simply looked at her, not saying a word, but the hostility was fading from his eyes.

"I'm not even sure I *want* to be friends with anyone," she added quietly. "It seems safer not to. But it can be very lonely." That was part of her dissatisfaction. She talked to dozens of people, but she rarely had a simple conversation. She had plenty of companionship in the form of no-strings-attached dates, but that was lonely, too, because there was no connection. No affection. No meaning.

"Is that what life boils down to for you?" he asked quietly. "Being safe? Not taking risks?"

"It's easier that way."

"No, it's not. Having someone to care for, someone who cares about you, someone who shares your life and your problems and your worries and your successes—*that's* easier, Beth. Sharing your life with someone else doesn't weaken you. It makes you stronger." He shook his head in dismay. "How can you live such different lives? You take chances professionally. As a lawyer, particularly as a female lawyer practicing criminal law, you take chances every day. But in your personal life... hell, you don't even have a personal life, because it's safer that way. It's easier."

Beth tore her gaze from his and turned to slip into her shoes. It was such a simple action, but it made her feel more secure. Better prepared to defend herself.

Except that she had no defense. Everything he'd said was accurate. Rather than admit it to him, rather than offering a defense when the only defense was the truth, she smiled coolly and asked, "So... do you want to have dinner?"

After a brief perplexed look, Zachary slowly smiled. It wasn't charming or boyish or sweet, but a bit rueful and a lot resigned. "I'll pick you up at home at seven."

She opened her mouth to tell him that she never made it home before eight, then closed it again. Seven would be fine.

That settled, he picked up the books and started toward the door.

"Where are you going?"

"Back to the motel."

"But it's only three o'clock."

"Good. I can avoid the traffic and still get some work done." With a wave, he disappeared out the door.

Beth slowly returned to her desk and sat down. Picking up the appointment book, she tossed it into the middle drawer, then considered the work in front of her. Maybe she should follow Zachary's example. There was nothing here that couldn't be done at home—letters to dictate, an expense record to update, three medical journal articles on spouse abuse to read. Why not, for the first time in her eleven years with the firm, go home early and finish her work there?

Without giving it further thought, she put everything in her briefcase and told her secretary where she was going. Half an hour later she was home.

The office there was the only room she really liked. The walls were painted a deep, rich teal, and oak bookcases filled every inch of available space. Her desk was an antique, big and heavy and solid, and the chairs, one behind the desk and two in front of the marble fireplace, were designed for comfort.

The grate was already laid with firewood. She lit the gas jets and set the wood ablaze, then kicked off her shoes and settled into one of the nearby chairs. It was nice working in front of the fireplace on such a cold day, she decided. Maybe she ought to try it more often. And after she got used to it, she could graduate to truly playing hooky from work, taking time off for nothing more important than shopping or a movie or no reason at all.

For the first time in weeks she quit working at quitting time and went upstairs for a leisurely bath. Afterward she dressed in black slacks and a silk tunic that matched her eyes. She reapplied her makeup, put on her favorite diamond earrings and dabbed perfume on all her pulse points. She was standing in front of the coat closet downstairs, wondering where Zachary would take her, debating whether to wear her simple wool coat or the luxurious long fur jacket she'd splurged on for her last birthday, when the doorbell rang. The wool if he was wearing jeans, she decided, and the fur if he was, by chance, in a suit.

The wool won out. This was the country lawyer, in jeans, a pale blue shirt and a silvery-gray corduroy jacket. As much as she loved her fur, she didn't mind.

"I half expected you to change your mind," he said in place of a greeting.

"I probably should have," she acknowledged.

"It's just dinner," Zachary said, his gaze slowly moving from her hair, gleaming and smooth and swinging free, all the way down to her feet. "You know, food? Sustenance? It's not a commitment."

Not that he wouldn't willingly accept one from her, he thought regretfully. Even a short-term something—relationship, affair, friendship—would be better than nothing.

Short-term was all they could ever have. Beth would never leave her city, her profitable practice and her prestigious firm for a nowhere town like Sweetwater. She would never give up her career to be anyone's wife or mother, but Sweetwater and the surrounding communities could never support two lawyers.

And he couldn't leave home for the city, not on a permanent basis. He couldn't cope with the crowds and the traffic and the crime. He couldn't live with the anonymity inherent in a city the size of Nashville. He couldn't survive away from his family, his farm and his mountains.

Not even for love.

Turning away from that depressing thought, he asked, "Do I ever get a tour of this place, or are you always going to keep me standing in the hall?"

She had one arm in her coat. She paused, then slipped it off and laid it over the stair railing. "There's not much to see," she warned as she led the way into the living room.

But she was wrong, Zachary thought. There was something to see from practically every room. The condominium shared the top two floors of a high-rise building, and the outer walls were primarily glass. The lights of Nashville spread for miles in every direction. It would be an impressive sight during the day.

As for the apartment itself, though, she was right. There wasn't much to see—just elegantly decorated rooms that would look just right in some fancy interior design magazine, but not in somebody's home. There were no homey touches, no personal flavor, no commonplace clutter, in any of the rooms—nothing that said Beth Gibson lived here. Nothing that said *anyone* lived here. Even her room, which he caught only a glimpse of, more closely resembled some luxurious hotel suite than a bedroom.

"Don't feel obliged to comment," Beth said as they descended the stairs. "The decorator went a little overboard, but I'm not here enough to mind."

He wondered if that was true. If she really didn't mind, she wouldn't even have noticed the chilly, unlived-in feeling of the place. "If I were decorating this place for you," he remarked, "I would use wood. Nothing exotic—cherry and mahogany and walnut. And stone—not marble, but granite. And lots of colors, bright ones, bold ones. No white, no pastels, no gray or black—although," he added with a grin, "I would probably keep those black sheets on the bed."

There had been just a hint of them where the white down comforter had snagged. What an image that created—Beth's red hair and delicate ivory skin against night-black sheets. It was enough to make him clench his teeth to keep a soft groan from escaping.

"My mother's decorator is responsible for this," Beth commented, completely unaware of the direction his thoughts had taken. "Maybe when I redo it, I'll send her to talk to you. Anything would be an improvement over this."

Yes, indeed, Zachary thought as he followed her out. Anything at all would be an improvement over *this*—this way he was feeling. These thoughts he was thinking. These needs she was arousing. All with no hope of relief. No hope of satisfaction.

He stepped out of the elevator and into the frigid garage with a muted sigh. There was no chance for a cold shower, but this was the next best thing.

Then the image returned once more: Beth naked and beautiful on those wicked sheets, not alone, but with him. Not passive but passionate. Not just lovely but loving.

A short walk in thirty-degree temperatures wasn't the next best thing for what ailed him, he admitted grimly. In fact, it was a depressingly poor substitute for what he really wanted.

For what he really needed.

For what he *had* to have.

Beth was feeling guilty.

They had lingered for two hours over dinner, and not once had she thought about all the work waiting for her at home. Not once had she wished, as she always did on dates, that she was someplace alone—in her office working, in her bed asleep or anywhere except where she was. Not once had she regretted asking Zachary out.

And for those reasons, she should regret it. Nothing but sorrow could come from getting involved with him, and it would break every rule she'd ever set for herself. They were simple rules: don't get personal with people you work with. Don't get personal with people so vastly different from you. Don't get personal with anyone you might care for. Don't get personal at all. She'd followed them for ten years, only to come perilously close to suddenly forgetting them all now.

Zachary was, for the time being, her associate. He always had been and always would be vastly different. He was definitely someone she could care for. He was a threat she couldn't handle . . . and a temptation she couldn't resist.

"Do you want dessert?"

She looked at the tray of sweets and pastries the waiter held. They all looked sinfully rich and delicious, but with a regretful sigh, she shook her head. Even if she liked to exercise, which she didn't, her schedule left precious little time for it. Spending so many hours at her desk meant watching her weight by watching her diet. "Just coffee, please."

"No sweet tooth, huh?" Zachary asked after ordering coffee, too.

"I have one. I just control it."

"You like being in control, don't you? And you don't like emotional extremes—anger, exhilaration, passion."

She studied him coolly. "We all took one or two psychology courses in college, Zachary, but it doesn't qualify any of us to practice."

He waved that off. "All lawyers analyze to some extent—clients, opposing counsel, judges. Tell me you don't know the strengths and weaknesses of every attorney you've ever faced in court."

"That's part of the job."

"So—"

"This isn't." She knew that would quiet him. He would be surprised into silence at her pointed reminder that this was a date. Personal, not business.

And he *was* silent, for all of sixty seconds. Then he returned to the subject. "You also like to control the conversation. You did it this afternoon and again just now."

After an uncomfortable moment of silence, she admitted, "You're right. I like being in control." Then, unexpectedly, she asked, "What's your earliest memory?"

"What does that have to do—"

She silenced him with a gesture, then waited.

He thought about it. "Fishing with my grandfather." The hint of a sweet smile touched his mouth and his eyes and her heart.

"*My* first memory is my parents fighting. I don't know how old I was, but I know I was afraid. They were shouting and swearing, and my mother was throwing whatever was handy, and I thought . . . I must have thought the world was coming to and end. I was terrified." She smiled, too, but knew it had none of the innocence of Zachary's. "I used to run and hide in my closet whenever they fought, but I couldn't block out the noise. I couldn't hide from the anger. I couldn't get away from the malice.''

She fell silent as the waiter served their coffee. Zachary sweetened his, but she took hers black.

''My parents never took me to church,'' she continued, ''but my great-grandmother was a religious woman, and she taught me little prayers to say at bedtime. Every night for years I prayed that they would get a divorce. That he would move out. That we would have one night a week, or maybe even two, of peace. That their battles—their disagreements—would stop. That was what Mother called them. Disagreements. 'Walter and I had a slight disagreement last night,' she'd say as the maid swept up five hundred dollars' worth of shattered crystal.''

She glanced at Zachary only obliquely, then turned her gaze on the other diners around them. ''By the time I was twelve or so, I'd decided God wasn't listening, or He just didn't care. I gave up praying, but they never gave up fighting.'' She tested her coffee and found it too hot. ''Yes, I like being in control. For eighteen years my parents controlled my life. Now *I* do. And no, I don't like emotional extremes. I find them unsettling.''

''But don't you find it tiring to always be restraining yourself?'' he asked softly. ''Just once, wouldn't you like to lose your temper? To jump for joy? To scream with excitement? To enjoy a wild and wicked affair? To love someone? To hate someone?''

To enjoy a wild and wicked affair? Even her affair with Philip couldn't be described as wild and wicked. Making love with him had been satisfying, but not steamy. Enjoyable, but not breath-stealing. No, her pleasure in Philip had been in loving him, in believing for the first time since her great-grandmother had died that she was loved in return.

She could learn to lose her temper and even to jump for joy. But to scream for any reason? To be wild and wicked? Those things weren't in her character. Neither was loving. And if she didn't care enough about any man to love him, how could she care enough to hate?

"This is who I am," she said, hearing the note of apology in her voice but making no effort to disguise it. Then she smiled lamely. "The personality I have has stood me in good stead for thirty-six years."

"If you don't mind being lonely. If you don't mind the idea of being alone for the rest of your life."

Six months ago she would have denied ever feeling lonely. She would have insisted that a lifetime by herself was exactly what she wanted. Six weeks ago she might have acknowledged the loneliness, but she still would have denied any desire to share her future with anyone. Now, she admitted, it looked a little bleak.

Safe, but bleak.

"You're a fine one to talk," she replied, turning the focus on him. "*I* never intended to fall in love or get married, so I can be excused for remaining alone. But *you've* always intended to do those things. Here you've spent the better part of the last three weeks in a city filled with single, marriage-minded women, and how have you spent your free time? Watching television, reading and sleeping. At the rate you're going, Zachary, you'll be spending the rest of your life alone, too. And that's not what you want." That would be too unfair, she thought silently—to the woman he would one day love, to the children they would someday have, and to himself.

They finished their coffee in silence; then Zachary paid the check, and they went out into the cold night. He remained quiet on the drive back to her condo. Was he thinking about what she'd said? Beth wondered. Realizing, maybe, that this was a perfect opportunity for him to meet some women, to look for that special woman he'd waited all his life for? How would she feel, spending every evening working alone in her office or moping alone in her house and knowing that he was taking other women to dinner and possibly to bed?

Relieved, she tried to tell herself, because the sooner he got out of her life, the quicker she could get him out of her mind.

Jealous, she finally admitted. Even if she couldn't have him herself, she didn't want to know he was with someone else. She didn't want to know that some other woman was receiving what he wanted to give, and giving him what *she* couldn't.

He parked on the top level of the garage and walked to the elevator with her. When the doors slid open, she turned to tell him that he didn't need to escort her upstairs, that they could say good-night right here, but he was standing so close, looking so sweet and handsome and so damn solemn, that the words simply wouldn't come. She entered the elevator, pressed the button for her floor and silently avoided looking at him until they reached the foyer that separated her apartment from her neighbor's.

"We're doing this all backward, you know," she remarked as she unlocked the heavy door. "I asked *you* out, so I should have picked you up and paid the check and taken you home."

"Then *you* should kiss *me* good-night."

She wasn't sure she wanted to do that, she thought, then silently scoffed. Of course she *wanted* to. She just wasn't sure it was wise. Safe.

But he was leaning comfortably against the doorjamb, and he showed no sign of moving until she had complied. Reluctantly she took a step toward him.

With just the faintest hint of a smile, he said softly, "That's okay. You come over, and I'll take care of the rest."

It took her four more steps to reach him. Slowly he straightened and raised his fingers to her jaw. His touch was warm and rough, and that—just his fingers grazing her skin—was enough to make her tremble inside, enough to make her want to turn and run and hide, the way she had when she was a child.

But she wasn't a child. She held her ground. She endured his touch. She *savored* it. And she waited for his kiss.

Cradling her face in his hands, he brought his mouth to hers. It could hardly be called a kiss, it was so light, so gentle. She'd been kissed dozens of times with more passion, more hunger, more demand, more strength, but never so tenderly. Never so soul-soothingly, so tenderly.

He released her and backed away, one slow step at a time. "Good night, Beth," he said softly.

Good night. Yes, she thought dazedly as she watched him step into the elevator, then disappear from sight. It *had* been a good night.

Maybe *too* good.

Zachary was a bit uneasy when he arrived at Beth's firm Friday morning. Tired after the long day, he'd gone straight back to the motel after dinner last night, but he'd been too restless to sleep. Packing in preparation for today's trip back to Sweetwater hadn't helped, and neither had reading more complicated case law. He'd needed physical activity—of the most intimate sort—but that, of course, had been impossible.

And so he had paced the small room. He'd stared at the television. He'd taken a long shower. He had tossed and turned in the bed, once comfortable, now too confining, too small.

Too empty.

It seemed that every time he had closed his eyes, he'd seen Beth's bedroom once again. The immaculate, impersonal place where she slept. The steel-gray carpet. The dove-gray walls. The black lacquered furniture. The stark white comforter.

The wicked black sheets.

All he'd been able to think about was the intriguing contrast of blazing red hair, soft ivory skin and smooth, sinful black sheets. All he'd been able to imagine was lying on those sheets with her, arms and legs entwined, mouths touching, bodies joined. All he'd been able to feel was desire, and all he had desired was *her*.

Thank God the weekend was here. He could go home, where he belonged, and shake off the city. He could forget about the case, about Carrie and all her problems, and he could, for two days, work Beth out of his system. He could wear himself out at the farm, hammering, sawing, chopping wood and doing whatever else needed to be done. He could have two nights of peace.

Then he shook his head grimly. He could tear his house down and start again from scratch and still not work her out of his system. He could cut down every one of the thousands of trees on his property and chop them into toothpicks and still have the energy to want her. To dream of her. To lust for her.

The stern Mrs. Taylor informed him that Beth was in a meeting with a client, but she'd left instructions for him to be shown to her office. Sometimes he forgot that she had other cases, he thought as he followed the secretary into the office. Where did she find the energy for Carrie's case and all the others? he wondered, then promptly answered that as Mrs. Taylor left again. From her personal life. She took the time and energy that she was supposed to devote to herself and gave them to her job. She gave everything to the job.

He shrugged out of his coat, returned the law books to their proper places on the shelves, then wandered over to the window behind Beth's desk. The air there smelled faintly of the fragrance she wore, as if she hadn't been gone long. He liked the scent, he decided. She had probably chosen it because it was suitable to a professional woman—light, pleasing and subtle. Not seductive. Not sexy.

But *he* found it sexy. It reminded him of cold nights and warm bodies. Of hunger and need and satisfaction. Of passion, sweet and hot, and pleasure, sharp and shattering.

He gave a sigh of resignation as his body responded all too quickly, all too pleasurably, to those thoughts. He was gradually becoming used to unsatisfied arousal. It was a condition he had never before endured for any length of time, but he could live with it. Until it was relieved or it died from sheer futility, he could endure it.

Leaning against the windowsill, he glanced around the office, his gaze finally settling on the portrait of Althea Townsend. He would have liked to have known the only member of her family whom Beth had loved unreservedly.

He would have liked to have her insight on how to deal with her great-granddaughter, how to earn her trust, how to break through her defenses.

The door swung open, interrupting his thoughts, and Beth came in, looking as lovely as ever. She was halfway across the room before she realized she wasn't alone, and she stopped suddenly, meeting his gaze for an instant before swiftly looking away. "Good morning."

Her greeting was stilted, formal, guarded. She was already regretting last night's date, Zachary thought, not surprised, but disappointed. She had already convinced herself that the dinner, the conversation and the kiss—especially the kiss—should never have taken place. She already had her defenses in place, fortified and unbreachable.

Beth stopped in front of her desk and simply stood there, the files she held forgotten. If she went around the desk to sit down, she would be too close to Zachary—simply being in the room with him was too close—and so she chose to remain where she was. Safe.

"What do you want me to do today?"

She considered the answers that came instantly to mind: I want you to go home and never come back. I want you to stop being so charming, so appealing, so damn tempting. I want you to stop disrupting my life, to stop invading my privacy.

I want you to make love to me.

She had to clear her throat before she could reply. "There's a list of people we still haven't talked to on the pad there." She nodded toward her desk and watched his gaze shift briefly from her to the legal pad, then back again. "Maybe you could start with them."

He looked tired, she thought, as if he hadn't slept much last night. Neither had she. She had sat up until well past midnight going through a small cardboard box she stored in the back of her closet. It was, she supposed, the equivalent of a scrapbook, an item she had only a passing familiarity with. It held photographs, souvenirs and little mementos from her time with Philip.

Her first impulse, when their relationship had ended, had been to throw it all away, but some perverse side of her nature had refused. Instead, everything had gone into the box, and the box had been tucked safely in the closet. It was there to remind her of how foolish she had been to trust Philip, of how easily he had deceived her, of how thoroughly he had broken her heart.

It was there to remind her not to make the same mistake again.

Before last night she had opened the box only once in ten years, and she still remembered the pain that had returned with those memories. Last night there had been pain, too, but of a different sort. The pain of disappointment, of loss. The pain of a future that stretched forty years or more ahead of her, a future as empty and cold as her house. As her life.

As her heart.

But the memories had served their purpose. They had strengthened her resolve. They had made her see once again that no relationship was worth the risk. No man was worth the pain. Not even Zachary.

He tore the page from the pad, skimmed over it, then folded it and slid it into his pocket. "I'll get to as many of them as I can this morning. I'm going home after lunch."

She didn't ask if he wanted to meet her for lunch. It wouldn't be wise, not yet. She might have strengthened her resolve, but she needed time for it to harden. Right now there were still weak spots that his smile or his charm or his blue eyes could penetrate.

"When will you be back next week?" she asked, trying to sound as if her only interest were professional. It was a short work week, due to the holiday, and they still had so much to do.

"I'll be in Tuesday and Wednesday."

"What about Friday?"

He shook his head. "Not the day after Thanksgiving. That's a holiday, too." He moved away from her desk, and she slowly edged into place behind it.

"All right," she agreed, summoning up a cool smile. "Then I'll see you next Tuesday."

He left without further farewell, leaving Beth with a sense of unfinished business. She wanted to call him back, to tell him . . .

What? What could she possibly say that would matter?

Slowly she sank into her chair and forced her mind back to business. She had plenty to keep her busy. After all, work was her life . . . wasn't it?

Chapter 7

Zachary was on the road to Nashville before the sun rose Tuesday morning. A light snow had dusted the mountains, and he'd spent a chilly fifteen minutes scraping the Cherokee's windows before setting out. The talk at Rosa's Diner at noon yesterday had centered on the weather and the old-timers' predictions for winter. It wasn't here yet, Leon Peters had insisted, but Henry Walters, always looking for an argument, had disagreed. There would be no more nice weather, he'd said emphatically.

Zachary had agreed with old Leon. He was looking for a few more pretty days—preferably on weekends, so work on the house could proceed—before the frigid temperatures brought their annual quota of snow and ice. But this morning, as the snow gave way to a misting rain at lower elevations, he had to admit that it looked as if Henry might have been right.

He'd had a reasonably good weekend. He was making progress on the house—by spring it should be livable—and he'd gotten some badly needed rest. But thoughts of Beth had overshadowed everything he'd done. He hadn't found a way to rid himself of her even for an hour.

This would be his fourth week in the city, but there was no suitcase in the back this time. Between work on the house, motels and a steady diet of restaurant meals, his savings account was quickly dwindling. For this week and next, until next month's rent had been paid by the bank and Dr. Haynes, he would have to keep his expenses to a minimum by commuting from Sweetwater to Nashville. He wasn't looking forward to it. A six-hour round-trip added to eight, nine or ten hours spent working made for very long days. But the only other options were not only to go broke but into debt, or to tell Beth that he couldn't afford to help out anymore.

Neither option, each for its own reason, appealed to him.

He arrived at her office shortly after eight-thirty and found her in conference with several of the firm's younger attorneys. She motioned to him to help himself to the coffee on her desk and have a seat with them. He refused with a shake of his head, hung up his coat and settled in on the sofa against the far wall.

They were discussing another of her cases, a new one, from the sound of it. Zachary listened with half a mind, paying little attention as Beth gave each of the two young men a detailed list of instructions. She talked to them the same way she talked to *him,* he thought, dismayed even though he shouldn't have been. Was he no different in her eyes than the dozen or so associates the firm employed?

No, she saw him differently. These two men, neither a day over twenty-seven, were up-and-coming legal eagles. They were hotshots, or soon would be. They were, like Beth herself, high-quality, high-caliber attorneys.

And *he* was a simple country lawyer. Small-time. Old-fashioned. Naive.

No wonder she wanted nothing more from him than this temporary working relationship, he thought morosely.

After she dismissed the associates, she brought two cups of coffee to the sofa and offered him the sweetened one.

"You're in early. Did you drive up from Sweetwater last night?"

"No." He didn't elaborate.

"I wasn't expecting you until noon, but I'm glad you made it early. I have an appointment in half an hour with Elinor Clarkson. She's the counselor at Tyler Lewis's school. Would you like to go along?"

He considered refusing. There were still quite a few names left on that list she'd given him last Friday. But it would be interesting to hear what Ms. Clarkson had to say.

And it would be a chance to spend a little time with Beth.

"Sure," he agreed, slipping into his coat as she got hers from the closet. "I talked to Carrie's parents this weekend. They're bringing the kids in tomorrow to see her."

"How are they?"

"Who knows?" he asked with a shrug. The little ones had seemed relatively normal during his visit, although the baby had clung to his grandmother the entire time. Tyler was the one who concerned him. He carried so much rage and bitterness. It had destroyed the child he'd once been, the child he should still be. He was already old at fourteen.

When they reached the garage, he offered to drive. No matter how much rain they were used to, people just didn't drive well in it. If he had to be on the highway, he preferred his sturdy four-wheel drive Jeep over Beth's car.

He had located the school on his last trip into Carrie's neighborhood, and he found it again with little trouble. Pulling his coat tighter, he stepped out into the biting drizzle and, sharing Beth's umbrella, hurried inside the building.

Elinor Clarkson was a young woman, auburn-haired and pretty, her manner as warm and bubbly as Beth's was controlled. She was a mothering sort—taking their coats, offering them coffee, fussing over the weather. She reminded him of every woman he'd ever been involved with. Sweet. Generous. Outgoing. *Real.*

She was nothing like Beth.

"You're here about the Lewises," she said, finally slipping into the seat behind her desk. "We had all three of the older children at this school. They're good kids—quiet, guarded, a bit secretive. Of course, the situation at home would account for that. Tyler's the only one we've ever had any problems with. That's how I happened to meet Mrs. Lewis."

She went on without prompting, telling them about Tyler's behavior problems. The school had let things slide until the day he'd blown up at one of his teachers. Although he hadn't made any actual threat, there had been such anger, such hostility in his manner, that she had felt obliged to bring in his parents.

"Did you meet his father?" Beth asked.

"No. Only his mother came. She said her husband couldn't come, that he'd told her to take care of it herself."

Beth glanced at Zachary, then away. He knew what she was thinking. To prevent an angrier, even more hostile scene with Del, Carrie had probably lied. She probably hadn't even informed her husband of the incident. If she had, he might have turned on Tyler. He might have blamed her, too, or prevented her from meeting Elinor Clarkson. His behavior had been so unpredictable that she'd been safer handling the problem on her own.

"What was your impression of Carrie, Ms. Clarkson?"

"I felt sorry for her. It was winter, and there was snow on the ground, and she had on this thin coat, and her legs were bare and her shoes were soaked. She said she'd had to walk because they had only one car, and her husband needed it for work. She had the baby all bundled up in blankets, but *she* was so cold. She didn't stop shivering the whole time she was in my office."

"Did she have any bruises? Any cuts?"

"None that I could see. But she acted odd—all stiff and sore. She sat with her shoulders hunched like this—" she demonstrated, then sat straight again "—and her breathing was shallow. It was like she couldn't catch her breath."

Being used as a punching bag could do that to you, Zachary thought grimly. "How did she behave?" he asked. "Was she nervous?"

"Oh, yes. She was on edge the entire time. Then, during our meeting, the principal came in, and she almost jumped out of her skin. He just wanted to meet her, because in all the years her children had been students here, none of us had ever met her. A lot of parents are uncomfortable with the principal when their kids are in trouble, but this was more than that. She was *afraid*." She grew silent for a moment.

"You gave her the number for a shelter for battered women," he reminded her. "Why? What made you think she needed it?"

"Instinct, I guess," she replied with a shrug. "She wasn't the first battered wife I'd had contact with through my job. The neighborhoods this school serves are working class. Some studies indicate a correlation between income and domestic violence, and an even higher incidence of violence among the unemployed. We have more than our share of both groups."

"Is it that simple?" Zachary wondered aloud. "Give them better-paying jobs and it stops?" His research didn't support that theory. Battered wives could be found in every income range, at every level of education, on every rung of the social ladder.

Elinor Clarkson laughed softly, humorlessly. "Of course not. There are probably more reasons why men beat their wives than there are sociologists and psychologists studying them. There are dozens of components to the problem. Low income is only one." She settled back more comfortably in her chair. "How are the Lewis children?"

Zachary glanced at Beth, but she left it to him to answer. "I suppose as well as could be expected."

"Are they here in Nashville?"

"No, they're with Carrie's parents."

She swiveled her chair from side to side. "I don't know what kind of services are available wherever they are, but they need counseling, not only to help them deal with their father's death and their mother's arrest, but also with the violence. It's been proved that family violence is often a learned behavior. The kids see the father abuse the mother, they see that she accepts it, and they grow up believing that it's normal. They may not become abusive themselves—not all children who grow up in violent homes exhibit that tendency as adults—but it's too big a risk to ignore."

Zachary looked thoughtfully at Beth. No, not all kids did. She was a prime example of that. Her parents had been emotionally violent, and in response she had become exactly the opposite—too calm, too controlled.

"Tyler and his brothers and sister have lived all their lives exposed to violence," Ms. Clarkson continued. "They've learned to associate it with love, that if you love someone, you can hit him or you can let him hit you. We all learn from our parents, and these are roles that *they've* learned—the man as abusive and dominating, the woman as helpless victim. Without professional help, they're at increased risk of carrying those roles into their adult relationships."

"We'll do what we can," Beth said quietly. "I have one more question about Carrie, Ms. Clarkson, and then we'll be on our way. Did you ever follow up on your meeting with her?"

"I called her house several times. I sent a note home with Tyler. I even went by there twice." She shrugged. "She refused to speak to me. She didn't want me to interfere any more. I suspected that her husband had somehow found out about our meeting and punished her for it."

After a moment of thanks and goodbyes, they left her office. Except for the echo of their steps, the broad hallway was quiet as they made their way back to the main entrance. There Zachary paused while Beth unfurled her plain black umbrella.

"What kind of social services are available in Sweetwater?" she asked as they left the warmth of the building for the icy chill outside.

"We have one social worker who's overworked, underpaid and, after twenty years on the job, undermotivated." He shivered as a gust of wind sent raindrops down his neck. Reaching back with one ungloved hand, he pulled the collar of his jacket closer. "I'll talk to the Morrises. Maybe we can work something out."

He opened the Cherokee's door for her, tucked the long hem of her coat inside, then slammed it. By the time he'd circled the car, there was a fine mist coating his hair and shoulders. Beth leaned across to unlock the door for him, and he climbed in beside her.

"This is depressing," she remarked softly as she gazed out the window.

Zachary started the engine and turned on the heat before looking at her. "The case?"

"That, too, but I mean the rain. I don't mind cold or snow, but rain like this makes me..."

"Blue?"

She smiled faintly. She'd been about to say melancholy, but she liked his word better. Yes, ugly gray mornings like this made her blue. "This started about ten last night, and it shows no sign of letting up."

"It snowed last night in the mountains."

Still gazing out the window, she smiled again, but this time with more feeling. "How long will it take you to get homesick for your mountains?" On Sarah's visits into the city, she usually lasted only a few days before she began longing for the peace and quiet for her mountaintop home. Daniel couldn't even make it that long. He endured the city only when the details of his business demanded it.

Zachary chuckled softly. "I get homesick as soon as I leave. Don't you miss Nashville when you travel?"

Even though the answer came immediately to mind, she gave it a moment's thought, anyway. What was to miss about Nashville? Her work? Like Daniel, she usually traveled only on business. Her family? What was to miss about anger, arguments and threats? Her friends? A sound of disdain bubbled up in her throat. *What* friends?

"I could leave Nashville tomorrow," she replied quietly, "and never miss it." Her statement sounded a little hard, she acknowledged silently, and a little cold, but it was true. She could walk away from the firm, from her family and her acquaintances, from the place that had been her home for most of her life, and never regret it.

"And where would you go?" he asked, driving out of the parking lot, his attention on the road instead of her.

"I don't know. I suppose I could live anywhere." She hadn't given the idea *that* much thought. In fact, it was only recently that it had even come to mind.

Only since she'd started working with Zachary.

And only as a lovely fantasy.

"How would you support yourself?"

Her first impulse was to answer him; her second was to put an end to the silly conversation. Surprising herself, she went with the first. "I could continue to practice law." Then she surprised herself even more. "Or I could live off Great-Grandmother Althea's trust and do nothing."

Zachary brought the Jeep to a stop at a red light, then gave her a long look. He was trying to judge if she was serious, Beth thought, keeping her gaze on the windshield wipers as they swept rhythmically back and forth across the glass. He was trying to reconcile the things she'd just said with the woman he knew her to be.

After a moment, she met his gaze evenly. "Of course, it won't ever happen. Someday I'll probably be the oldest practicing partner in the firm. And like all the Gibsons and Townsends before me, I'll live and die in Nashville."

That seemed to be more what he expected to hear, she thought. But for a moment, just one brief, gone-too-quickly moment, she thought she saw disappointment in his eyes. She *knew* she felt disappointment—her own—deep down inside.

"Why don't you drop me off at the office?" she suggested, turning away once again, uncomfortable with the disquieting feeling inside. "Then you can get started on your interviews."

He didn't protest, didn't suggest that they have lunch together, didn't do anything at all but nod. Just like an associate. A strictly business partner. That was exactly the relationship she wanted with him.

Wasn't it?

Zachary walked into his mother's house Thursday morning and immediately inhaled deeply. There was no sweeter aroma than the one that filled this house on holidays. He separated and identified each scent—the turkey roasting, rolls baking, pies cooling, coffee perking. Individually they were enticing. Together they were heavenly. They brought back memories of Thanksgivings past, of holidays when his grandfather had still been alive, of football games and hiking through the woods and too much food.

They reminded him of family.

His father, uncles and male cousins had been banished to the living room to talk fishing and weather and politics until dinner was ready. He knew as he hung his coat in the hall closet that he would find the women of his family in the kitchen, each skillfully performing her own special task in spite of the crowded conditions and the numerous small children running around. It was controlled chaos, but he couldn't think of any other place he would rather be.

He waved hello to his father and Daniel, then headed down the hall to the kitchen. He'd seen many of these relatives as recently as Sunday morning in church, but he wanted to say hello before he settled in the living room with the men.

His grandmother was seated in the place of honor at the breakfast table, out of the way of those working but close enough to supervise. Zachary greeted her first, then found his mother as she rolled out piecrusts. She barely paused in her conversation with one of his aunts, but took notice when he dipped his finger into the baked meringue topping of a nearby pie. She slapped his hand, shook her head and sighed. ''You're just like your father.''

With a grin he kissed her cheek, then moved on to the sink to deliver the last of his personal greetings. There Alicia and Sarah worked together to diminish the steadily mounting stack of dirty dishes.

"How's Nashville?" Sarah asked.

Alicia was more direct, more sly, more teasing. "How's your new boss?"

He'd never confided his attraction to Beth to anyone but Sarah and Daniel, but his younger sister wasn't as naive as he sometimes wished. She'd certainly guessed right in this instance. "Nashville is cold and wet," he replied, "and Beth is fine, I suppose. She's having dinner with her family."

"Then she won't be fit for human company for a few days," Sarah replied. "You should have brought her here, Zachary—shown her how a *real* family celebrates Thanksgiving."

For all his invitations to dinner, he hadn't once considered asking Beth to spend the holiday with his family. What would she make of the crowd, the noise, the cramped quarters? He would guarantee that she'd never washed dishes after dinner for fifty, or eaten turkey and dressing off paper plates while sitting—or standing—wherever she could find an empty space, or met anyone who even remotely resembled the characters a few of his older oddball relatives had become.

No, her holiday meals, he was certain, were formal affairs, with damask cloths and heirloom silver and delicate crystal goblets, with a seven-course dinner prepared behind the scenes and served by stern-faced employees who'd had to forgo dinner with their own families in order to wait on hers. Attire would also be formal, of course. Jeans would be frowned on, and overalls, like Uncle Milton's, would be forbidden. Everyone would be civil, even to their most hated enemies, and enjoying oneself would be strictly prohibited.

He wouldn't trade his place on the living room floor, eating dinner at the coffee table, for any of it.

And Beth probably felt the same way.

He let the women shoo him out of the kitchen, giving a piggyback ride on the way to one of his young cousins. He didn't try to keep track of exactly how he was related to all of the younger Adamses. A cousin was a cousin, whether directly or three times removed.

In the living room he found a place on the sofa near Daniel and joined in the conversation. They had already covered politics once, he suspected, but a newcomer meant new opinions and a second going-over. And, of course, once the subject had been played out again, it wasn't much of a leap at all from that to the justice system, then to Carrie Lewis's case. He begged off on the questions, claiming client confidentiality. When that didn't slow the conversation, he used the holiday as an excuse. No one really expected him to discuss business on Thanksgiving, did they?

More than an hour had passed before he was able to talk quietly, privately, with Daniel. He had always been merely casually acquainted with the man until Katie's birth had brought so many changes into both their lives. Since then, a deep friendship had developed between them, until there was nothing they couldn't discuss with each other.

"I got a letter from my mother yesterday," Daniel said when they were alone in one corner of the room.

"What did she have to say?" Zachary remembered Patsy Ryan only vaguely. She had said goodbye to Sweetwater and Daniel when he was only a teenager, leaving for a new husband, a new life and a new family in Florida. She'd had little room in that new life for her first son. She hadn't once come to see her only grandchild when Daniel had been given custody of Katie, and she hadn't yet met her only daughter-in-law. Zachary didn't need to know anything else about Patsy to dislike her.

"She and her husband are traveling to Chicago next week, and she plans to stop by Sweetwater and meet Sarah and Katie." He looked down at his daughter cradled in his arms, asleep and snoring softly. When she was a baby, Zachary recalled, she had looked like a tiny doll cupped in her father's big hands. She was bigger now but, compared to Daniel, still so small. And still so precious, he thought with barely controlled longing.

"Nice that Tennessee just happens to be on the way," Zachary replied with a hint of sarcasm.

"Yeah." Daniel sighed softly. "Sarah and Katie deserve better."

"So do you."

Suddenly Daniel grinned. He did that a lot more since Sarah had come into his life. "I've got more of a family than I ever thought I'd have. I don't need my mother. Besides, Katie thinks your folks are her grandparents. She won't be interested in these strangers who are coming by for a couple of hours." He shifted the sleeping girl effortlessly, then asked, "How are things going with Beth?"

"We had dinner last week, but that's about the extent of anything personal." Dinner and a kiss. He smiled solemnly. Was that all he would ever have? Just that one sweet kiss?

"What if it does get personal? What if you and she...?" Daniel let his question trail off, trusting Zachary to understand. "You couldn't leave the mountains, and I can't imagine Beth leaving the city."

"I don't know. I guess that's something we would have to deal with when the time came. And right now..." He shrugged. "I don't know if that time is ever going to come."

Beth accompanied an executive from one of her father's companies into the dining room, the polite smile pasted on her face concealing the taut line of her jaw. She had been here at her parents' home for exactly one hour, and already her head ached, her neck was stiff, and her jaw hurt. She had avoided all but the most public exchanges with her parents. She had been miserably polite to their friends and had even pretended not to notice the executive for the obvious setup that he was. Her father had never been able to bully her into the family business; now, she suspected, he was considering trying to marry her into it.

Not likely.

Dinners with her parents were excruciatingly formal. Well aware that her mother would detect the slightest flaw in her appearance, she had dressed more carefully for this dinner than for her most important court dates. She had changed outfits a half dozen times, knowing that nothing would satisfy Francine, and sure enough, the first words out of her mother's mouth after "hello" had been critical. "That color really doesn't flatter you, dear."

Beth had smiled, but her temples had begun to throb. "Thank you, Mother, for telling me that," she'd said politely before escaping. Thanks for nothing, she thought now as she slid into the seat her escort held for her.

There were twenty guests at the mahogany table and half that many servants on hand. What a shame that they couldn't spend the day with *their* families, she thought as she laid the linen napkin across her lap. But what did servants' families matter when Walter and Francine Gibson wanted to throw a party?

There weren't any servants at Zachary's parents' house, she was sure. She had experienced a bit of the Adams family hospitality at the reception following Sarah and Daniel's wedding. Mrs. Adams had probably been up since dawn cooking, baking and cleaning. The tables and counters would be filled with food, and everyone would help themselves, and they would all have a good time laughing and talking and eating.

While she sat there in physical pain, wishing she were somewhere else. Home alone. In her office—yes, even on Thanksgiving.

Or maybe in Sweetwater.

"So...you're a lawyer," remarked the executive at her side.

She reached for her water goblet, sipping slowly from it to control her annoyance at both the comment and the man. When she trusted herself to be polite, she smiled coolly at him and replied, "Yes, I am."

"What's your specialty? Corporate law? Tax law?"

Her smile slowly began slipping. "Trial law. I defend murderers."

He laughed as if she'd made a joke, and Beth rigidly focused her attention inward. She let the conversation continue, making the appropriate responses and showing the appropriate interest, but none of it registered with her.

She had asked Zachary to return to the city on Monday. The trial was scheduled to start two weeks later, and they had set aside several hours each morning for an in-depth interview with Carrie. Beth didn't like surprises in the court room and went to great lengths to avoid them. When they went into court for the jury selection, she wanted to know every detail of Carrie's life as well as she knew her own.

She made a mental note to get in touch with Darla Newman and make sure she could join them in court for the jury selection. Beth considered herself a good judge of character, but she'd found the psychologist's help invaluable in determining which jurors were more likely to be sympathetic to her presentation. The one time she'd disregarded Dr. Newman's recommendation, she had seated a juror who'd wound up casting the deciding vote against her client.

She also had to find time to put together her opening statement, to review all the research and interviews Zachary had done, to interview all the witnesses they would put on the stand, to say nothing of keeping up with her regular workload....

Briefly she closed her eyes and rubbed the bridge of her nose. She always felt she'd taken on too much just before a trial started, and this time was no exception. Even though she had Zachary's assistance, that provided a problem in itself. He was as much a distraction as a help.

"Have a headache?" the executive beside her asked.

Beth glanced at him, then around the table. Everyone was laying napkins aside, sliding chairs back, standing up—everyone but her. She had just eaten a dinner prepared by some of the best cooks in Nashville, and she couldn't remember even one bite of it.

She looked back at the man. For the life of her she couldn't remember his name or his title or exactly which company it was he worked for. She suspected that, as nice-looking as he was, she would forget his face and the time spent in his presence as soon as she walked out the door.

And yet she remembered every moment—every pleasant, easy, serious, uncomfortable, awkward, intimate moment—spent with Zachary.

There was no sense lying to herself. Her parents, dishonest and phony even with themselves, had taught her to value the truth.

She was in serious trouble. In spite of her rules, in spite of her self-control, in spite of her determination to never let another man into her life, she had done just that. She had told herself that her relationship with Zachary was strictly business, but when was the last time she'd let a business associate kiss her? When was the last time she'd fantasized about making love with one of her co-workers? When was the last time she'd wanted to run away with one of them and never come back?

"Yes," she answered the question her companion seemed to have forgotten asking. "I have a headache." One that aspirin could do nothing for.

One that could only lead to heartache.

After the cold and rain of the past week, Saturday dawned still and sunny and relatively warm. Zachary stepped out onto the front porch in jeans and nothing else and judged the temperature to be at least forty degrees. That meant he could forgo the thermal underwear and heavy socks and gloves while he worked at his new house.

He went back inside and finished dressing, pausing only briefly to call the Morris farm. Their place was on the lower slopes of Laurel Mountain. He wanted to stop by and talk to Ruth and Dutch about getting help for the kids. Ruth answered on the second ring, said they would be glad to see him and why didn't he plan on having breakfast with them?

It beat cooking his own, he thought with a grin, or spending money he couldn't afford to buy it at the diner. He accepted and hung up, then shrugged into his coat. He'd chopped wood all day yesterday at the farm, and the muscles in his shoulders were tender, making him wince with the movement.

He sang along with the radio all the way to the Morrises' house. He was in a good mood this morning. On a bright winter morning like this, nothing seemed impossible.

Not even winning Carrie's case.

Not even winning Beth.

The farmhouse was small and shabby, but clean and in good repair. Unlike Carrie's neighbors in the city, no matter how tough things got out here, Dutch and Ruth never quit caring. They never gave up hope, and they wouldn't let their grandkids quit, either. For the girl, Becky, and the two little boys, there *was* still hope. But Zachary wasn't sure about Tyler.

Ruth greeted him at the door, an apron around her waist and the baby on her hip. Breakfast was already on the table, and they ate and talked about everything in the world but Carrie's trial. Afterward, Ruth sent Tyler to help the younger kids get dressed, and Zachary told her and Dutch what he'd come to say. He'd expected some resistance, particularly from Dutch, but the old man simply nodded.

"We'll find a way," he said quietly.

"Start by seeing Miss Agnes in town," Zachary suggested. "She's a social worker, and she should be able to steer you in the right direction." He gazed through the open door as Tyler entered the next room. The boy went straight to a chair by the window, where he sat down and stared out the glass. "If he'll come with me," he began thoughtfully, "do you mind if I take Tyler up to the farm for a few hours?"

When they both agreed, he thanked Ruth for the breakfast, then went into the living room, pulling on his jacket as he went. "Tyler, I'm building a house up the mountain a few miles. Want to go up there with me to do a little work this morning?''

At first the boy gave no sign of hearing him. Then, when Zachary was about to walk out, he stood up, took a thread-bare jacket from a hook behind the door and pulled it on. As Zachary followed him to the truck, he wasn't sure what he'd hoped to accomplish by convincing Tyler to come along, but whatever it was, he'd succeeded at the first step. Now, he wondered ruefully, what was the next one?

Beth slowed her car to a stop and shut off the engine just as Sarah Ryan came out of her house onto the broad porch. Her friend looked surprised, she thought as she reached for her suede jacket and climbed out. Of course, why shouldn't Sarah be surprised? Beth rarely dropped in unannounced to visit anyone, even her best friend.

"What are you doing here?" Sarah asked, coming down the steps with a small cooler in her arms. She set it down long enough to hug Beth, then picked it up again and put it in the back of her Blazer. "Not that I'm unhappy to see you—I wish we could spend more time together—but this is a bit unexpected."

"Would you believe I was in the neighborhood?"

Sarah looked at her, then laughed. It was such a pleas-ant, happy sound. Beth envied that laugh, that pleasure, that happiness. She envied Sarah's home and her husband and daughter. She envied Sarah's life.

"In the neighborhood?" Sarah echoed. "Three hours away? Well, you've got good timing. Daniel's working to-day, and I was just on my way to take him some lunch. Ride along with us."

Beth hesitated, then agreed. This wasn't exactly what she'd planned when she'd gotten up this morning. She'd dressed for the office, then decided that what she *really* wanted was to see Sarah. To spend time with her friend. To chat. To take advantage of her gentle heart and her wom-an's understanding and her shoulder to cry on.

Not that Beth ever cried, of course. Not since she was eight years old.

But, she thought philosophically, if you showed up unexpectedly on someone's doorstep a hundred and fifty miles from home, you had to be satisfied with what you got.

The screen door closed with a thump, and Katie came to the top of the steps. Clutching a teddy bear, she stared down at Beth, showing no hint of curiosity, pleasure or even recognition, not even when Beth offered her a stiff smile and a stiffer greeting.

Sarah followed her daughter down the steps, a large brown bag in her arms. Beth placed the bag in back with the cooler, while Sarah lifted Katie and fastened her securely in her safety seat.

"How was Thanksgiving?" Sarah asked as they settled in the front seat.

Beth gave her a dry look. "I'm considering making plans to be out of town for Christmas."

"That bad, huh? We had a nice day."

She didn't elaborate, and Beth didn't question her. She knew the Ryans spent a great deal of time with Zachary's family. She knew they'd shared in a real holiday celebration—a real *family* celebration. The less she heard about it, the less she would envy them.

"So what brings you out here?" Sarah asked as they started down the mountain.

Beth sighed softly. She turned her gaze out the window, to the woods full of trees that had lost their leaves for the winter, their bare black limbs a stark contrast against the evergreens here and there. This was a pretty place when the meadows were filled with spring wildflowers, or when the changing leaves were a hundred different shades of red, orange and gold. She imagined it would be pretty, too, when snow covered the ground.

The city was never pretty—*really* pretty. Not even when the azaleas were in full delicate-hued bloom. Not even when the crepe myrtles and redbuds and dogwoods blossomed.

Then she glanced at her friend, who was waiting patiently for a response to her question. Sarah had always been incredibly patient. It had made her an outstanding teacher and an extraordinary mother. It had helped her become Beth's best friend. Her *only* friend.

"I just needed to get away," she finally replied, sighing softly as she did. "Between work and Thanksgiving, I haven't had much time for myself. With Carrie's trial starting in two weeks, this is probably the last chance I'll have to do anything for myself."

"How is the case going?"

"I don't know. There's no way the jury could not be sympathetic to Carrie, but there's still the minor fact that Del was asleep when she killed him. That weakens our claim of self-defense."

"At least she's got a good lawyer," Sarah said with a smile as they reached the highway. When the road was clear, she pulled away from the stop sign, but not toward town. Instead, she crossed the highway and continued on the same narrow dirt road. Her forehead wrinkled into a frown, Beth considered what her friend had said earlier: Daniel was working, and she was taking him lunch. But Daniel's only work was his furniture business, and his workshop was only a few yards from their house.

As the road began to climb, she felt a sinking sensation deep in her stomach. They were climbing steadily. Up a mountain. And the new house Zachary was building was on a mountain.

Maybe she was jumping to conclusions. Just because Daniel had chosen to work away from the house today didn't mean that he had to be working at Zachary's. Since Sarah had come to Sweetwater, since she'd helped Daniel to become more comfortable with people, he had gotten involved in all sorts of short-term projects. He had helped with the town's annual Harvest Festival and the county fair. He had volunteered his services in the construction of a new classroom at the elementary school and worked on the renovation of the old Baptist church in town.

And he was helping to build Zachary's house.

She had something suspiciously close to butterflies in her stomach.

"Sarah," she began as the road snaked around a jutting rock wall, then wound across a rapidly flowing brook, "where exactly is Daniel working today?"

Her friend glanced at her, then directed her attention back to the road. "On Laurel Mountain." Then she clarified that. "At Zachary's new house."

Chapter 8

Twenty yards before the road ended in a grown-over clearing, Sarah turned into a driveway, slowing almost to a crawl as she drove through the gate. Beth entertained a brief, silly notion about stopping her friend and jumping out there. She could swear Sarah to secrecy, then wait until she and Katie were ready to return home. She could count the different varieties of trees that grew on both sides of the road. She could watch the birds flying overhead. She could sit on that tree stump and wonder why in the world she'd left Nashville this morning.

She could avoid seeing Zachary.

Then common sense reclaimed her. She would end up making a complete and utter fool of herself, and she wasn't about to do that, not even with her best friend.

And so she sat stiffly as they followed the rutted trail that was apparently Zachary's driveway, and she gathered her self-control more closely. She would be calm, she decided. Polite and collected. She wouldn't let him know how frequently he'd been in her mind these last few days. She wouldn't let him guess how thoroughly he'd woven his way into her life.

She wouldn't let him see how much she'd missed him.

Then they topped a rise and she saw the house, and everything else was forgotten. It was simple, nothing fancy, nothing grand. It wasn't large—three, maybe four bedrooms, she estimated. But it was beautiful. It was perfect for Zachary. She could easily see him living there, surrounded by meadows and woods and a gorgeous view in every direction. She could imagine him sitting on that broad porch, watching the sun set, enjoying the quiet evening.

The only thing she couldn't imagine was the woman sitting at his side. The woman who would live in this beautiful home with him. The woman who would share his sunsets and quiet evenings. The woman who would have his love and sleep in his bed and bear his children.

The woman who wouldn't be her.

Sarah parked beside Daniel's pickup and cut the engine. After freeing Katie from her seat, she picked up the cooler, Beth took the bag, and they both followed the little girl across the porch and inside the house.

Beth fell behind, gazing down the wide hall, up the gracefully curved stairs, around the two rooms in front. The Sheetrock was up, the fireplaces completed, the wires for lighting hanging from the ceiling. She wondered what colors he would paint the smooth walls, whether he would opt for carpeting or wood flooring with cozy rugs.

She wondered if she would ever see the house completed.

Shaking away the thought, she followed the sounds of hammering down the hall to the back of the house. There she found Sarah and Daniel, Katie perched on his shoulders, in what was apparently the kitchen. The whine of a power saw outside indicated Zachary's whereabouts.

She exchanged greetings with Daniel; then she and Sarah began spreading out lunch on a makeshift table. They had just finished when the noise of the saw stopped. Beth straightened, rubbed her damp palms on her slacks and took a deep breath just as Tyler Lewis and Zachary walked through the door.

He was wearing jeans, a flannel shirt and those sturdy hiking boots she associated with him. There was sawdust on his jeans and in his hair, and his jeans bore an L-shaped tear in the knee. A streak of dirt was smudged across his jaw, and she thought for an instant that he had never looked more appealing.

This was where he belonged—in his country home, in comfortable clothes, with good friends. This place where she felt awkward and overwhelmed. This place where she felt so out of place.

He grinned when he saw her, said hello to Sarah and gave Katie a kiss, then crossed the room to the table where she still stood. He didn't ask what she was doing there, didn't express any surprise that she'd chosen to spend today with Sarah instead of shut up inside her office. He simply grinned and said, "So, you survived Thanksgiving."

"Barely." She gestured to the house around her. "You have a lovely place."

"It will be if we ever get it finished. We're building cabinets today." Then his grin turned sheepish, and he corrected himself. "Let me rephrase that. *Daniel* is building cabinets today. Tyler and I are helping and learning."

She forced her gaze from him to the room. The lower cabinets, minus the countertops, were already in place. They were pine—Daniel's favorite wood—and they were beautiful.

"Come on," Zachary invited, drawing her attention back to him. "I'll give you a tour."

She didn't consider refusing. She didn't think about the hazards of being alone with him. She simply moved around the table and followed him out, greeting Tyler along the way.

The first room he showed her was the living room, dominated by a huge window and a slightly smaller-scale fireplace. The smaller room at the front, connected to the kitchen, would be the dining room. He wasn't yet sure what the room across the hall would be, he told her with a grin. Maybe an office, since he and Daniel had already built bookcases along two walls.

She had been right about the bedrooms upstairs. There were currently three, with one large enough to divide into two smaller rooms if it became necessary. If he and his future wife had enough children to need the extra room, Beth translated with a tinge of uneasiness.

The master bedroom was the last room he showed her. In spite of its unfinished state, she knew immediately that it was going to be perfect: beautiful, cozy and welcoming, with a breathtaking view. What a great place to lie in bed and stargaze or watch the sun rise . . . or to forget about the view outside and concentrate on the one inside. On the *man* inside.

He was leaning against the half wall where the bed would stand. She turned from her place beside the window and faced him as he talked about paint and wallpaper and rugs.

Zachary trailed off in the middle of a description of the deep, rich Colonial crimson that he intended to paint this room and for a long moment simply looked at her. She looked so *right* here. In spite of the bare flooring, the unpainted Sheetrock, the unfinished air of the room, she looked as if she belonged right here. In his house. In his bedroom. In his life. Was it just an illusion, something that he wanted so much that he made it seem real? Could illusions be that powerful, that enduring?

Slowly he crossed the room, joining her at the window. The sun was already high overhead, but it took little effort to imagine the strong morning rays touching her through this window, setting her red hair afire, warming the cool porcelain of her skin. It took no effort at all to imagine the desire he would feel seeing her like that. It was the same desire he felt now. The same need.

The same hunger.

Nervously she took a step back, then turned away, facing the window and the woods and the mountain again. "You have a gorgeous view here. I can see why you chose this place. It's really—''

He touched her, brushing a strand of her hair back, catching it behind her ear, and her words stopped abruptly. He took advantage of her sudden silence to speak. ''I know you didn't come to Sweetwater to see me,'' he said softly. ''I know Sarah somehow coerced you into coming over here. However she did it, I'm grateful. I've missed you, lady.''

Slowly he moved his hand from her hair, soft and silky, to her jaw, turning her to face him. Her skin was cool, her muscles tight. But she didn't pull away. He gave her plenty of time to push his hand back or to walk away, but she didn't. She simply stood there, her green eyes dark and heated, and waited for his next move.

He brushed his lips lightly across hers. She tried to remain unresponsive, but he felt the slight shiver that rippled through her. Slowly, deliberately, he touched his mouth to hers again, this time exerting more pressure, this time moistening her lips with his tongue, teasing, tantalizing.

Beth raised her hands to his chest. They hovered there for a moment, close enough to feel his warmth, but not actually touching him. What was she going to do? she wondered dimly. Push him away? Or pull him closer? Then he brought his other hand up, too, cradling her face in his warm, rough palms, and began a third kiss, a *real* kiss, the kind of kiss that she had dreamed about, the kind of kiss that made her heart thud and her legs go weak and caused her brain to shut down so her body could savor the sensations without the distraction of thought.

And that settled the dilemma of what to do with her hands. Pushing him away was an impossible idea that made her breath catch in her lungs—or was it the kiss that did that? She settled her hands on his chest, her fingers curling around the softness of his shirt, her right palm feeling the soft, rapid beat of his heart.

When he encouraged her with the gentle caresses of his fingers, she opened her mouth to his tongue, and intense satisfaction gave way to intense need. It had been years since she'd been kissed like this. Then some part of her amended that. She had *never* been kissed like this, not with tender touches and soft sighs and throbbing passion. Not with hunger and need and caring. Not with such frightening sweetness.

Zachary gently drew her closer, wrapping his arms around her, molding her body to his. He could lose himself in just this—touching her, tasting her. He could simply hold her, touch her, glide his hands down the long line of her spine and stroke the gentle curve of her hips, while his tongue explored the dark warmth of her mouth. He could stay like this forever... if not for his body's insistent swelling demand.

He guided her a step back, then another and another, until she was leaning against the broad wooden window frame. Then he shifted against her, letting her feel the strength of his arousal, and he felt her swift intake of air. Reluctantly, calling on every ounce of willpower he possessed, he ended the kiss and raised his head for a long, strengthening breath of air. He didn't move away from her, though. He couldn't give up everything.

Bending his head once more, he pressed a kiss, light and fluttery, to her eyelid, following with another on her other lid. Then he softly commanded, "Look at me, Beth."

She swallowed hard, touched her tongue to her lips, tightened her hold on his shirt, then finally forced her eyes open, forced them to focus on him. His smile was small, secretive, as he read the emotion there. Passion. For *him*.

"You're a beautiful woman," he murmured, covering her hands with his, gently working her fingers free of the flannel. He raised her hands, palms up, to his mouth for a brief, moist kiss, then clasped them in his own. "I'd like to think that I could make love to you now if the others weren't downstairs," he said with a solemn smile. "But since I don't want to know if I'm wrong, I guess it's lucky that they *are* there."

Color filled her cheeks, staining them a pale rose. She drew a deep breath—calming herself? Zachary wondered.

Preparing to speak? To tell him that he *was* wrong?—then let it out all in a rush.

She was flustered, Beth privately acknowledged—a condition as alien to her as the passion she had just experienced. As the need that still made her tremble. As the knowledge that Zachary was right, that if they'd been alone in the house, they would have finished what they'd started. She would have allowed him—no, pleaded with him—to make love to her. Being too practical, she might have regretted it later, but she would have enjoyed it while it happened. She would have reveled in it.

She would have reveled in *him*.

But they weren't alone, and the passion was fading, and the realization was becoming clear that neither of them was in any condition to join their friends downstairs. Zachary looked fine except for that wistful little grin and the arousal that pulled his jeans taut, but she was still unsteady, her lipstick had been kissed away, and her clothes were liberally dusted with sawdust, courtesy of their embrace.

Almost as if he'd read her mind, he gestured for her to move away from the window frame; then he dusted her suede jacket and brushed the worst of the fine particles from her black slacks. Her sweater was a different problem. After fingering the intricate knit for a moment, he ruefully shook his head, then turned away.

She was disappointed, she realized as she turned once more to face the window, brushing away the dust with quick, purposeful strokes. Her breasts were sensitive and aching for the pleasure only he could bring them. But this wasn't the time or the place. She wondered briefly, sadly, if the time would ever come.

Reflected in the glass, she saw Zachary standing in front of the fireplace, gazing down at the cold stone hearth that had never held a fire. One part of her wanted to go to him, to tell him that he'd been wrong, that she did want him, that she would have made love with him. The stronger part knew that would be a mistake, just as the kiss had been. Just as working together was a mistake.

Everything in her life was a mistake, it seemed, and Zachary was the biggest one of all. One that she couldn't correct.

One, she admitted with a defeated little sigh, that she wouldn't correct even if she could.

Thursday was cold and dreary—a good day to stay inside, Beth thought as she glanced out her office window. That was what she and Zachary had done all day. They had worked, eaten lunch at her desk, discussed the upcoming trial and the jury selection and their list of witnesses.

They *hadn't* discussed last weekend.

They *hadn't* discussed Saturday's kiss.

She had been uncomfortable when Zachary came into the office on Monday. She hadn't been able to look him in the eye or to get even remotely close to him. But he'd acted as if nothing had happened between them, as if nothing had changed, and gradually she'd begun to relax. She'd slipped back into her comfortable business-as-usual manner.

Except when she remembered the feel of his mouth on hers.

Except when she sometimes looked up unexpectedly and caught his gaze on her.

Except when she recalled the extent of his arousal, when she occasionally felt again the extent of *hers*.

Today had been simply business. They had kept busy all day and now were waiting for their last appointment. Then Zachary would leave and return to his motel, and she would stay here and try to work while wondering what he was doing and wishing that, whatever it was, she was doing it with him.

She fingered the report Dr. Newman had asked her to prepare. The more information the psychologist had about the case, the better prepared she would be to assess each potential juror. The assistant prosecutor who was handling Carrie's case had in the past scoffed at the idea of enlisting a psychologist to assist in jury selection. He trusted his own judgment, he had boasted to Beth. Maybe he would change his mind when the jury in this trial accepted Carrie's plea of self-defense.

Taking the file with her, she crossed the room to where Zachary was lying on the sofa, a law book braced against one bent knee. He looked so relaxed, Beth thought a bit jealously, so comfortable in this room where she always had to be on her most professional behavior. She wouldn't dare to kick off her shoes, stretch out on the sofa and work. All it would take was for one person—one partner, one associate, one secretary—to see her that way, and her carefully maintained image would suffer.

"Zachary, do you mind taking a look at this and—" She stopped abruptly and looked more closely at him. His eyes were closed, and his chest rose and fell with long, even breaths. "Zachary?" When there was no response, she bent closer. "Zachary?"

Relaxed? He was *asleep*. She waited for her natural indignation that her partner had fallen asleep on the job, but it didn't come. In its stead came the realization that soft, smudgy shadows darkened the skin underneath his eyes and that there was a strained, weary look about him. He had seemed unusually tired the last few days, she thought, remembering several times when she'd caught him hiding a yawn, times when she'd had to repeat things to him. But she had simply assumed that he wasn't sleeping well, that maybe working here all week and at his farm all weekend was more than he was used to.

Bending, she removed the book from his loose hold and laid it on the table. Then, returning to her desk, she found the number of the motel where he'd been staying and quickly dialed it. "Can you tell me if Zachary Adams is registered there?" she asked when the desk clerk answered. A moment later, she quietly thanked the man, then hung up.

No, ma'am, we don't have anyone by that name.

Had he chosen to stay at a different motel this week? she wondered. But if that was the case, surely he would have told her. Unless he wasn't staying at a motel at all. Hadn't she encouraged him to take advantage of his time in the city to look for a woman? Maybe he'd found one and was . . .

Pursing her lips, she shut off that train of thought. If Zachary had been seeing someone else, he never would have kissed her the way he had. *Never.*

Before she could consider the matter further, the intercom buzzed. "Dr. Newman is here," Loretta announced. "She's on her way in."

The last word was barely out when the door opened and Darla Newman walked through. She was an older woman, probably about her mother's age, Beth estimated, although she couldn't imagine anything else the two women might possibly have in common. Darla was gray-haired and plump, and her face was lined with some sixty years of living. She cared little about opinions, but a great deal about people. She was warm, disarmingly friendly and unfailingly optimistic.

"How are you, Beth?" she asked, offering her hand.

Beth shook hands with her, her fingers gliding across powdery-smooth skin. "I'm fine, Darla. You?"

"I can't complain. I'm running on a tight schedule today, though—had an emergency call from one of my patients—so if you'll call your associate, we can get right to work."

With a faint smile, Beth gestured toward the couch. "I don't think he'll be joining us."

The doctor put her briefcase down, then looked curiously at Zachary. "He doesn't look like the typical stuffed shirt who holds such appeal for your partners. Are you sure he works here?"

"Actually, he doesn't. He's just helping with this case." At Darla's questioning look, she felt compelled to continue. "He went to school with our client, and he's handled a few things for her parents, and . . ." She gestured awkwardly. "It doesn't really matter."

"He's nice-looking."

Even though she didn't need confirmation, Beth glanced at him before silently agreeing. He certainly was that. And

Darla was right, too, about the stuffy part. In his wheat-colored jeans and blue plaid shirt, he bore no resemblance to the other men in the office. But he could, she reminded herself. The suit he'd worn to Carrie's preliminary hearing had proved that.

"Okay, let's let Sleeping Beauty snooze and get down to business." Darla seated herself in front of Beth's chair and pulled a pair of glasses from her briefcase. "Did you prepare the report I asked for?"

Obediently, Beth handed it to her.

The doctor scanned the notes while Beth waited silently. She knew better than to interrupt Darla's concentration. If the woman had questions, she would ask them when she was ready. If she had comments, she would make those, too.

It didn't take long. In only a few minutes Darla closed the file and removed her glasses. "Interesting family. Too bad your client had to resort to murder to get anyone's attention."

"If they had come to you, could you have helped them?"

"I don't know. Men like Delbert Lewis are usually resistant to outside interference. They don't believe they have a problem. They think it's all right to knock their wives around. It gives them a sense of power. Lewis may not have been a very strong man in character, but physically, he could beat and control and terrorize his wife, and that made him stronger than she was. Never mind that she was a thin, frail woman. He could still feel superior to *her.*"

"So he wouldn't have accepted your help," Beth said thoughtfully. "What about Carrie? Could you have convinced her that her life was in danger? That she could build a life for herself and her kids away from him?"

"She knew her life was in danger for a long, long time, Beth. She didn't just suddenly reach that realization a month ago, when she killed him. She had lived with that fear longer than you and I can imagine. As far as her leaving him . . ." The doctor sighed softly. "It may sound strange, but most abused wives don't want out of the marriage. Most of them still love their husbands, even after all the beat-

ings, all the broken bones, all the degradation and humili-
ation. They simply want the abuse to stop. They want to
stop being afraid. They want a normal marriage and a normal life *with* their husbands.''

''And those who do leave?''

''You're the one in the legal profession. You probably
know the answer to that better than I.''

She did. Too many women who left abusive husbands and
went into hiding got found. For too many of them the abuse
continued. For far too many it ended in death.

Darla slid the file, along with her glasses, into her atta-
ché, then stood up. ''I'll go over this again and do some
reading of my own over the next week.''

''Thanks. We'll see you in court a week from Monday.''
Beth politely got to her feet as the doctor left, then sank into
her seat again when the door closed once more. Her natural inclination was to turn her thoughts to Zachary once
more, but she used every bit of her self-discipline to chan-
nel her energy toward work instead. There would be plenty
of time to think about Zachary later. When she was alone
in her big, empty condo. Alone in her big, empty bed. Lying between those black sheets that had caught Zachary's
fancy. Remembering the way he'd kissed her last weekend.

For a long, drawn-out moment, the only sound in the
room was a soft, stifled, frustrated groan.

Zachary came awake slowly. His first thought was that he
was still fully dressed. His second was that he needed at least
twelve more hours of sleep to feel human. He stretched
slowly and started to roll over, then realized where he was:
on a couch, not a bed. In Beth's office, not his house.

The room was dark except for the lamp on her desk. She
sat there working, a stack of papers and a yellow pad in
front of her, her glasses slipping down her nose. Behind her,
the sky outside was black. He should have been on the road
hours ago, he thought, squinting to make out the numbers
on his watch. It was nearly nine o'clock. That meant it
would be midnight before he got home, which meant he

would get maybe five hours of sleep before he had to get up again, which meant . . .

He didn't want to think about how tired he would be in the morning. He didn't want to wonder how long he could function like this, adding the stress of a six-hour commute to already-long days. But he *couldn't* consider quitting.

Slowly he sat up, stretched, then reached for his shoes. Noticing he was awake, Beth pushed everything away and came to sit on the low table in front of him. She seemed more serious than usual, and he wondered why. Had something happened to Carrie, to their case? Had he talked in his sleep? Had he somehow offended her by falling asleep here?

"You must have been tired," she remarked evenly. "You've been asleep for at least five hours."

He knew his responding grin was unsteady, that it was threatening to slip away any second now. "What can I say besides it won't happen again?"

"It's all right. You still look half asleep. Tell me where you're staying and I'll give you a ride tonight. You don't need to be driving like this."

Why did he have the funny feeling that she already knew where he was staying? Had she called the motel where he'd spent the first three weeks and found out he wasn't registered? Did she know his money was about to run out? Did she think that *he* was about to run out, too, leaving her to finish this case alone? Was that what displeased her?

She waited patiently, her cool emerald gaze on him. He ran his fingers through his hair, then grinned again. "I'll be fine after a cup of coffee."

"Where *are* you staying, Zachary?"

"Someplace comfortable."

"Where?"

He sighed. "My house."

His suspicion had been correct. She didn't show even the slightest surprise. "You're driving back and forth from Sweetwater every day."

"Look, I already told you this won't happen again. I'll get caught up on my sleep this weekend. I'm just cutting back on expenses."

She didn't say anything for a long time. She just kept giving him that long, steady look that made him want to squirm like a naughty little boy caught in the middle of his latest mischief.

"It won't be a problem, Beth," he said, smiling his most charming smile, hoping to coax a returning smile from her. "I'm not going to run out on you. I just need to economize a bit. My income's not used to building a new house *and* out-of-town living expenses. But this won't change the time I can spend here or the work I can do."

She stood up and returned to her desk, clearing it, placing this folder in her briefcase, that one in the bottom desk drawer. When she was finished, she put on her suit jacket, then took her coat from the closet and shrugged into that, too. She looped a long, black knitted scarf around her neck, tugged on a pair of black gloves, then faced him again. "I have four extra bedrooms." She sounded stiff, awkward, ungenerous. "You can use one of them until the trial is over."

Now it was Zachary's turn to stare in silence.

She shifted from side to side. "I realize it doesn't have all the comforts of your home, but it's not a hundred and fifty miles away, either. And it's free. I'm hardly ever there, so you'll have plenty of privacy. You'll have the kitchen, if you like to cook, and—"

Slowly moving nearer, he interrupted her. "Have you thought this over?"

"Of course." She sounded defensive. "I don't act impulsively."

"You acted impulsively Saturday when you let me kiss you," he reminded her. "If you'd thought about it, you would have remembered that you don't get involved with men you work with, or with men who don't meet your very narrow requirements. You would have remembered that you don't get involved with men, period. But you didn't think it over. You acted on impulse. You let me kiss you, and you kissed me back. You—"

"I'm offering you a place to sleep," she said sharply, her cheeks flushing pink. "Not a woman to sleep with."

"And I'm warning you it won't stop there." Now he was standing directly in front of her, close enough to see the anger and annoyance—her defenses—in her eyes. He shook his head regretfully. "I appreciate the offer, Beth, but—"

Again she interrupted him. "You have no choice but to accept it. You can't continue commuting. You've already had snow up in the mountains. What if it snows again and you can't get into the city?" She didn't wait for him to respond. "You fell asleep reading this afternoon. Driving can be just as monotonous as reading, but a hell of a lot more dangerous. This is the only reasonable alternative."

He knew she was right. He was running a big risk of falling asleep at the wheel and driving right off the side of a mountain. But what kind of risks would he run if he accepted her offer? If he moved into her house? If he spent every night in a bed just down the hall from hers?

She didn't want a relationship with him. She didn't want to spend the rest of her life with him—although Saturday, he dryly acknowledged, she'd seemed pretty interested in a few hours with his body. But *he* wanted it all—an affair, a romance, a future. How painful would it be to live with her and have nothing?

But what if this was his chance to get *something,* anything that she could be persuaded to give him? At the very least it was a chance to spend more time with her. Even though she had said that she was hardly ever home, when she was, *he* would be there, too. When she went to sleep at night, when she awoke in the morning, he would be there.

He dragged his fingers through his hair once more, then slowly, solemnly nodded. "Okay. Thanks, Beth."

After he got his coat, they left the office, walking past empty offices, taking the elevator to the garage, which was empty except for their cars. Silently they separated there, Beth climbing into her import and Zachary walking to his

Jeep. Once the engine was warmed up, he followed her in a wide loop to the ground level, then through nearly empty streets to her condo.

The condominium was utterly silent, he marveled as he waited in the entry while she hung up their coats. The normal creaking, settling sounds of a house were absent. The clocks, including the tall antique grandfather clock in the entry, ticked silently. Even the kitchen appliances and the heating system seemed to make no noise. He'd never been aware of such stillness before, but Beth lived with it. No wonder she rarely spent any time here.

She approached him, her heels tapping loudly on the marble floor. "I'll show you the guest rooms, then we'll see about dinner."

With a nod he followed her up the stairs and down the hall past her own room. She pushed open the doors and flipped on the lights of each of the empty bedrooms, then waited silently for his choice.

Zachary didn't care about the interiors of the rooms. He simply chose the one farthest from Beth's. It was decorated in a pale blue that reminded him of ice, and all the accessories were snowy white: white carpet, white pillows on the chaise, white glass shades on the bedside lamps. He would like to see a lemon-yellow vase on that pale wood table, or some fiery crimson flowers on the marble mantel, or a bright-colored crazy quilt on the bed. None of that was likely in Beth's house.

But she did have those black sheets.

He'd brought nothing from home, since he had intended to return, but Beth supplied him with all the necessities—toothbrush, shampoo, razor, shaving cream—from a linen closet bigger than his bedroom in Sweetwater. He left them in the adjoining bathroom, also ice blue and white, then went in search of the kitchen.

It was gray—he remembered that from his previous visit. Everything except the gleaming steel of the sink, the cook top and the refrigerator was the same bland shade of gray. And there were no sharp corners, he noticed as he looked around. The island in the center of the room was oval-shaped. The corners of the cabinets were softly rounded, as were the edges of the counters and the small table and even the chairs in the breakfast nook.

The freezer door was open, and Beth was standing in front of it, sorting through an assortment of frozen gourmet dinners. She offered one for his approval, chose another for herself, then closed the door, read the instructions and stuck them in the microwave.

"You don't cook much," Zachary commented when she took a moment to figure out how to operate the microwave.

"Not at all. I buy these dinners for the occasional times when I'm too tired to go to a restaurant or order out. But my refrigerator is bare, more or less."

She opened it to reveal a six-pack of diet soda, a half-empty carton of bottled water and two bottles of imported beer. He knew she wasn't much of a drinker, and he certainly couldn't imagine her choosing beer when she did drink. Who, he wondered, had she bought those for? Which one of her diverting, unentangling gentlemen friends?

Common sense told him to forget them, but he was too curious. Too nosy. Too jealous. "Who's the beer drinker?"

She closed the refrigerator and leaned against it. "Someone I used to see."

"Let me guess. He's . . . a lawyer? A banker? A broker?" Shrugging as if it didn't matter, he moved to lean against the wall near the table. "A business whiz." That covered them all. "He's older than you. He drives an imported car, drinks imported beer and lives in a place like this. His income is in the mid six-figure range, his family is old, his style is impeccable, and his blood is blue—but not so blue that he's unimpressed by Walter Gibson and Bill Townsend." He smiled cynically. "And he wanted nothing but the pleasure of being seen socially with you. And you wanted . . . what? A diversion? You traded a few hours in public for a few hours in bed? No ties, no responsibilities, no obligations?"

Beth stared at him for a long moment, her expression unreadable. Then she moved away from the refrigerator and began gathering napkins, place mats, silverware. Her movements were jerky, uncoordinated, and her voice when she spoke was brittle. "He was an executive with one of the record companies here. You're right about the rest—*all* of it. We were together for two months, and we got exactly what we wanted from each other. You want to be judgmental with your small-town morals and your old-fashioned values, go right ahead. Say what you're thinking—that that's cold. That it's little better than prostitution. Trading services for sex."

She slapped the place mats on the table, tossed a napkin, knife, fork and spoon on each one, then stood in front of him. "Tell me that you've loved every woman you've been to bed with. Tell me that you've never taken a woman out, bought her a nice dinner and shown her a nice time, with the expectation of getting a little nice sex when it was over."

He gazed down into her angry green eyes, feeling as if he could lose himself in them. "I've never been in love with any woman," he said softly. "But I've never made love to a woman who I didn't care about, who I didn't have something—some romance, some relationship—going with. And I've never traded anything for sex."

Her laughter was soft, bitter, painful. "Of course not. I forgot. You're the romantic who believes in commitment and the healing power of love."

She was mocking him, but this time, Zachary acknowledged, he deserved it. He'd had no right to question her. He'd certainly had no right to criticize her. If she wanted to make love—*have sex,* the little voice in his head amended—with every man she knew, that was her business, not his.

He couldn't even tell her why he'd done it, couldn't explain the jealousy that had pushed him. He hated knowing that there were other men, men she hadn't cared deeply about. He hated knowing that she had so casually given this record company executive the very thing that *he* would cherish, that he ached for.

Gently he touched her, just his fingers to her cheek. She flinched, but she didn't pull away. "I'm sorry, Beth," he said quietly.

Finally she took a step back so that his hand fell away. Then she nodded curtly and turned toward the microwave as it dinged.

Watching her go, Zachary sighed deeply. "Oh, lady," he murmured softly. "I *am* sorry."

Chapter 9

Giving up any pretense at sleep, Beth opened her eyes and gazed into the cool darkness of her room. She didn't need to look at the clock to know it was late—the last time she'd checked, it had been one-fifteen—but her mind wouldn't let her body relax.

She'd given up berating herself for inviting Zachary to stay here. She had made the offer, he had accepted, and now she was stuck. Besides, she'd told him the truth. She spent very little time here, and most of that was asleep—or it usually was, she thought with a scowl. Tonight was an exception. Most mornings she was gone by seven, and she rarely got home at night until after eight. She spent evenings in the office downstairs, Saturdays at the firm and Sundays... Well, Sundays she could go shopping, or visit what few friends she had or, God forbid, even her parents.

It wouldn't be so bad having Zachary here, she told herself, and she even tried for a moment to believe it. Deep down inside, though, she knew it wasn't true. She didn't have to see him to know he was here. His mere presence seemed to change the aura of the house. He made it less empty. Less lonely. Less cold.

So it wouldn't be easy. Dinner had proven that. After that little scene, they'd both been uncomfortable. They'd eaten without speaking, although she had occasionally felt his regretful gaze on her. She hadn't relented and looked at him, though. She hadn't wanted to see that he truly was sorry for what he'd said. She hadn't wanted to hear him call her lady again in that soft, sad voice. She hadn't wanted another apology for words that she had provoked with her lies.

Her relationship with Gregory Hampton hadn't been as cold and emotionless as she'd made it sound. She had known from the start that nothing substantial would develop between them. She hadn't been looking for permanence, and neither had he. But it hadn't been a simple exchange of her company for his body. She had liked him—and, in fact, still did. She still occasionally went out with him, although they no longer went to bed afterward. He was one of the few men who she had become friends—of a sort—with.

But she had deliberately made it sound worse and had made herself sound sordid. Maybe she had wanted to warn Zachary away. Maybe she had wanted to convince him that she wasn't the kind of woman he wanted an affair with... before *he* convinced *her* that she was. It was only fair. After all, he had given a warning of his own in her office this evening. When she had told him that she was simply offering him a place to sleep, he had replied that it wouldn't stop there. If they were living together, they would probably end up sleeping together. No, making love together—that was how he would phrase it.

She smiled in the dark. It was a funny phrase, one that she seldom used and never with any real meaning. But when Zachary said it, it sounded different. Serious. Lasting. Erotic. He believed in it. He believed there was a difference between having sex and making love. He believed two people really could create something special and gentle and enduring.

Wouldn't it be nice if that were true? If she didn't have to spend the rest of her life alone? If she could one day find the courage to love someone, to someday be a wife and maybe even a mother?

That last thought made her scoff. It would take a miracle to transform the person she had become into mother material. She didn't even know how to relate to Tyler Lewis, and he was fourteen years old—hardly a child. Even Katie, her best friend's daughter, who greeted everyone with sweet smiles and kisses, generally met Beth with a solemn look, no more. And in spite of her parents' best efforts to get her to say Beth's name, the only thing Katie had ever called her was "Hey."

But Zachary was wonderful with children.

With a harsh groan, she rubbed her eyes. Enough was enough, and fantasies of motherhood were more than enough. She had other things to think about—Carrie's trial, all the other cases on her schedule, getting some sleep.

With her luck, she thought as she settled deeper beneath the covers, sleep would come…and bring with it dreams of Zachary.

Sweet dreams.

Although he hadn't liked Beth's condo from the first moment he'd seen it, Zachary found over the next few days that he didn't mind living there at all. The kitchen was stocked with every time-saving appliance conceivable, the bathtub in his private bathroom was just the right size for stretching out and relaxing, and the giant-screen television hidden inside an inlaid-wood cabinet in the corner of the living room certainly made Saturday afternoon sports more interesting to watch. Now that he had extra clothes and all the other essentials, courtesy of a quick trip to Sweetwater yesterday afternoon, he was as comfortable as he would be at home.

Beth had asked him to stay in the city this weekend so they could work. They had done just that well into the afternoon today; then she had gone on home while he'd stopped off to do a little grocery shopping. He wasn't a great cook, but he knew a dozen recipes for chicken, his chili rated at least three alarms, his roast was almost as good as his mother's, and his spaghetti would please any Italian. Right now a big pot of beef stew, just the thing for a cold, drizzly evening like this, was simmering in the kitchen. In another hour or so, when this football game was over, he would put a pan of cornbread in the oven and see if he could lure Beth out of whatever room she was hiding in for dinner.

The grandfather clock in the hall interrupted his thoughts, chiming seven times. As the last tone faded, he heard footsteps in the foyer and turned to watch as Beth entered the room. For a moment he simply stared; then the satisfaction he'd been feeling turned to a cold emptiness.

She was dressed for an evening out. She wore a black dress with a beaded bodice and a slinky, silky skirt and impossibly high black heels. Her hair was twisted in some complicated style that was at the same time sophisticated and softening. She was carrying a black handbag and, draped over her arm, a gorgeous black fur.

She had a date.

With one of those men she preferred.

"Whatever you're cooking smells delicious," she said, laying the bag and coat on the sofa beside him, then securing the back of one of the diamond earrings she wore. After fiddling with it for a moment, she sat down on the giant leather hassock at the opposite end of the couch and slipped off her shoes.

"Don't you think you're a little overdressed for an evening at home?" he asked, but his effort to inject a little teasing into his voice fell flat.

"One of my clients invited me to his anniversary party. I accepted weeks ago."

"How long has he been married?" An outfit like that deserved a really special occasion, something like the golden fiftieth, he thought morosely.

"Five years." She smiled, the practiced kind of smile she gave the people in the office. "I handled his first two divorces for him and drew up the prenuptial agreement for this marriage. Since he can walk away with practically everything he owns, it probably won't last another five.''

Zachary knew he was scowling, knew his displeasure was too apparent, but he wasn't as phony as Beth. He couldn't smile on command. "I thought you big-city lawyers specialized. Why is a trial lawyer handling divorces?''

"I did divorces when I first joined the firm. Some of my clients continue to request my services.'' She hesitated briefly over that word, and Zachary remembered the way she had used it only two nights ago—*trading services for sex*—and clenched his jaw. "I don't know how late I'll be. If there's someone you'd like to invite over while I'm out, feel free.''

She seemed relieved when the doorbell rang then. Quickly she scooped up her shoes and bent to put the first one on. She wasn't intending to invite her escort inside, Zachary realized. She wanted to meet him at the door and whisk him away before *he* got a look at him.

But he was quicker on his feet—not having to worry about shoes helped—and he was closer to the door. "Take your time,'' he graciously told her as he entered the foyer. "I'll get the door.''

The man waiting there was about what Zachary had expected. Smelling of cologne and looking entirely too perfect, he could have stepped right off the cover of some ritzy men's magazine. If he was surprised to find another man answering Beth's door, he hid it well behind a familiar smile—the male counterpart of Beth's—and said, "Good evening. I'm here to pick up Beth.''

Good evening? "Hey,'' Zachary greeted. "Come on in. She'll be ready in a minute. You must be—''

"Martin Hamilton.''

Where had he heard that name? he wondered. On the evening news? In the Sunday paper?

Before Zachary could say anything else, Beth joined them. He caught only a glimpse of her frown before she replaced it with a welcoming smile. "Hello, Martin.'' She raised her cheek for his kiss, then said, "This is Zachary Adams. He's in Nashville temporarily. We're working on a case together."

She barely gave them a chance to acknowledge the introduction, Zachary thought with a scowl, before she was continuing. "We'd better be on our way. I'll see you later, Zachary. Have a pleasant evening."

Hamilton reached for the fur she still held, but Zachary smoothly intercepted it. It felt... His grin was faint and whimsical. It felt the way fur was supposed to feel. Smooth. Silky. Luxurious. The way Beth's skin felt when his fingers came in contact with her bare neck. He lingered a moment in spite of the warning in her green eyes.

Then, suddenly, he stepped back. "Nice to meet you, Hamilton," he lied. "Have a good time, Beth."

The next five hours passed interminably slowly. He watched television. Ate dinner. Cleaned the kitchen. Wandered around the apartment. Finally he went to bed, but he couldn't sleep, not until he heard the front door open, then close, followed by footsteps on the stairs—a single set of footsteps.

He was annoyed with her for not mentioning her date earlier.

He was jealous of Hamilton for being the kind of man who appealed to her.

He hoped she'd had a rotten time.

And he was glad she was home. Safely. And alone.

"Do you want to go out to lunch?" Beth asked the question reluctantly. It was raining once again, and she had no desire to leave the dry warmth of the condo just for food, but she'd needed some way to break the silence that had existed between her and Zachary ever since she'd gotten up this morning. She knew he was angry about last night—well, maybe that was a little strong. He was irritated, and it made her feel unreasonably guilty. After all, just because she'd let him move in here temporarily didn't mean he had any say over her life. She could go out with whomever she wanted whenever she wanted, and she didn't need to clear it through him first.

But maybe she should at least have mentioned it to him. Apparently he had thought they were in for the evening. She suspected he might even have fixed that big pot of savory stew with the intention of sharing it with her. But if that was the case, he should have asked first. She was letting him live in her house, giving him free access to everything in it; did she have to provide him with company, too?

He was lying on his stomach on the floor, sections of the Sunday paper scattered around him. He seemed to find the newspaper that she usually only scanned extraordinarily interesting . . . but then, he lived in a town where the only paper was a weekly that did a less-efficient job of providing news than the rumor mill.

Or maybe the paper provided an easy excuse to pretend that she wasn't here.

Finally he rolled onto his side, resting on his elbow, and looked at her. "Lunch?" he repeated, considering it for a moment. Then he shook his head. "Go ahead. I'd rather stay here and have a bowl of stew."

If it tasted half as good as it had smelled last night, so would she, Beth thought. Pushing aside the knitted throw that covered her feet, she stood up from the sofa. "I'll put it in the microwave—"

"You don't have to stay here because of me."

She hesitated. "Would you prefer that I go out?" It was going to hurt if he said yes, she realized, even though it shouldn't. Hadn't she already planned to spend today away from the condo, away from him?

He sat up and began neatly stacking and folding the newspaper. "It's your house, Beth."

"That doesn't answer my question."

He rose to his feet in one fluid movement and stopped in front of her. For a moment he simply looked at her, letting her read his eyes. He was more than annoyed about her date last night, she saw. He was jealous—jealous that she'd willingly gone out with Martin while it seemed that nothing she did with *him* was done willingly. Impulsively, maybe, but not willingly.

"No," he said finally. "I don't want you to feel as if you have to leave."

That wasn't what she wanted. Stubbornly she waited, and, after a deep exhalation, he said what she needed to hear.

"No. I don't want you to go out today."

It wasn't fair to want him to feel that way when she was giving him nothing in return, but it pleased her, anyway. It made her feel warm and tingly deep inside. She tried a smile, a tentative one, a genuine one, and found it shaky. "I'll put the stew in the microwave now," she said softly and turned away.

Part of her hoped that he would follow her, but he didn't, so she busied herself with lunch. She wrapped squares of cornbread in foil and placed them in the oven to heat, then spooned several big helpings of stew into a bowl for the microwave. While everything cooked, she set the table and poured two glasses of tea, then called Zachary's name.

He appeared in the doorway. "Do you have a tray?"

She gestured to the niche in the island that held a variety of serving trays, and he pulled one out and began placing the butter, dishes and napkins on it.

"I've built a fire. Let's eat there."

She didn't need to ask which room. There were a number of fireplaces in the house, but only one was ever used: the one in her office. Agreeing, she added the food to the tray, then followed him down the hall.

The fire was bright and hot, and it filled the room with a warm, woodsy fragrance. Zachary sat down in front of the hearth and began ladling the thick stew into their bowls. At first Beth sat in the closest chair, but when he offered her a napkin, with silverware rolled inside, she slid to the floor across from him before accepting it.

"I take it you only eat at the table."

She shrugged.

"And you don't go on picnics. You don't have lunch on the floor. You don't stretch out on the sofa to watch TV with a big bowl of popcorn."

Feeling a little wistful, she shook her head. "I don't get casual."

"Is that a conscious choice or a result of the way you were brought up?"

She complimented his cooking before considering his question. "The way I was brought up, I suppose," she replied slowly. "About the only thing my parents ever agreed on was how they thought a proper little girl should behave. I always wore dresses. I never spoke to an adult—except my great-grandmother—unless they spoke first. My manners were impeccable. I never had outbursts, I was never rude, and I never talked back."

"What else did you never do?" Zachary asked. "Did you never have fun? Did you never get to be a little girl? Did you never get loved?"

She bit into a piece of cornbread, savoring the warm, buttery flavor. The crumbs that broke off fell into her bowl, soaking up the rich, dark juices. "My great-grandmother loved me," she said with a smile of remembrance. "Althea spoiled me. I was her favorite of all the children. I missed her so much when she died."

For a moment she fell silent, listening as the rain outside picked up in intensity, the fat drops splashing against the windowpanes. Inside it was countered by the crackle and hiss of the fire. "When I was little, I used to make these elaborate plans to run away with Althea. I knew we couldn't stay at her house or my parents would find us, so I thought maybe we could go to New York or California, someplace far away."

"Why did you want to run away?" Zachary asked so softly that she barely heard him.

She looked at him and smiled, this time a little shyly. "The point wasn't simply running away. It was doing it *with* Althea." Then her smile faded. "I wanted to get away from all the fighting and the screaming. I wanted to escape being put in the middle, used by my mother to anger my father and vice versa. I wanted to go off and live someplace quiet with the only person I was absolutely sure loved me.''

Zachary set his dishes aside, then settled down comfortably, his head pillowed on his arm, and watched Beth. He was half afraid that if he spoke too loudly or moved too suddenly, she would realize that she was telling him things she had probably never shared with anyone, and the mood would be broken.

He ached for the little girl whose parents had neglected her emotional needs as surely as they had provided for the physical ones. He wished he could protect her from ever being hurt, ever being unloved, again. He had the love to give, the gentleness she needed, the tenderness she'd never known except for those few short years from that one old lady. It was simply a matter of acceptance. Could she accept love, gentleness and tenderness from a man who was so obviously not her type? And could he accept that whatever she took from him would only be temporary, ending when he returned to Sweetwater?

Wasn't it better than nothing?

Wasn't loving somebody once, even only temporarily, better than going through life wondering how it would feel?

"Why do you see your parents now?"

She busied herself for a moment gathering everything onto the tray once again. She was searching for an answer, he suspected, and couldn't find one she felt was satisfactory. "They're my family," she said finally, with a helpless shrug.

"It's your duty as their daughter," he replied, and got a confirming nod from her. "Daniel's mother left him on his own when he was a kid so that she could concentrate on her own needs. In all the time Katie—her only grandchild—has lived with him, Patsy has made no effort to meet her. She's shown no interest in Sarah. But now that she and her husband just happen to be passing through Tennessee on their way someplace else, she wants to stop by for a few hours. And because she's his mother, because he's been a good son even if she hasn't been a good mother, Daniel feels obligated to let her put in an appearance in their lives, even though he knows she'll disappear again until they're convenient for her."

"Do you think he's foolish for that?"

"No. I think the importance of *family* takes deeper root in some people than others. I think it means more to Daniel than it does to his mother. I think it means more to you than it does to your parents."

"But that's foolishness," Beth persisted. "Logically, Daniel should want nothing to do with his mother."

He noticed that she didn't include herself in that supposition. But inside, he suspected, she did. She knew that her parents had long ago abused whatever special treatment being family accorded them. They no longer deserved forgiveness or tolerance. They no longer deserved their daughter. "Logic has nothing to do with it, Beth. We're talking about families. That's emotion, and emotion is very rarely logical." *He* was living proof of that.

"Don't you find this subject the slightest bit depressing?" she asked, forcing a smile that lacked pleasure.

As a matter of fact, he did, but he didn't say so. He simply offered the change of subject that she wanted. "What do you normally do on Sundays?" Then, before she could answer, he gave her his most charming grin. "And please don't say work."

Beth responded with a grimace. "Only when I have to. I go shopping or run errands or read."

"And what do you read? Law books? The U.S. Code?"

He wasn't far off the mark, she thought. She didn't often read fiction. Grim stories with unhappy endings filled her workdays; she didn't find pleasure in reading them on her weekends. She didn't have the imagination for science fiction, didn't enjoy mysteries, didn't believe in the happily-ever-after of romances. "Biographies," she replied. "History."

"What else do you do for pleasure?"

She gave it a long moment's thought. She had devoted herself so completely to her career that she'd never found time to develop other interests. She'd never found a need. There really wasn't anything else in her life that qualified as pleasure...except Zachary.

Trying to blame the heat that flooded her face on the fire, she rose to her knees, picked up the tray and started to stand up. But he stopped her, gently pulling the tray away and setting it on the hearth. He spoke her name softly, hoarsely, and took her hands in his, drawing her closer, slowly closer, until all she could see was him. All she could feel... All she could want...

Snatching her hands away, she jumped to her feet and picked up the tray. A glass fell, sloshing tea over the butter dish, spilling ice cubes into an empty bowl. "I—I have things to do," she said abruptly. "Make yourself at home, and I—I'll see you later."

"What do you think?"

Zachary hadn't been in Beth's office more than sixty seconds when the question came. He silently groaned. His head was hurting, he was tired, and he would have given anything for a few quiet moments alone before he answered any questions.

The last five days had been difficult ones. The closer the trial had moved, the harder they'd worked, and the more stressful life had become. He wasn't cut out to handle this kind of case, he'd acknowledged. Talent, money, prestige—all those things that usually figured into career decisions aside, he didn't have the make-up for such pressure. Everyone was short-tempered. He and Beth hardly spoke to each other anymore outside the office, and even Carrie had blown up, then burst into tears, during this afternoon's interview.

Of course, his personal feelings for Beth weren't helping an already-tense situation any. He was tired of her stubbornness, tired of getting nowhere with her, tired of the walls she kept throwing up between them.

He was tired of wanting her and never getting what he wanted.

With a sigh, he finished removing his jacket and gloves, then turned his attention to her. She waited near her desk, holding a green dress with black trim in front of her. "It's not your style," he said after a moment. "Or your size. But the color's nice."

She gestured impatiently, unamused by his response. "It's for Carrie. For the first day of her trial. I don't want the jurors to see her in a jail uniform."

He studied the dress more closely. The style was simple—long sleeves, a rounded neck, a full cut to allow for Carrie's pregnancy. The fabric was cotton, the color brighter, probably, than anything she'd ever chosen for herself. "It'll be fine." As she folded it back into the box on one chair, he sprawled comfortably in the other. "I took Dr. Vega back to her hotel after she finished interviewing Carrie. She said she'll meet us here tomorrow morning at ten."

Beth nodded as she sat down. She removed a pair of black shoes—also for Carrie, he assumed—from her desk, then folded her hands together and looked at him. "You don't like her, do you?"

"I thought I'd done a pretty good job of hiding that," he remarked flippantly, then sighed. Psychologist Marian Vega was one of the foremost experts on battered woman syndrome in the country. She was intelligent, shrewd and sympathetic. She was also sharp-edged, blunt almost to the point of offensiveness, and a die-for-the-cause feminist. The woman had taken an immediate liking to Beth, an independent career woman dedicated to helping a sister in need. Her dislike for Zachary had come just as quickly and, as far as he could tell, for reasons just as superficial: he was a man. Marian Vega saw men as the enemy. It was a male-dominated society that had allowed Carrie's situation to exist and a male-dominated justice system that had failed to intervene until it was too late. He was judged guilty by association.

"She is a little too much, isn't she? But she's testified in a lot of similar trials, and she's usually very effective."

"She's sincere," Zachary admitted. "She believes what she says one hundred percent, and the jury can see that. As long as that's all they hear—and not her speeches on the evil of men—she'll be effective." He gestured toward the legal pad in front of Beth. "What else do we have to do today?"

She consulted the list. "The witnesses have all been subpoenaed. Dr. Newman will meet us in court Monday morning for the jury selection. Mr. Morris will bring Tyler in as soon as we notify him."

"So you're going to make the kid testify." He had hoped she would change her mind, had hoped they could build a strong-enough case without Tyler. The way things were going, he might as well give up hoping—about anything.

"What do you want me to do? Put on the rest of our defense, wait until the jury finds her guilty, then say, 'Oh, wait, I have one other witness who just might change your mind'?" she demanded sarcastically. "I don't *want* to put that boy on the witness stand. I don't want to make him get up there in front of a roomful of strangers and tell them what an awful man his father was. But even more, I don't want to miss even the slightest chance of keeping his mother from spending the rest of her life in prison."

Zachary didn't argue with her. How could he, when he knew about her own unhappy childhood? When he knew that she would do anything—except sacrifice her client—to protect a child from being hurt?

"If it makes you feel any better," she continued stiffly, "you'll be the one questioning him. He relates to you better than to me."

"Fine," he said just as stiffly. "It's been a long day, and we have to meet Dr. Vega tomorrow. Let's go home."

Her gaze locked defiantly with his as she said, "I have a date tonight."

Again. He wasn't even surprised. Just annoyed—and so jealous that his teeth ached with it. "Then *I'm* going home."

Grabbing his jacket he walked out, closing the door quietly when all he wanted was to slam it.

When he reached his Jeep, he tossed his coat in the back seat, climbed in and simply sat there. He didn't want to go home. If Beth had come, even if they had spent another awkward, silent evening together, he could have managed it. But going there now, knowing she would soon follow, but only to get ready for her date, having to see the man she'd chosen instead of him—that was more than he could bear.

Late Friday afternoon wasn't the best time to be driving aimlessly around Nashville, but his timing was never great, anyway. If he were home in Sweetwater, he would drive up to the farm and chop some wood. Just a walk through his house would calm him. The closeness he always felt to his grandfather would soothe him.

But he was hours from his mountain and a lifetime away from his grandfather, and here in the city he had no place to go. And so he went for a drive.

He found himself in a neighborhood he'd never seen before, one that he had looked up on his city map out of curiosity but had never intended to visit. It was the neighborhood where Beth's parents lived. Where she had grown up. He had come across the address by accident while looking for a number in her Rolodex, and somehow it had taken root in his memory. That brief search for the street on the map had registered, too, so that he'd driven here without consciously intending to.

He drove along the street until he found the house that matched the number in his mind; then for a moment he simply sat there and stared. There were no tall security fences here. From what he'd heard of Francine and Walter Gibson, they seemed the type to take pleasure in their wealth and in displaying it for all the world to see. And there was certainly a lot here to display.

The drive wound through a beautifully landscaped lawn, passing by the broad main entrance, then curved around to the garage behind the house. The lawn easily covered six acres, and the house itself seemed practically as large. It was probably twenty rooms, he estimated, maybe more. It was far beyond the dreams of the average person and twice that far out of reach for someone like him.

It had been, for eighteen years, Beth's home.

And he'd thought her condo was too big, he thought with a touch of self-mockery. It must have seemed like doll's quarters to her after growing up in this place.

With a sigh, he checked over his shoulder, then pulled into the street again. Thoroughly depressed, he drove away.

Beth dressed as carefully as she did for every date, but this time her heart wasn't in it. As she surveyed herself in the mirror, she admitted that she didn't really care how she looked. She would settle for "passable" tonight.

Still, the outfit she'd chosen—a velvet off-the-shoulder blouse and a slim-fitting skirt—was nice, and its emerald-green color complemented her eyes. The skirt was shorter than she ordinarily wore, but she had the legs for it. She liked the rich texture of the velvet and the way the neckline of the blouse slipped off her shoulders as if by accident and not by design. She liked the way the outfit looked and the way it made her feel and . . .

Sighing, she swept her hair back and fastened it on both sides with heavy gold combs. The only thing wrong with her plans for this evening, she admitted as she scowled at her reflection in the mirror, was the man she'd made them with. She was going out with the wrong man, while the right one waited here at home.

It was as if the mere thought of Zachary brought his presence right into the room with her. Well, almost. She saw with a sideways glance at the open door that he was standing in the hall, his hands shoved into his hip pockets, his displeasure evident even though his face was in shadow.

Directing her gaze back to the mirror, she picked up a pair of diamond earrings. Each stud measured a full two carats and was flawless. More than once she'd been told that diamonds suited her nature: icy and cold. Did Zachary also hold that opinion? she wondered as she inserted first one, then the other.

Aware that he was still watching her, she slipped into her heels and started across the room. She reached the hallway just as the doorbell downstairs chimed, but for a moment she stood motionless, simply looking at him. He looked angry, as if he'd somehow been cheated.

He looked hurt.

He looked—heaven help her—too precious. Too perfect. Too desirable.

The doorbell sounded again, but she ignored it. Instead, she spoke his name and reached out hesitantly, wanting only to touch him, to somehow tell him that she was sorry for everything. But he shied away as if her touch was unwelcome, and with a pang of regret, she started to turn away.

He moved quickly, unexpectedly, blocking her way. His hands came up to cup her face, and his mouth came down to cover hers. It was a quick kiss, hot and demanding and relentless, and it made her crave more—more touching, more kissing, more everything—until she'd taken all he could give. She didn't care that it had begun in anger. It mattered only that it ended in passion. In need. In a bone-melting groan that was part her name, part pure desire.

Before she could reach to pull him back, he was out of reach, wiping her lipstick from his mouth, giving her another of his long, hard looks. *I'll cancel my date and spend the evening with you,* she was about to offer, but she clenched her jaw to keep the words in. If she stayed here tonight, they wouldn't have any trouble finding something to occupy the hours, as they had the previous nights.

They would make love.

Zachary wanted it.

She wanted it.

As the doorbell rang for a third time, Zachary glanced down the stairs, then back at her. "You'd better get that."

Confused and off balance, she remained where she was. More than anything in the world she wanted to stay here and explore that kiss—to explore *him*. Knowing that they would make love if she canceled her date, she wanted to do just that. Knowing that it would be a mistake, she wanted to do it anyway. If only Zachary would ask... He wanted her—she only had to look in his eyes to see that. She only needed to remember the insistence of his mouth on hers.

But he didn't ask, and she couldn't offer.

It was that simple.

She was halfway down the stairs when he spoke. "Hey, Beth."

Her fingers clenched around the railing, she turned and looked at him. He was smiling, but it wasn't pleasant or sweet or any of the other qualities she associated with his smiles. It was sarcastic, just as his voice was when he continued.

"Have a nice time."

Nine.

Ten.

Eleven.

Twelve.

Zachary paused in front of the grandfather clock, listening to it chime the midnight hour. He'd done this—stopped and counted—every hour since Beth had left with her date. All four of them.

Four hours wasn't so long for a date, he kept telling himself, especially not for the kind of formal affairs Beth preferred. But surely by midnight even Nashville's hardiest socializers had to think about calling it a night. Surely she would be home soon, and he could go to bed and stop worrying and wondering. Unless...

Unless she was already home—at her date's home—and already in bed. He knew that was a possibility. She'd never said she would be home late. She'd never said she would be home at all. Maybe she was spending the night with the guy. Maybe she would come home at three or four in the morning, fresh from his bed to hers. Maybe...

Muttering a curse, he went into the dimly lit living room. He couldn't deal with the idea of Beth making love to someone else. In the past, sure. He had no problem with that. Virtually everyone had past affairs, past lovers. But not now. Not while he was here. Not while he would sell his soul to make love to her, to love her. Not while he was willing to trade his future for a present with her.

If it weren't so damned painful, it would be funny, he thought as he stared out the window at the city lights. He had never been less than level-headed, had never shown anything but common sense in his relationships with women. He had never lost his temper or his patience with a woman. He had never experienced even the slightest twinge of jealousy, to say nothing of the kind that made him feel sick inside.

Until Beth.

How had he ever fallen in love with a woman so different, so obviously not meant for him? How had he forgotten level-headedness and common sense? How had he ever expected to make any kind of relationship work with a woman who wanted no relationship at all?

For a moment he forgot the city and focused on his reflection instead. His expression was bleak, the set of his mouth grim. Two perfect words to describe the mess he'd made of his life. And he grew even bleaker, even grimmer, as he asked the next silent questions.

How was he going to get through this?

How could he make her want him?

How could he make himself stop wanting her?

And, most important of all, how could he stop loving her?

Chapter 10

He must have dozed off, Zachary realized the instant he was awake. He was sitting on the couch, his head tilted back, his feet propped on the coffee table. His neck was stiff and his bare feet were cold, but none of that mattered, because outside the apartment, through the partially opened door, he could hear Beth's voice and her laughter, soft and sexy.

He could also hear the lower, masculine sound of her companion's voice.

"Not tonight, Jason," she replied in response to his mumbled question. "I had a lovely evening. Thanks."

There was a moment's silence—a kissing type of silence, Zachary thought with a scowl—then Beth said good-night and closed the door. He heard the lock click; then she came into sight, pausing at the bottom of the stairs to remove her fur and drape it over the banister. She braced herself with one hand on the rail while she removed first one shoe, then the other, leaving them standing neatly on the bottom step.

Then she turned toward the living room, probably intending to shut off the lamp he'd left burning. That was when she saw him.

"So... tell me about Jason," he requested, picking up a small throw pillow and propping it behind his head. "Is there anything to tell, or is he a carbon copy of all your other dates?" He put all his anger and frustration into that last word, making it sound as unflattering as he could.

Beth slowly entered the room, but she didn't come close. Given his mood, he didn't blame her.

"Waiting up for me?" she asked coolly.

"Why didn't you invite him in? That was what he wanted, wasn't it? To have a drink? To maybe spend the night? Or did you already get that part out of the way?"

She took a seat on the edge of the coffee table. Now she was close enough that he could smell her perfume. He could feel her anger. And he could see all too much of her long, sexy legs. He let his feet fall to the floor with a dull thud, then sat up, fully intending to rise from the couch and shut himself away in his room, where he could go insane in private. But sitting up placed him even closer, and it robbed him of the desire to go anywhere.

"What do you want, Zachary?" she demanded. "Do you want a blow-by-blow description of my entire evening? Do you want a detailed account of everything we did, every time he touched me, every time he kissed me? Well, you're not getting it because it's none of your damned busi—"

He interrupted her quietly. Solemnly. Honestly. "I want *you.*"

Beth stared at him, remembering after a moment to close her mouth on the words she'd never finished. *I want you.* It sounded simple enough. She'd heard the words from other men. She had even said them to one or two. But coming from Zachary they meant something entirely different. Not sex. Not mere physical pleasure. Not a few hours tonight that would be forgotten tomorrow.

He was talking about making love. About sharing. About committing. About caring.

About things she'd sworn she didn't want in her life. About things she wanted so badly right now that she ached with it.

"Beth?" His whisper sounded raw, filled with equal measures of need and despair, and his blue eyes searched her face for some clue to her feelings.

But she had no answers for him, none for herself. Could she make love with him tonight without hating herself for it in the morning? Could she survive loving him and knowing that it was only temporary, that when Carrie's trial ended, he would go back to Sweetwater, back to his life without her, and leave her in this life without him?

But if she turned him down, if she chose to protect herself, could she live with that? Could she face every day of the rest of her life regretting her decision here tonight?

Could she pass up the opportunity to be Zachary's lady, even if only for a while?

He must have seen something encouraging in her eyes because he touched her—the gentlest, sweetest, most endearing touch she'd ever felt—and she gave up thinking, considering, deciding. *This* was what she wanted—this man, this gentleness, this caress. For as long as it lasted, whether it was one night or more, a few hours or a few weeks, this was what she needed.

"All right," she whispered so softly that the words faded before they were fully formed.

He slid his fingers behind her neck and drew her closer, until their mouths almost touched, until their breaths combined, until she could almost taste him. "Are you sure?" he whispered. "Are you sure you want this?"

Her eyes closed, she sought for some way to convince him and settled for the simple honesty he'd given her earlier. "Yes, Zachary." She leaned toward him, and her next words were lost in his mouth. "I'm sure."

They had kissed before—once outside the door, once in his house, once upstairs—but each time was different. This kiss was almost leisurely, a slow savoring of tastes and textures, a slow feeding of the passion she'd tried too long to deny. It heated her body, made her clothes unbearably warm, her skin unbearably sensitive. Every place he touched her, she throbbed—as well as the places he didn't touch, the parts of her that longed for his kisses, his caresses.

Zachary slowly ended the kiss, then looked at her, half afraid he would see rejection in her eyes. But when he looked, he saw only the soft haziness of arousal. Desire.

At some point while he was kissing her, he had moved from the sofa to his knees on the floor. Now he stood up and offered both hands to Beth. "Will you come upstairs with me?" he asked hoarsely.

The formality of his request made her smile as she placed her hands in his. "That's a good idea," she replied, her voice husky, too. "You see, I have these black sheets...."

The mere mention of the sheets was enough to make him groan. Did she have any idea how often he had fantasized about her lovely body on those wicked sheets? Clenching his jaw, he released her hands and followed her up the stairs, bypassing the heels and the rich black fur.

He stopped in the doorway while she crossed the room to turn on a lamp. For a moment, they simply stood there, a room apart, looking without touching. Feeling. Needing. Longing. Then he approached her, and she met him near the bed. He removed the combs from her hair, letting it fall over his hands, gliding his fingers through the silky strands, tangling his hands in them to hold her still while he took her mouth with his once more.

Shifting restlessly, Beth moved closer, bringing most of her body in contact with his. All that work at his farm had left him in better shape than any other lawyer she'd ever known—than any other man, period, she amended. His muscles were solid and taut with need, and if there was an ounce of fat on his body, she hadn't found it yet—not that she intended to quit looking.

Then she moved her hips against his and felt his arousal, long and hot and thick, against her belly. When was the last time, she wondered dimly, that she'd felt such satisfaction, such power, over the hunger she'd aroused in a man?

The last time she'd made love with a man like Zachary. Never.

Abandoning her mouth, he left a long trail of kisses down her throat, stopping only at the barrier of her blouse. Raising his head, he gazed at her, the look in his eyes so intense that it made her shiver, and while he looked, he raised his hand to her breast, and that made her shiver, too. He stroked across the velvet, finding her nipple, already full and hard, for the first time. He stroked it, gently pinching, and she whimpered. It was a helpless sound, foreign to her own ears, full of everything she wanted from him.

"You are so beautiful," he murmured as his fingers disappeared inside the rounded neck of her blouse. She shuddered again and tried to speak, but the only sound she could form was a gasp as he rubbed her tender breast with his callused fingers.

Zachary tugged, and the blouse slipped far enough to reveal one bare breast. He liked the contrast of his fingers, dark from so much sun and rough, against the velvet, rich green and soft, and Beth's skin, ivory pale and the softest of all. He liked the way her nipple, the color of a dusky pink rose, responded to the slightest touch of his fingers. He liked the way her heart pounded beneath his palm, matching the same relentless throbbing that he felt within himself.

Supporting her with one arm, he ducked his head to taste her nipple, tugging it into his mouth, gently suckling and making her moan, making her fingers clench helplessly on his shoulders. When he nipped the hypersensitive crest, tremors raced through her, and she groaned aloud, trying to form his name but settling for a throaty sound of pleasure.

Pulling her blouse back in place, he guided her to the dresser a few feet away, giving her the solid wood for support and freeing his hands to stroke and tease and caress her. He glided his fingers over the bare skin of her shoulders and rubbed slowly, sensuously over the rich nap of the velvet. His hands slid along the slick fabric of her skirt, past the hem that ended mid-thigh and over her stockings, both sensuously coarse and soft at the same time.

Settling his hands at her waist, he simply looked at her. Her head was bowed, her hair falling forward to hide her face, but after a moment, almost as if drawn by his gaze, she looked up at him. Her eyes were smoky and shadowy, a passionate contrast against her fiery hair and delicate fair skin. The lipstick was gone from her mouth, kissed away, and her lips were slightly parted. Her hair, always sleek and smooth, fell in fragile tangles where he'd wrapped his hands in it, and one thick strand was caught on the cold glimmer of the diamond stud she wore.

She was beautiful. Heartachingly, unforgettably beautiful.

And that was what he was setting himself up for tonight. Heartache. A lifetime of not having and not forgetting. Never forgetting.

But not for a minute did he consider walking away.

Still holding her gaze, he began unfastening each button on his shirt. After only two, Beth pushed his hands away and took over the task, working slowly, sliding her fingers between the buttons for light, insubstantial caresses that made his skin tingle. When she reached his jeans, her fingers hesitated, and he squeezed his eyes shut. She was so close to touching him more intimately than they'd ever touched, and he swore he could almost feel her hand there. His body grew heavier with anticipation, and heavier still when she prudently returned her attention—and her hands—to his shirt, pulling it from his jeans, undoing the last two buttons, guiding it off his arms.

In much the same way that he had caressed her a moment ago, she stroked him, but he had the advantage of feeling her long, talented fingers on his bare skin instead of through heavy clothing. His muscles tightened with every light touch, every scrape of her nails, every moist kiss. Finally, when his skin rippled at her barest touch, when his breathing was uneven and harsh, when he feared he couldn't endure much more, she stopped and pulled off her blouse. She didn't step away from him when she did it, so that he felt the touch of her arms, the brush of her breasts, the coolness of her skin, against his chest.

Then she began unfastening his belt, and he *knew* he couldn't take much more. Suddenly she had become clumsy, having problems with the belt buckle and the metal buttons of his jeans. She had to search, to probe, to awkwardly fumble with every fastening, until his restraint was worn thin, until his need was too powerful, too raw, to control.

"Damn it, lady," he growled, pushing her hands away and drawing her whisper-close for a kiss. His tongue filled her mouth, demanding, stroking, mimicking, and his hands made short work of the zipper that secured her skirt.

Without breaking the kiss, they somehow finished removing their clothing, then moved the few feet to the bed in a passionate embrace. Blindly Zachary followed her down to the mattress, covering her slender body with his, settling between her thighs, sheathing himself in the tight, warm welcome of her body.

For a moment he held himself rigid, adjusting to the heated feel of her flesh, marveling at how perfectly they fitted together, savoring for just one moment the sheer pleasure of being like this with Beth. Then his body protested the demands he'd placed on it, protested being joined so intimately with such a beautiful woman and being unable to seek completion, and he gave in to the need.

Beth struggled to keep her eyes open. Too often she'd completed this act in the dark with some uninspiring man and lukewarm feelings. She had never before experienced this level of need, this kind of pleasure, this intense sort of torment, and she wanted to see the man responsible. She wanted to watch Zachary, to see the passion that shadowed his blue eyes and held his muscles so tight. She wanted to see his face when he reached fulfillment, when the release of his desire flooded into her, when everything, for that long, endless moment, ceased to exist except this.

She wanted to see the caring.

Each thrust he made was long and deep and filled her more surely than she'd ever thought possible. The empti-

ness and the coldness she'd harbored for so long faded away,
and the dissatisfaction that had tormented her disappeared, too. There was no place inside her that wasn't filled
by Zachary. No emotion that wasn't tuned to him. No need
that wasn't met by him.

She arched her back to meet him, wondering dimly how
sensation could be so painful, how pain could be so pleasurable. The need that had begun in her soul and spiraled
outward now filled her entire body, and every touch—his
mouth against hers, his hands on her breasts, his hips
rhythmically brushing hers—fed that need. She burned with
it, ached with it, even—to her dim surprise—cried with it,
until it consumed her. Her heart was pounding, her body
throbbing, as tremors rippled through her, causing her
nerves to tighten reflexively, bringing her breath in empty
gasps, drawing a cry from deep inside her throat. A moment later she was aware of Zachary's own release, of the
muscles deep in her belly tightening helplessly around his
hardness, of his harsh groan, of liquid fire and potent satisfaction.

Such satisfaction.

He sank against her, his body slick and hot and comfort-
ingly heavy. His breath tickled her ear, and she turned her
head to the side so that she could press a kiss to his mouth.
Then, smiling sweetly, she closed her eyes.

She'd seen what she'd wanted.

When he found the strength to move again, Zachary
pulled the covers down. Beth's eyes were closed, her
breathing heavy, her body limp, and she grumbled softly
when he dragged the comforter from underneath her. He
started to lie down beside her, but for a moment he hesitated and instead simply looked at her. The sight was even
better than he'd fantasized: midnight-black sheets, pure
blazing red hair, smooth ivory skin. Add to that the things
he'd had to guess at before—the soft, full curves of her
breasts, the narrow line of her waist, the slender flare of her

ips, the dusting of red-gold curls between her thighs and those sexy, long legs—and the picture was perfect.

Their loving had been perfect, too, so perfect that he'd thought he just might die from it. He had never experienced anything like it, and it would be a long time before he would recuperate enough to try it again.

Or so he'd thought. But his body was proving him wrong. Simply looking at her was making him hard again—not with the unbearably desperate need that had seized him before, but simply, comfortably, hungrily hard. The kind of arousal that could be enjoyed or ignored.

And since Beth seemed to be sleeping, it would go ignored tonight.

After turning off the lamp, he lay down beside her and drew the covers over them. She hadn't suggested that he should return to his room, and he certainly wasn't volunteering. He wanted this night with her, wanted her to snuggle into his arms as she'd just done, wanted to spend an entire night knowing she was just a few inches away.

She settled in next to him, her head pillowed on his arm, her knee bent across his, her arm across his... He stiffened as she moved it from his chest to his stomach, then lower still. Her hand was across his groin now, unmoving but innocently touching. Innocently arousing.

Zachary swallowed hard and tried to ignore the swelling there, but it wouldn't be ignored. Worse, it brought other sensations clearly to mind: how smooth and soft her skin was, how clearly defined the muscles in her thighs were, how warm and heavy her breast felt against his ribs.

He swallowed again, then whispered, "Hey, lady."

There was a long silence, broken by a soft, "Hmm?"

"You want to roll over the other way?"

"Not now," she murmured sleepily. "I've got my hands full."

"Not yet," he disagreed, "but you will in a minute if you don't move."

"I don't want to move." Sighing softly, she pressed a kiss to his chest, then rubbed her cheek back and forth in a sleek, sensuous gesture. "That was nice, Zachary."

He slid his fingers into her hair. "Thanks a lot," he replied, sounding chagrined. "That's just what every man in the world wants to hear after making love to a beautiful woman. *That was nice.*"

She laughed softly. It was a sound he'd heard so seldom from her, and rarely for him. He liked it that she was able to laugh here, now, after what had just happened between them. "It was wonderful. Fantastic. Unequaled."

"Unequaled. I like the sound of that."

"The male ego," she said, her mocking sigh whispering across his nipple. One more moist little whoosh like that, he thought, and that small part of his anatomy would be as erect as another was quickly becoming.

"You say that as if there is no female ego. Aren't you the least bit interested in whether *I* thought this was 'nice'?"

She brought her knee up to press gently against him. "Even if you were terribly bored the entire time, you're too much of a gentleman to say it was less than perfect."

The only light in the room came from the wall of windows, and it was too weak for him to see her face. Still, he reached out unerringly and wrapped a strand of her hair around his finger before giving it a tug. "Maybe it wasn't perfect," he said thoughtfully. "But it *was* the best time in my life. We'll work on perfect later."

She gave up her pretense at disinterest and with tantalizing caresses began exploring the treasure beneath her hand. "How long until it's later?" she asked huskily.

Zachary caught his breath as she cradled him in her hand. "How long will it take you to slide over here?" he replied, his voice just as husky.

She moved gracefully into position above him, taking him deep within her, then leaned down to kiss him. He tasted her mouth briefly, drew away, then returned. His words were mumbled against her lips.

"Now it's later."

* * *

It had been a very long time since Beth had been forced to deal with a lover the morning after. The few men in her life since Philip had known they weren't welcome to spend the night, and so they had left soon after. But Zachary wasn't like those men. She doubted that it had even occurred to him that maybe he should go to his own room when they were finished last night. Even if it had, she wouldn't have wanted him to go.

She'd been up for more than two hours, had drunk a cup of coffee and showered and gotten dressed for this morning's meeting with Dr. Vega, but Zachary was still asleep. He slept deeply, peacefully, as if he didn't have a care in the world. She had sat here on the edge of the bed for the last thirty minutes, watching him, wishing he would awaken, wishing she knew what to say to him when he did.

Several conflicting responses came to mind. We can't do this again. When can we do it again? I want you. I don't need you. I love you.

That last one drove her away from the bed and to the window. Wasn't she the one who had sworn she would never fall in love again? The one who didn't want a man in her life on a steady basis? The one who rarely had the time for an affair, much less a relationship?

Her life simply wasn't compatible with love. Any man, even Zachary, had to come in a distant second to her career. Children, if there ever were any, would place third. She was too busy, too involved, too preoccupied with her job, to give anything to a man.

Then she turned and looked at Zachary again. He had rolled onto his stomach, the covers slipping down to his waist, and his face was turned toward her. He needed a shave, and his hair was boyishly tousled. Heavens, he was so endearingly handsome. And *she* was too busy with a job she no longer loved, with a job that no longer satisfied her, to give anything to this man?

Something was wrong with her priorities, she thought grimly. Something was wrong with her *life*.

The alarm on her nightstand began beeping, and she went to turn it off, then bent over and gave him a shake. "Time to get up, Zachary."

"If I wake up, will you come back to bed?" he grumbled, turning his face into the pillow.

"Not this morning. We're supposed to meet Marian Vega in a little over an hour. Come on and get up." She started to rise, but his hand snaked out from beneath the pillow and closed around her wrist.

Pulling her closer, he gave her a long, leisurely, breath-stealing kiss. "Hey, lady," he greeted her softly.

She wiped lipstick from his mouth, then smiled uneasily. "Good morning."

He studied her face, and she knew what he was looking for: regrets. Indecision. Sorrow. Rejection. She waited patiently, letting him look, wondering what he saw. Was it fear? Uncertainty? Confusion?

Love?

Not that, his question seemed to indicate. "Sorry?"

Again she smiled edgily. "About a great many things."

"About last night?"

"No. Never about that."

He looked for another moment, then threw the covers back and swung his feet to the floor. "I'll be ready in twenty minutes."

She couldn't resist watching him walk naked across the room, stopping at the dresser to scoop up the clothes she'd picked up earlier. He was definitely a sight worth waking up to, she thought with an admiring smile as he left the room. What would it be like—a lifetime of sharing his bed, of seeing him first thing every morning?

Heaven.

Not that he'd given her any indication that he wanted anything more than a short-term affair, she thought, a scowl replacing her smile. She got up and tossed the pillows onto the floor, then began making the bed. Yes, he was interested in getting married and filling his lovely farmhouse with children, but he wanted to marry the *right* woman. He'd known her for a long time, and he'd never considered her even close enough to right to ask her for a date until he'd found himself stuck and homesick in Nashville. Here she was agonizing over their future, and the odds were high that they didn't even *have* one. Not as a couple. Not as husband and wife. Not as parents.

Not as anything but temporary lovers.

She spread the comforter over the bed, then on second thought turned it down so that the sheets showed. If Zachary liked those sheets, he could see as much of them as he wanted while he was here. And when Carrie's trial was over, when their affair was over, she would throw them away and never again buy anything but plain, boring white.

"Tell me again what kind of juror we're looking for."

Zachary leaned against the wall while Beth and Dr. Newman talked at the table. It was early Monday morning. He'd skipped breakfast because Beth was too nervous even for coffee; the jury selection phase of Carrie's trial was scheduled to start in fifteen minutes, and already the tie he wore was choking him. All things considered, he would rather be home.

In Sweetwater.

In bed.

With Beth.

But that hadn't been one of the options she'd offered him this morning, and so here he was. He'd met Darla Newman only moments ago, when she'd greeted him with some comment about Sleeping Beauty that had made Beth smile for the first time all morning. But he liked the doctor, much better than her counterpart who would testify for them later in the trial.

"The juror to look for in this case," the psychologist said, "is a woman, preferably college-educated, in her twenties or thirties, ideally with some feminist tendencies. Of course, that's exactly the kind of juror the prosecutor will want to avoid. With the male jurors you'll be better off with young professionals or possibly older men—the protective father type, the kind who would want to kill any man who did this to their daughters.''

''Is there anything in particular I should ask the prospective jurors?'' Beth asked.

''What kind of questions do you intend to ask?''

''If they've ever been the victim of an assault, if they've ever been involved in or witnessed an incident of domestic violence—that sort of thing.''

The psychologist shook her head. ''I don't have anything special for you. Just stay away from any questions regarding women's rights.''

It would be interesting to see how Beth picked out jurors with feminist tendencies without asking any questions about their beliefs on feminist issues, Zachary thought. Moving away from the wall, he pulled out the chair at the end of the table and sat down. ''What do you base your recommendations on, doctor?'' he asked curiously.

''Partly instinct, of course. Woman's intuition.'' She smiled as if to take the sting out of that. ''I consider their opinions and study their actions, their reactions, their attitudes. Most people are fairly transparent and easy to read. You can learn from what they say, how they say it, what they don't say, personal quirks, habits.''

Maybe he ought to invite the good doctor to dinner, he thought ruefully. Maybe she could help him read Beth. He'd been trying for three days now to figure out exactly where he stood with her. Did her decision to make love with him Friday night—and Saturday and Sunday nights, too—mean they had moved one step ahead in their relationship, or were they merely having an affair? Had she wanted to go to bed with him because she felt something special for him, or had it been merely a desire for sex? Were her feelings for him even one-tenth as strong as his for her?

Could she ever love him?

He knew the obstacles to a permanent relationship so well that he could list them in his sleep. Her big-city home versus his small-town life. Her thriving, high-powered career versus his laid-back country lawyering. Her sophistication

and glamor versus his old-fashionedness and simplicity. Her
hunger for independence versus his desire for a woman who
was strong enough to occasionally be dependent. Her casual affairs versus his need for a lifetime commitment.

Her lust versus his love.

Beth checked her watch, then stood up and announced,
"It's time." She looked at him for the first time since they'd
entered this small conference room. There was uneasiness in
her eyes, uncertainty, a request for assurance that he
doubted anyone else could see. He didn't dare touch her—
she still wasn't comfortable with casual displays of affection—but he almost smiled, just almost, and nodded. She
would be fine. Everything would be all right.

Beth nodded, too, just a slight bob of her head, then led
the way out. Zachary waited at the door for the doctor to
precede him, and her smile warned him that the subtle exchange hadn't gone unnoticed.

"Sleeping Beauty, indeed," she murmured as she passed
him.

Zachary followed them down the hall and into the courtroom, taking the end seat at the defense table. Beth had
warned him that jury selection, important though it was,
could be tedious and boring. He wouldn't be bored, he'd
assured her. After all, he had never argued a case before a
jury, so he had never participated in selecting one. She had
stared at him in disbelief, echoing, *"Never?"*

It was seldom necessary in the minor criminal cases he'd
handled, he had explained. His clients were usually guilty,
and they rarely pleaded otherwise. Besides, putting together an impartial jury in a place like Sweetwater wouldn't
be an easy task, not with everyone knowing everyone else.
She had simply shaken her head in dismay, and he'd regretted pointing out one more difference between them.

The selection got underway a few minutes after they were
seated. Each potential juror was sworn under oath, then
asked a variety of questions, some by the prosecutor, an arrogant, self-important man if Zachary had ever seen one,
and others by Beth. The prosecutor rejected one woman for

her blatantly feminist opinions, another for her volunteer work with abused children. In turn, Beth refused a rough, plain-talking man who reminded Zachary eerily of Del Lewis, another man who'd grown up watching his father beat his mother and a former police officer.

Using one of her peremptory challenges to unseat a cop was a tough decision to make, she'd told him last night. You could reasonably expect someone who'd chosen a career in law enforcement to be hard-line law and order, right or wrong, black or white, with no shades of gray. On the other hand, who knew better than police officers how many times the system had failed women like Carrie? It was cops who received the calls and broke up the fights. Cops who arrested abusive husbands night after night, only to see them home again the next day. Cops who interviewed bloodied, battered women in emergency rooms and shelters. Cops who investigated their deaths.

Still, when someone's life was at stake, she couldn't afford the risk.

By the end of the day, they had seated a full jury: the twelve who would actually decide the case and the alternates. It had gone quickly and smoothly, he thought when he and Beth were home again, shoes kicked off and feet propped on the coffee table while they shared a pizza straight from the box.

"Are you happy with them?" he asked as he pinched off a trailing string of cheese, then bit into a slice.

Beth dabbed at the corners of her mouth with a linen napkin. She ate daintily, he thought with a grin, never dropping a crumb of crust, a dab of tomato sauce or a piece of onion. She was undoubtedly the neatest person he'd ever met. "I think we'll do all right," she said cautiously. "I don't like the last two men we seated, but I'd used all my challenges, so we were stuck. But I think we did okay on the others. Dr. Newman was pleased."

"So what's next?"

"Opening statements tomorrow, then the prosecutor will present his case. He doesn't have much *to* present, so it shouldn't take long. Then we put on our witnesses, and then we wait."

"That will be the hardest part, won't it?"

She nodded. "I always find myself wondering if I handled it right, if maybe I should have tried this angle instead of that, if I presented the facts as clearly and yet as emotionally as possible. If my client is convicted and goes to jail, is it because I wasn't good enough? Because I didn't try hard enough?" She carefully separated two slices of pizza, then lifted one, balancing it in both hands. "By then, I usually have a case of heartburn that started the first day of the trial and a world-class headache that just won't quit."

"Have you ever considered that maybe your body's trying to tell you that this job isn't good for you?" he asked quietly.

She smiled tautly. "What would I do if I gave it up?"

He suggested an answer she'd given him to a similar question not too long ago. "Live off Great-Grandmother Althea's trust and do nothing. Maybe enjoy life. Take a long vacation. Learn to relax." He swallowed hard. "Fall in love."

She looked up sharply, her gaze locking with his, her cheeks burning. She seemed shaken, although she quickly covered it with a low, phony laugh. "I don't need to give up my job to do any of those things."

After a moment's uncomfortable silence, he asked, "What *do* you do with Althea's trust?"

"It collects interest. I was going to use some of it once to buy a car, but..." She finished with a shrug.

"You have a car."

"I have a status symbol," she corrected him with a haughty air, then suddenly wrinkled her nose. "I wanted a *car*—a sports car. Something small and flashy and incredibly fast. In fire-engine red."

Flashy and fast wasn't a concept he could easily apply to Beth, but he liked trying. And anything, he admitted, would be an improvement over that sedate import parked downstairs in the garage. "So why didn't you get it?"

Her sigh was wistful. "It didn't fit my image."

"*I* don't fit your image, Beth," he reminded her quietly, painfully. "Does that mean you're going to walk away from me, too?"

She closed the box on the uneaten crusts, then dropped the linen napkins on top and started to stand up. For a moment, though, she hesitated and looked at him, the green of her eyes turning liquid with emotion. Then she got up and walked out, leaving him alone in the big room. Her answer was no answer at all.

And he found it all too painfully clear.

Chapter 11

Beth looked at Carrie, seated between her and Zachary at the defense table, and quickly sized her up. The green-and-black dress she'd bought for their client was a little too big, but that was good; it emphasized her pregnancy and her waifishness. She had pulled her hair back, fastening it with a black clasp that let it fall, straight and limp, down her back. She wore no makeup, nothing to soften the lines of her face, nothing to camouflage the small scars left by her husband.

Her appearance was fine, Beth decided, and even her demeanor might work in their favor. All these weeks of interviews by detectives, lawyers and doctors, all these days of sharing a cell with other women, of spending virtually twenty-four hours a day with strangers, hadn't lessened her shyness any. It hadn't eased her fear. She looked like a frightened little rabbit longing to hide away from the world. She *didn't* look like the cold-blooded murderer the prosecution was making her out to be.

The testimony had been going on since nine o'clock, with a brief recess for lunch. So far Duane Misner, the prosecutor, had interviewed every policeman who had been at Carrie's house the night of Del's death, and he had asked them very narrow questions designed to support his case. It was a weakness in his strategy that Beth had recognized right away. In cross-examining, she had been able to draw out the information that these same officers had been called to that neighborhood, to that house, time after time in the past, that they were aware of Delbert Lewis as a violent man, that the neighbors had feared he was going to kill his wife. She'd gotten them to talk about the disarray inside the house—the broken dishes stacked by the sink, the badly mended furniture—that had nothing to do with Del's death. She'd asked them to describe the blood splattered on the ceilings and walls that didn't belong to the victim. She had asked for and received detailed descriptions of Carrie's condition when the first officers arrived.

The end result had been a vivid portrait for the jurors of what had gone on in the Lewis house that night. A side benefit was the little niggling doubt that she'd hoped had been planted in their minds about the prosecution's integrity: *if he doesn't want us to know this, what else might he be keeping back?*

After Beth finished with the last cross-examination, the judge called a recess until the next day. She was grateful for the break. Trials were always tiring, and she had several upcoming cases that needed her attention this week. As soon as court was dismissed and Carrie had been led away by a bailiff, she began stuffing her notes and files into her briefcase.

Zachary slid into the seat beside her. "Misner would have been better off if he'd been upfront about everything, but downplayed the stuff about Carrie."

She nodded her agreement. "Let's hope he keeps going this way. It'll make our job easier."

He watched the spectators file out of the courtroom before asking softly, "Want to go home?"

"I'd like to, but—"

"You have to work." He smiled a regretful sort of smile that made her feel guilty. Before she could apologize, though, he went on. "Do you need me for anything?"

This time it was Beth who smiled—slowly, slyly, lasciviously—and a faint blush colored his cheeks. "For anything besides that?" he clarified, his voice hoarse.

"Do I need your help in the office? No. There's nothing that concerns Carrie. I just need to get caught up on a couple of other things. Why don't you drop me off, then take my car and go on home? I'll catch a cab when I'm finished."

"I'll drop you off, and I'll take your car," he agreed. "But call me when you're done, and I'll pick you up."

Closing her briefcase, she accepted his offer merely to placate him. But she knew she would be working late, and she saw no reason for him to come out again in the cold when she could easily take a cab home.

It was only a few blocks from the courthouse to her building. Zachary pulled over in a loading zone and waited for her to get out. She opened the door, then turned back, leaned across and kissed him—nothing intimate, nothing toe-curling, just a brief unimportant little kiss. It made him smile, though, because she rarely touched him and never kissed him outside the privacy of her apartment. But he knew she was working on overcoming what she had once considered her natural reticence but had lately decided was totally *un*natural. All she needed was time...patience...him.

"I'll fix something for dinner," he said when she drew away. "Call me when you're ready for me."

After a nod, she left the car and hurried inside the building without looking back. She didn't want to see him driving away.

In her office, she put away her coat and her briefcase, got the case files she needed from her bottom drawer and settled in to work. But no matter how she tried, she couldn't concentrate on drunk driving or assault charges. All she could think about was Zachary. Herself. Her life.

After a moment she removed her reading glasses and left her desk for the comfortable sofa across the room. She didn't sit down with her legs demurely crossed, but removed her heels and stretched her legs out the length of the cushions. She propped the extra pillows behind her and tilted her head back to stare at the ceiling.

Ten years ago, building a new career and ending a bitter relationship, she had set a few goals for herself: success. Respect. A partnership. Power. She had achieved all of them, and now there were no new career goals to set. What else could she aim for? Senior partner? No thanks. Establishing her own high-powered firm? Not interested.

No, the things she wanted now had little to do with her career. More satisfaction in the cases she handled. Less pressure to meet others' expectations. Happiness. Friends. Family. And since her own family was so inadequate, the only way she knew to get a good one was to marry into it— or have her own.

She could gain the career satisfaction she sought if she left the firm. If she forgot about partners and billable hours and corporate reputations. If she took only cases that interested her. Cases that she cared about.

She could also forget about having to live up to the image she had constructed for herself. She could quit striving to be the hotshot attorney, the cool, aloof woman, the perfect daughter. She could remove everyone from her life who didn't mean *something* to her. She could restructure her life, with no more boring social functions simply because her presence was expected. No more miserable holidays because her presence was demanded. No more meaningless affairs because that was all she had allowed herself to want, to have.

She could reserve her time—her life—for people she cared about: friends like Sarah and Daniel Ryan. Lovers like

Zachary. No, she quickly amended. Lover. Singular. Only one. Because she could have so much more than a meaningless affair. In spite of her family, in spite of Philip, she *could* love someone. Zachary was proof of that.

She could get married. She could have children. She could learn to relate to babies and toddlers and teenagers. She knew she would never be as warm and loving and affectionate as Sarah was, or Zachary's mother or his sister Alicia, but she had learned to be one of the best damn attorneys in Nashville for no reason other than to defy her father, so she could certainly learn to be a good mother. After all, she wanted *that* not for her father or for Zachary, but for herself.

What would she do if she gave up law? she had asked just last night. But she didn't have to give it up. She just needed to reorder her priorities, to refocus her direction. It wasn't as if she needed the income to survive. All these years she had considered her inheritance from Althea a nice little gift, a secured income for someone who would never need it. A pile of money she could never manage to spend that would grow and multiply and earn even more money she could never spend.

But it was more than that. It was a gift of independence. It was freedom to do whatever she wanted. To walk away from this job and into one she could love. To help women like Carrie. To live in a place where she couldn't earn a living.

Suddenly she covered her face with both hands. That was what she wanted, wasn't it? *Yes.* But she wanted all those things with Zachary, not with some man whom she hadn't yet met, but with the one man she'd been certain was all wrong for her. The only man, she knew now, who *would* be right for her.

But what reason did she have to believe that *she* was who *he* wanted? Yes, he made love so tenderly to her. He treated her as if she were the only important woman in his life. He was considerate and charming and gentle. But he was that kind of man. He would exhibit those qualities with any woman he got involved with. It meant he cared for her.

It didn't mean he loved her.

What if she made all these changes—left the firm, cut her ties to her family and the casual acquaintances who had passed as friends, took off from Nashville and turned her entire world around—and he didn't care? What if he wanted no more than this affair they were having now? What if he wanted to go home to Sweetwater after the trial as free as when he'd left it?

Then where would she be?

Alone.

Then she smiled whimsically. Could it be worse than where she was now?

"We need a break."

Beth, seated at her desk with her reading glasses on, looked up from the notes she had made through the week's testimony. "What kind of break?"

Zachary fully expected her to refuse his suggestion. Beth Gibson give up a Saturday in the office? Worse yet, give it up to take a mini-vacation? In the middle of a trial? But he took a deep breath and made it anyway. "Let's go home."

She looked at him without comprehension. "Go to the condo?"

"To Sweetwater. *My* home. Let's forget about work and witnesses and juries. We'll take a long walk in the woods. We'll have dinner with Sarah and Daniel. We'll stop in and see my folks. We'll act like normal people whose lives aren't ruled by their jobs."

Any minute now, he thought, she would open her lovely mouth and say, "Sorry, this is more important, but you go ahead."

But she sat there for a moment, then another, before finally taking off her glasses, swiveling her chair around so she could cross her legs, and studying him thoughtfully. "All right," she said at last. "Let's go."

He was surprised...but not so much so that he hesitated. He left her to clear her desk and went to get their coats from the closet. By the time she was finished, he was standing at the door, his jacket on, hers in hand.

They returned to the condo long enough for her to pack an overnight bag. As they were walking out the door, Zachary remembered one last thing he wanted to take. Returning to the closet, he slipped the fur from its padded hanger and draped it over his arm.

Beth watched him with a knowing smile. He hadn't tried to hide his fascination with the rich, extravagant garment. Much like the black sheets on her bed, he found the black fur erotic. The stuff fantasies were made from.

They took his Cherokee and headed south, out of the city, eventually turning back east. They talked a little, but not much. Even after weeks of togetherness, they rarely indulged in idle conversation. Occasionally he pointed out something special—the tiny cafe that made the best fruit cobbler in Tennessee, the scene in a valley that dipped below them to the south, the area where some of the earlier Adamses had settled.

The three hours passed quickly. At the last town before Sweetwater, he stopped at a tiny mom-and-pop grocery and stocked up on fresh bread, locally made cheese, sliced meat and fresh-out-of-the-oven cookies. No need to head straight into town, he thought with a grin, where the only place for lunch was the diner. Where he would see at least two dozen people he knew. Where his time with Beth would have to be shared.

Maybe she had the same idea, because as they drew closer to Sweetwater, she asked, "Can we go to your mountain first?"

His grin widened. "I only own twenty acres of it," he reminded her.

She simply shrugged. "Can we?"

"Sure." He slowed at the turn and left the highway for the rougher dirt road. When they reached the end of the road, he stopped to open the gate, pulled through and closed it again, then followed the driveway to the house.

"This is a nice place," she said softly, almost to herself.

It was, he agreed. It was even nicer when she was there. After getting the food from the back, he followed her onto the veranda. Beth took the bag while he unlocked the door, then stole a cookie before giving it back.

The house was cold and quiet inside, and it smelled of wood. It was a strong aroma, pleasant and clean, one that clung to his clothes and his skin when he worked here. As they walked through the rooms, he could easily imagine the house completed, with rugs scattered over the pine floors and the walls painted in rich crimson, forest green and teal blue. The furniture would be slightly battered—the stuff from his house in town, along with a few antiques his grandmother was saving for him—except for the bedroom. Daniel was going to make him a bed, a massive four-poster hand-carved with an intricate design.

The only thing he couldn't imagine was a woman living here. There was only one he wanted to share the place with, but how could he ask her to give up her entire life to come live on the mountain with him? The likelihood that she would ever agree was too remote to even fantasize about.

"Let's eat outside," Beth suggested, stopping in front of the French doors that led to the deck.

Zachary agreed, and, after retrieving a six-pack of soda from the kitchen, he joined her out there. It was a bit chilly for an impromptu picnic, but he was used to the cold, and Beth didn't seem to mind.

"It's so quiet here," she murmured. "The city is never quiet. Even in my office or the condo, I can still hear the traffic."

"I've come up here a lot since my grandfather died, to camp and to hike through the woods. In the spring that meadow out there will be covered with wildflowers, and in the summer you can sit here and watch the deer. In the fall the squirrels collect the nuts from these trees and stash them for the winter.'' The echo of his words made him stop. He knew *he* would be here to see the wildflowers and the deer and the squirrels, but Beth wouldn't. They'd been keeping long hours in the courtroom and had already presented the majority of their witnesses. Only two—Tyler and Carrie— remained to testify on Monday. The case would go to the jury by Wednesday; with any luck they would come back with a verdict on Thursday.

And he would come back to Sweetwater on Thursday. Christmas Eve. Funny. He hadn't realized Christmas was so near. He usually looked forward to the holiday, but not this year. Not knowing that he couldn't have the one thing he wanted most. Not knowing that it would mark the resumption of his life without Beth. Already he dreaded the long nights alone and the months that would pass between brief glimpses during her visits to Sarah. He would miss the sound of her voice and her rare smiles and her rarer laughter. He would miss making love with her and talking to her. He would miss touching her. Looking at her.

She moved the leftovers from their lunch to the opposite side of the bench and moved to snuggle in beside him. ''Want to take a walk?''

Wrapping his arm around her, he gave her a measuring look that took in her dark wool slacks and low-heeled boots. ''You're not exactly dressed for a hike. Don't you own any jeans?''

''I did once in college. My mother said proper young ladies didn't wear jeans and threw them away.''

''I thought you were rebellious in college. Did you make a point of wearing nothing but jeans around your mother after that?''

''I could only stand up to one parent at a time, and in college that was my father. He was so determined to make me go to the school of his choice to study for the career of his choice. Right up to the day I accepted the job with the firm, he thought he could change my mind. If I ever have children . . .''

She let the comment trail away as Zachary slid his hand
beneath her sweater to rest on her flat stomach. The image
of her pregnant came too easily, too wistfully, to mind. "If
you ever have children . . . what?"

But she shook her head and refused to answer. "Do you
have electricity in the house yet?"

With a sigh he let her change the subject. "Just water so
far. Everything's been wired, but we probably won't actually hook up to the power lines until spring."

"Do the fireplaces work?"

"Uh-huh."

She was looking up at the master bedroom. Suddenly she
shifted her gaze to him. "Do we have to go into town? Can't
we just spend the night here?"

He leaned back so he could study her more thoroughly.
The idea wasn't as far-fetched as it sounded. He had an in-
flatable mattress in the back of his Cherokee that was as
large as a double bed and nine inches thick, and an air
compressor that would pump it up in fifteen minutes. There
was also a blanket or two back there, left from his last
camping trip, and there was more than enough firewood to
keep them comfortable.

Logistically, it would be no problem. But did he want her
to spend even one night in this house? Did he want to make
love to her here? Did he want to have to deal with memories of her later?

Ignoring his doubts, he simply nodded. "Sure. We can
spend the night here."

As Zachary had suggested, they went over to the Ryans's
house for a visit, and, of course, Sarah invited them for
dinner. It had been a lovely evening, Beth thought as they
drove up the mountain one more time.

It had been a *normal* evening, she corrected herself.
Friends enjoying one another's company. Two couples
sharing a meal and a good time. And for the first time ever,
Katie had approached her without that wary look and

greeted her the same way she greeted everyone, with a little-girl soft, wispy, "Hey, Bef."

Even as she thought about it, Zachary commented on it. "I heard Katie call you Bef. Sach and Bef. She has a way with words, doesn't she?"

As they crossed the brook, she glanced at him. "You know, I used to wonder sometimes just how far back she could remember. She's always been so leery of me, and I've never done anything to her. I sometimes thought maybe she remembered that I was the one who took her from her mother and brought her here to live with a stranger. But, heavens, she was just a baby. She couldn't possibly remember that."

"I think you probably just intimidate her a little," Zachary replied.

He got points for diplomacy tonight, she thought with a small smile. He could have reminded her that she simply wasn't the sort of person that small children warmed up to. But how could she be expected to interact well with little kids when she'd never been around them? Even as a child herself, she'd never been allowed to play in the rough-and-tumble way Katie did.

But she would learn.

This time when they reached his place, she offered to get the gate, but he was already jumping out. The few seconds the door was open let a blast of cold air into the truck. She was looking forward to a warm fire and a night in Zachary's arms.

Although the moon was full, the house was dark. Zachary pulled a flashlight from the glove compartment, then hustled Beth inside. He had inflated the air bed earlier and carried it, along with a sleeping bag and one blanket, upstairs to the master bedroom. Together they had carried up armloads of wood, and he had laid the kindling. Now he started the fire while she waited in a shadowy corner.

She had taken advantage of his busyness to change from her short leather jacket into the longer, heavier fur. It encircled her with warmth, but she still shivered. She had been anticipating this all day, and now her body trembled, her muscles were taut, and her breasts had already grown heavy.

And he hadn't even touched her.

The woodpile Zachary had taken these logs from was made up of the trees he'd cut down nearly two years ago, he'd told her. The wood was dry and well-seasoned, and it burned with a steady, heat-giving glow. He watched it for a moment, then stood and brushed his hands on his jeans before turning around. "It's not fancy, but it's..."

He broke off, and she saw him swallow as she stepped out of the shadows. She crossed the room to him at her own leisurely pace, cupping his face in her hands when she reached him and giving him a slow, leisurely kiss. She moistened his lips with her tongue, coaxed his mouth open and lazily dipped her tongue inside. He tasted of Sarah's coffee, warm and dark and rich, and of something else, something sweet, something mysterious. Something pure Zachary.

For the first stunned moment he simply stood there, his arms at his side, letting her kiss him. She finished the kiss, reluctant to break the contact but wanting more. She reached for his hands, letting her fingers brush innocently across his groin. Like her, he was already aroused. With one kiss, he'd grown hard and heavy and hot. Knowing that she could do that, could arouse him with just one kiss, made her feel more feminine, more passionate, more *real*, than she ever had before.

It made her feel loved.

She twined her fingers with his and lifted his hands, then laid them on her breasts. Between her flesh and his were the thick nubby knit of her sweater and the weight of the fur, but the sensations were no less than exquisite. Already she ached for his hands, for his mouth, for his hardness.

Slowly Zachary rubbed her breasts, his hands gliding over the fur. He couldn't find words to describe the way it felt—the tingling in his palms, the utter *richness* of the coat, the sheer pleasure of touching Beth.

Still caressing her, he bent his head for a second kiss. Just as she had filled his mouth, now he took hers, stroking and thrusting, suckling, nipping. He couldn't remember how many times they'd touched, kissed, made love, in the past week, but this time was going to be different. Already he was so needy that he ached. Already his blood was pumping and his breathing was ragged and his body was throbbing as if it had never known satisfaction. Already he wanted to strip off her clothes and this coat that gave him such pleasure and bury himself deeply inside her, too deep ever to be apart from her again.

Just as she had guided his hand to her breast, now he drew hers to his hardness, folding her fingers over the swelling, pressing her palm against it. She squeezed gently, and a low moan caught in his throat. Then she unfastened his jeans—quickly this time, with no fumbling—and slid her hand inside to stroke his bare flesh, and a tortured groan escaped him. For a moment he caught her hand, holding it in place, unsure if he could bear one more caress, certain he couldn't bear giving up this touch.

Then she pulled away, but only to undress him. She dropped his jacket on the floor, tossed his shirt beside it, guided his jeans and briefs down his legs to join the rest of his clothing. Then she knelt in front of him, and her mouth touched him in a kiss so intimate that he shuddered. He tangled one hand in her hair and braced the other on her mink-clad shoulder while she teased and tantalized and tormented him.

Groaning her name, he forced her to her feet, then pushed the coat off her shoulders and dragged her sweater over her head. She was naked underneath, as he'd known she would be, naked and beautiful. He wanted to kiss her breasts, to make her moan and tremble, but first he had to be inside her, needed to be before he was driven over the edge by the sheer overload of sensation. He pulled her slacks down, taking her narrow, lacy panties with them, then came to the barrier of her boots. With a throaty laugh, she unzipped first one, then the other, and kicked them both off, and he pushed the rest of her clothing out of the way.

He didn't even wait until they were on the bed, but simply lifted her, then settled her easily, heavily, on his hardness. When she'd taken every bit of him, he groaned, his frantic need somewhat abated. Holding her tightly, he found the hearth behind him and carefully lowered himself until they were seated on the stone.

"Nice fire, counselor," she whispered, shifting against him so that her breasts rubbed his chest and her body did all sorts of wicked things to him.

"You started the fire," he whispered back. He covered her breasts with his hands and studied the contrasts between his skin and hers, now colored creamy gold by the firelight, and the shadows they created. Slowly he rubbed her, the calluses on his palms abrading her delicate skin, making her nipples even harder, swelling her breasts even more. "Do you have any idea what you do to me, lady?"

She shifted her hips, withdrawing until only the barest contact remained, then taking him in again. "I think I have a glimmer. Why don't you show me?"

He chuckled softly, then suddenly grew serious. He raised his hands to her face, cupping her jaw, and looked intently into her eyes. "Beth—" And just as suddenly he stopped. She had made it clear that she didn't want a man in her life, that all she was looking for was companionship. Lovemaking. And he had accepted those terms the first time he'd made love to her. There could be no declarations of love now, he reminded himself. No pleas for forever. No attempts to draw promises of something more, something always, from her.

Instead he kissed her with all the need, all the passion, all the love, he felt for her, and he guided her against him, matching her rhythm, feeding her hunger, sharing her desire. Then in one soul-shattering moment it ended. Her body shuddered against his, her cries mingling with his groans, and he filled her.

He completed her.
He loved her.

They made love again on a mink-covered mattress, this time without the desperation, without the frenzy or painful, clawing need. When Zachary awoke a few hours later to a chilly room and warm embers, he stoked the fire, piling on log after log, then returned to bed to find Beth once more awake and waiting, tempting, teasing, pleasing.

After the last time she fell asleep in his arms, and he held her close, lightly stroking her. She would probably never come to this house again after this weekend. He would never make love to her in this room again. But no matter what happened, no matter if he never saw her again, if he married and finally learned to love someone else, he knew he would never forget this night.

He would never look at that fireplace without remembering her here.

He would never walk into this room without feeling her presence.

He would never make love to another woman without wishing she were Beth.

And even if he did learn to love someone else, he would never, as long as he lived, stop loving Beth.

They returned to Nashville on Sunday afternoon, Zachary driving, Beth staring quietly out the window. There had been a subtle change in their relationship last night, she acknowledged as she watched the countryside give way to the city, and she couldn't quite explain it. Somehow she was sure it had to do with their lovemaking. That first time had been so...*intense*. As if they had, in the truest sense of the words, been joined together and become one. As if their souls had bonded.

Then she smiled at the outrageousness of that idea. She wasn't sure she believed in bonding. She wasn't even sure she believed in souls. All she knew was that *something* had happened, and now Zachary was drawing away from her as a result. It wasn't anything overt—only someone who had studied him as long and as hard as she had would notice—and even she couldn't put her finger on it. He was a little more distant. A little less ... connected.

Maybe he was worried about appearing in court tomorrow. Their first witness was going to be Tyler Lewis, and Zachary was going to question him. He'd already questioned several of Carrie's neighbors and had done an excellent job, but Tyler was a little different. Zachary knew that, along with Carrie herself, Tyler was their most important witness, but he didn't want the boy called. He didn't want to subject him to the gawkers who crowded into the courtroom, to the sensationalism that surrounded the case, to the ordeal of getting up in front of a roomful of strangers and condemning his father, blaming him for his own death.

Or maybe his withdrawal was something more personal. Maybe his interest in her was waning ... although last night certainly seemed to indicate the opposite. Or maybe this spur-of-the-moment trip to Sweetwater had been some sort of test, some trial to see how she fit into his world, at his house, with his friends and, at one of those old-fashioned Sunday dinners he'd told her about, with his family. She had thought the meeting had gone rather well. His parents had been friendly and warm, his grandmother had seemed to like her, and *she* had liked *them*.

But maybe in Zachary's eyes it hadn't been such a success. Maybe somehow she had failed his test.

She sighed softly, and he glanced at her, but he didn't ask what was wrong. Was she being oversensitive in thinking that a few days ago, he would have?

Of course, *she* could ask *him* what was wrong. She was a lawyer, paid to ask questions, to dig up answers. Why not use some of her much-acclaimed talent on her own behalf?

Because she was afraid of the answers she might find.

Zachary left the interstate and followed the maze of streets to her condo. In the garage, they silently unloaded the Jeep—she took her mink, he took the overnight bag—and entered the elevator. He seemed so distracted on the ride up that she suspected he wouldn't notice if she appeared in front of him naked but for the fur.

Just before they reached her floor, she spoke his name at last. "Zachary? I—I had a nice time this weekend. Thank you."

He gave her a preoccupied look, then smiled faintly and nodded. As soon as the doors opened, he stepped off and walked down the hall to her door.

Feeling troubled and just a little bit despairing, Beth followed. She'd waited all her life to have a few nice times with a man. Now that she finally had, it seemed they were coming to an end almost before they'd started.

Maybe she'd been right all along.

Breaking the rules she lived by had been a mistake.

Getting involved with Zachary had been a bigger mistake.

And falling in love with him just might be the biggest mistake of all.

"Good thing we have reserved seats," Zachary muttered as they pushed their way through the crowd in the courthouse hallway Monday morning. "If we didn't, we couldn't get in to see this circus."

Beth touched his arm when they finally made it inside. "Don't worry," she said softly. "You'll do fine."

"I'm not worried about myself, counselor. I *am* worried about what we're going to do to that fourteen-year-old boy."

"Look at it this way—it's nothing compared to what his father put him through. And it's nothing compared to what losing his mother for the rest of his life will do to him. Besides, he might be Carrie's best chance."

"Yeah, sure. Anything for the client, right?"

She didn't like this cynicism in him. *She* was supposed to be the cynic, right? Zachary was supposed to be the romantic. The charmer. The easygoing, warm, supportive lover.

Not last night. He'd gone to bed before her, and he'd pretended to be asleep when she had joined him an hour later. She had wanted to touch him, to arouse him, to make him respond to her on that level, at least, but she had let him pretend. If she had pushed the issue, who could say that he wouldn't have retreated to the privacy of his own room down the hall? At least this way she had been close to him. She'd fallen asleep to the steady, even sound of his breathing, and she had awakened this morning with his arm around her waist. It wasn't much, but it was something, when soon she would have nothing.

The bailiff called the court to order, and the defense called their next witness, Tyler Lewis. At Beth's side, Carrie stiffened, then clutched her arm. "You can't do that," she whispered. "You can't make him testify."

Beth patted her hand reassuringly. "I've already explained this to you," she whispered back. "We need his help, Carrie. He's the only person, besides the victim—Del—and the defendant—you—who knows what happened that night. The jury needs to hear what he can tell them."

Tyler, accompanied to the courtroom by his grandfather, looked longingly at his mother as he made his way to the witness stand. It was the first time Beth had ever seen the child in him, the first time anything besides anger or hostility had filled his eyes. He was dressed in a white shirt that was too big for him and black trousers that were too long. The clothes made him look even thinner than he was, although she could tell that he'd put on a few pounds since moving in with the Morrises.

He was sworn in and seated before Zachary approached him. He asked a few unimportant questions first—how old Tyler was, how many brothers and sisters he had, their ages. His manner was kindly but not condescending, and it worked well with Tyler. Of course, Beth thought dryly, that day spent working together at Zachary's house was probably much more responsible for Tyler's receptiveness than anything on Zachary's part today. That was a bonus for them, since Duane Misner hadn't had that opportunity.

Zachary might never have argued a case before a jury, but he did it well. He was careful to stay out of their way, to do nothing to draw their attention from the boy to himself. His questions were unobtrusive, simply tools to prompt Tyler's story when necessary, and they were carefully phrased to draw the exact answers he wanted from the boy.

He guided Tyler through his recitation of his parents' last fight, including a description of his own injuries. Tyler was particularly graphic in describing Carrie's injuries, speaking in a flat, blank tone that was all the more effective for its lack of emotion. The jurors couldn't help but be impressed by his story, by the details of the life he'd lived, by the horrors he'd witnessed for as long as he could remember.

Zachary finished with one last question. "Do you miss your father, Tyler?"

He looked at his mother, then sought out someone among the spectators—his grandfather, Beth suspected. Then he turned his ancient gaze on Zachary and answered simply.

"No. I don't."

The impact of his three words was visible on every juror's face. Beth looked at each one, then settled back in her chair and silently applauded Zachary. There wasn't an attorney in Nashville who could have handled it better.

Softly, in the seat beside her, shoulders hunched, hands over her face, Carrie Lewis started to cry.

Misner's cross-examination of Tyler didn't take long. He emphasized the fact that Del had been asleep when Carrie had killed him, that it had happened several hours after the fight, that she had appeared calm when she'd gone to awaken Tyler to tell him what she'd done. He left the rest of the boy's testimony alone—wisely, Zachary thought. Del's violent behavior was documented fact. Trying to challenge it now would be an amateur's mistake.

Now it was Carrie's turn to testify. She rose from her chair at Zachary's urging and crossed the few feet to the witness stand with shuffling steps. She kept her gaze down while she was sworn in, and her hand when she raised it for the oath trembled visibly. She was scared half to death. She had never spoken in front of so many people, and she had never spoken for so important a reason.

She was wearing a maternity dress that he'd picked up at her house last week, a shapeless brown garment that made her look drab and pale. It had deep pockets, and as she seated herself, she shoved her hands into them to hide their shaking.

Beth began the questioning much the same way he had with Tyler—with simple questions, unimportant ones. While that went on, he watched the jury, wondering what they thought, what they felt, how they would vote. Including the alternates, there were nine women and five men. For the most part they were young to middle-aged. There was one housewife; occupations for the rest ranged from school teacher to nurse to construction foreman to accountant. They had watched the scenes played out for their benefit, had listened to the testimony, had looked at photographs of Carrie's injuries and of the walls at her house, splattered with her own blood.

Some part of him believed that they were sympathetic to Carrie. How could any human being not feel sorry for everything she had endured? But some other part wondered if they could possibly be sympathetic enough. Could any strong person truly understand what motivated a weak one? Could those women, with their careers and their jobs, their incomes and their independence—could they understand Carrie's helplessness? Could they—strong, rational women—adapt their way of thinking to match hers?

Beth led Carrie through a brief description of her life with Del, from the first beating to the last. Then she asked quietly, "What happened that first Sunday night in November, Carrie?"

Slowly Carrie forced her gaze to Beth's face. "He was drinking. He—he did that a lot. When he got drunk, he got mean, so we always tried extra hard not to upset him. But..." She sighed softly, a lost little sound. "He got upset, anyway."

"What upset him, Carrie?"

"We were out of beer, and he was mad 'cause he said I hadn't got enough when I went to the grocery store. I tried to calm him down, but he just got madder, and then he slapped me with the back of his hand."

Zachary was still watching the jurors, and he saw one of the women grimace. It wasn't a pretty image—Del, over six feet tall and more than two hundred pounds, backhanding his thin little pregnant wife.

"I got up then," Carrie continued, "and went into the kitchen to get the kids some supper. I was feeling kind of tired because of the baby, and so I was just fixing sandwiches and potato chips and soup. Del came in, and he started in again. He said his kids wasn't eating bologna sandwiches and soup out of a can, and he told me to cook a real meal for them. I told him that it would take a long time for anything out of the freezer to thaw, and the kids were hungry now. I promised that I'd cook a big meal the next night, but he didn't want to hear that. He picked up the pan of soup off the stove and threw it all over the floor."

"Where were the children when this happened?" Beth asked softly.

"At the kitchen table watching."

"All four of them? Including the little ones?"

"Yes."

"How did they react?"

"The three-year-old and the six-year-old both started to cry sort of—you know, whimpering and sniffling. Becky was holding both of them, trying to calm them down, because she knew their crying would just make their daddy even madder.''

''What happened next?''

Carrie sat silently for a moment, gathering her thoughts. ''Del pushed me down to the floor on my knees and told me to clean up the soup. When I bent over to do that, he kicked me right here.'' She touched her hip gingerly, as if feeling again the pain that had long since faded. ''I fell and got soup in my face and hair, but he wouldn't let me wash it out. He was making fun of me, about how clumsy I was, how dirty I was. When I finished cleaning the floor, he grabbed my hair and lifted me to my feet. Then he shoved everything off the table—the sandwiches, the chips, the milk— and he ground it all into the floor. Then he shoved me down again and told me to clean it up.''

Zachary had heard these details before. Each time he listened to them, he despised Del Lewis even more. Wasn't it enough that he'd beaten her nearly half her life, that he'd beaten her into the same kind of cowering, helpless submission that you got from an abused dog? Did he have to humiliate her in front of her children? Did he have to degrade her?

Carrie went on with her story, telling how she had cleaned the ruined dinner from the floor. She had taken a package of chicken from the freezer and placed it in a sink of cold water so it would thaw faster. Then she'd asked Del if she could get the kids, still seated around the table, a snack until dinner was ready—just a peanut butter sandwich or a cookie, she had pleaded.

Sure, he'd said, but when she had finished making the first sandwich, he pulled it apart and rubbed the peanut butter over her face before forcing it into her mouth, gagging her, choking her.

Then he'd gotten *really* angry.

Holding her by her hair, he'd slammed her face into the counter, then pushed her to the floor. He had kicked her, shoved her, hit her, and every time she fell, he lifted her up and knocked her down again. Then he'd begun hitting her face until she was bleeding from her mouth, her nose, her cheeks. Every time he hit her, the blood splattered onto the surrounding walls. And when her blood stained her dress and coated his hand, when she was standing simply because he was holding her up with his other hand, when he had beaten her almost into unconsciousness, Tyler had interfered.

And his father had turned his anger on him.

"Del hit him and knocked him clear across the room, but Tyler kept coming back," Carrie said, her voice so low that everyone in the courtroom strained to hear her. "The kids were crying, and I was screaming and trying to help Tyler, and finally Del stopped all of a sudden. He looked around at the mess in the kitchen—there were broken dishes, and things had been knocked off the cabinets and the stove, and there was blood on the walls—and then he just turned and walked out. He went into the front room and lay down on the couch and went to sleep."

"And what did you do?"

"I made sure Tyler and the kids were all right, then I went into the bedroom and took a bath. And then I just sat there shaking. I was so afraid. It was like my heart was going to pound itself right out of my chest."

"But your husband was asleep," Beth pointed out gently. "Why were you afraid?"

"Because he would have killed me if Tyler hadn't stopped him. I knew it was only a matter of time until it would happen again, until Tyler wouldn't be able to stop him." She breathed deeply. "Until he did kill me."

Beth walked back to stand beside the defense table, only a few feet from Zachary. Slowly he shifted his gaze from the jury to her. "Was that the first time Del had ever hurt one of the children?" Beth asked.

"Yes. But I knew he would do it again, and—"

Misner objected that she couldn't possibly have known
what her husband would do in the future. Carrie flinched at
the sound of his voice, then drew her hands from her pockets and clenched them tightly together in her lap. After the
judge upheld Misner's objection and the room was quiet
again, she haltingly rephrased her reply.

"I—I was *afraid* he would do it again. That was how it
started with me. He just hit me once or twice, then weeks
would go by with nothing happening. Then he started hitting me more and more until it was happening a couple of
times a week, sometimes even every day, and he broke my
arm and my ribs, and I had to have stitches, and—" She
broke off in an effort to control the rising hysteria evident
in her voice. When she spoke again, she was quiet. Firm.
Determined. "I wasn't going to let him do that to my kids.
It was bad enough that they had to watch what he did to me,
but I wasn't going to let him hurt my children."

Beth waited until the courtroom was perfectly still again
before she asked her next question. "When did you decide
to kill your husband, Carrie?"

She tilted her head to one side, a confused look on her
face. The jurors were waiting stiffly, as were the prosecutor
and the judge. If the answer she gave indicated a signifi-
cant passage of time between the decision and the stabbing,
Zachary knew their case would be irreparably harmed. That
would be all Misner needed to show premeditation. Self-
defense couldn't be planned in advance.

"I didn't," she said at last.

"Didn't what?"

"I didn't decide to kill him. It was just something that I
had to do to protect my kids. To protect myself."

"All right. The fight ended, and Del went into the living
room where he fell asleep on the couch. You went into the
bedroom to clean up. What happened next?"

She had heard the children moving around in the kitchen.
Tyler fixed sandwiches for them; then he bathed the kids
and put them to bed. It was about eight-thirty when he went

to bed. During that time, she'd sat huddled in the corner in her bedroom, trembling and crying.

She was tired and aching and wanted to just stay right there where she was, where she was safe, but she had known that Del would be furious if he woke up in the morning to the sight of that kitchen. Getting drunk the way he did always left him with bad hangovers, and he was almost as mean then as before. She'd known that she had to clean the kitchen before she could even think of getting any rest.

She had washed dishes, swept up broken glass and replaced everything that had fallen. She'd mopped the floor and tried to scrub the blood from the wall, but it had soaked into the porous paint. It had taken her more than an hour, but finally, except for the bloodstains on the white wall, the kitchen was neat and clean again, a stack of broken dishes waiting to be carried out to the garbage the only evidence of the fight.

Then she had sat down at the table, resting her head on her arms. She had vomited earlier and was worried now about the baby she carried. It wasn't due until next March, but she honestly didn't believe she would live that long. Del's outbursts had been increasing in both frequency and violence, and she had known as she'd sat there that night that soon he was going to kill her, and the baby would die with her.

And the other four kids would live with their father.

She couldn't remember how long she'd sat like that, all numb and empty. She did remember thinking that dying wouldn't be so bad. At least she wouldn't be afraid all the time. She wouldn't be hurting all the time. But how could she ever find peace when her children were with Del?

That was when she saw the knife. It had fallen from the counter when Del had shoved her and she'd grabbed frantically for something to stop her fall. Her fingers had closed around the dish drainer, pulling it to the floor with her. The few glass dishes had broken, the plastic ones had bounced and rolled, and the silverware had scattered everywhere. The knife had fallen into the crevice between the stove and the cabinets.

She had gotten up from the table and retrieved the knife, but instead of taking it to the sink, she had walked into the living room with it. She had gone to the sofa where Del was asleep on his back, his mouth open and snoring, and she had smelled the liquor on his breath, and she'd known that soon he would get drunk again and, unless she stopped him, he would kill her. Maybe not the next time or the one after that, but soon.

Soon.

And so she had stabbed him.

Chapter 12

The judge delayed the prosecution's cross-examination until Tuesday morning and dismissed court for the day. Zachary and Beth walked out side by side and silent, except for the occasional "No comment" she gave to the reporters gathered in the hall.

"Home or office?" Zachary asked as they started toward the car. He fully expected her to choose her office, but she surprised him, picking the condo instead. It wasn't an entirely pleasant surprise, either. It was hard being with her, but not really *with* her. It was for his own good—this distance he'd placed between them—but it ate away at him. In a few more days, at most, he would be out of her life and back in Sweetwater. It wouldn't be an easy adjustment to make—living alone, sleeping alone, facing a relentlessly long future alone. He needed to use these last few days together to start trying to get her out of his system.

Even if it was an impossible challenge.

"You did a good job," she told him as they got into the car. "You'd make a hell of a trial lawyer if you ever decided to go that route."

"No, thanks. I'm happy doing what I do." At least, he would be if she were there with him. But how could he ever expect someone who was already one hell of a trial lawyer to give it all up to be his wife? To trade respect and prestige and power and money for the only thing he could give her: love? "What do you think Carrie's chances are?"

"I don't know. Tyler was a good witness, and so was Carrie. It's a tough case, though. I'm sure the jury's sympathies lie with Carrie. I mean, here was this big, brutal, violent man who was beating this pathetic little woman half to death on a routine basis, who even gave his kid a few punches. The man deserved to die. Still, did he deserve to die like that? Did she have the right to be judge, jury and executioner?" She shrugged. "I wouldn't want to be making the decision that they're faced with."

Zachary didn't reply. He wouldn't have any problems acquitting Carrie if *he* were on the jury. She had suffered enough in the last fourteen years. She had paid the price long before she'd committed the crime.

When they reached the garage beneath Beth's condo, Zachary hesitated near the car. "Why don't you go on up?" he suggested. "I'd like to take a walk."

Beth opened her mouth, then closed it again. Had she been about to protest, to suggest another, much more satisfying form of exercise? He didn't wait to find out. Touching her shoulder as he passed, he said, "I'll be back soon." Then he disappeared down the steps that led outside.

He'd spent more hours than he could begin to count tramping through the woods up on Laurel Mountain. Whenever he had a problem, whenever he was simply tired or looking for peace, that was where he went. These city streets were a poor substitute. Still, the walk met his greatest need at this moment: it got him away from Beth.

He had prided himself on reaching the age of thirty-four without suffering a broken heart. Now he was facing the granddaddy of all heartaches, and it just wasn't fair. People shouldn't be able to fall in love with people who were so different from them. It hadn't happened that way with his grandparents. They'd known each other all their lives, had loved each other all their lives. It had been that way for his parents, too. And even though Daniel had fallen in love with a woman from the city, Sarah had been willing, even eager, to take up country life. Even if she and Daniel hadn't gotten married, Zachary believed she never would have left the southeast Tennessee mountains.

Just as Beth would never leave her high-rise condo for high-rise mountain peaks, her congested city streets for lazy country roads, her sophisticated social life for backyard barbecues and picnics alongside babbling streams.

He walked until his dress shoes began to pinch his feet, then turned back toward the condo. Back to a long evening with Beth. To withdrawing from her when all he really wanted was to hold her close. To protecting himself from further heartache instead of loving her and storing up memories for the future.

He let himself in with his own key and went straight upstairs to the room he shared with Beth. There he changed into a plaid flannel shirt and jeans and thick sweat socks. Then he went downstairs again, took a can of soda from the refrigerator and started toward the living room. When he passed the office, where he knew she would be, he knocked on the door and called, "Hey, I'm back."

He was stretched out on the sofa, with the television cabinet open and using the remote control to flip through the channels, when Beth came into the living room. She started to sit at the end of the sofa near his feet, but on second thought went to a nearby chair. He'd made her uncomfortable, he realized with regret. Just when she'd started making a few unexpected overtures, he'd had to withdraw from her. Now she didn't quite know what to say or do around him.

Oh, lady, he thought with a sigh. I *am* sorry.

"What do you want to do about dinner?" she asked, her manner a little stiff.

"I'll put something together in the kitchen. But if you want to go out, go ahead. Don't stay home on my account."

She sat motionless for a long time. Then slowly she smiled. "I think I will. I had an invitation from Martin for this evening, but I didn't want to leave you here. Since you don't mind, though, I think I'll call Martin and accept. It'll be nice to get away from business for a while."

He couldn't keep the jealousy from flaring in his eyes. If she thought she was going out with another man while *he* was still sleeping in her bed, she could just . . .

She could just do it, he admitted grimly. Besides, wasn't that what he'd wanted—to push her away?

But not into another man's arms, he argued. He didn't want to ever think of her with another man, and certainly not while he was here.

"Thanks for being so sweet, Zachary," she said, brushing her fingers across his hair as she passed. "I'll see you later tonight. Don't wait up."

He continued to stare at the television, although nothing registered in his mind except the sound of her steps on the stairs. He was still staring half an hour later when she came down again. Stubbornly he refused to look at her. He didn't want to see her wearing some gorgeous outfit for someone else.

He didn't want to see if she was carrying her fur.

"Good night, Zachary," she called from the doorway.

Not trusting his voice to work, he looked harder at the television and lifted his hand in a careless wave. But as soon as the door closed behind her, he forgot the TV. Weariness settled over him, particularly heavy around his heart. It was something unfamiliar, something he'd never experienced, but he suspected that he would soon get to know it very well. It was going to be with him for a long, long time.

Because Beth wasn't.

Beth let herself into her office, crossing the dark room with the assurance that nothing was in her path. She turned on the small lamp on her desk, then slipped off her fur. With a sigh, she sat down on the sofa, then propped her feet, one ankle over the other, on the coffee table.

She felt foolish for having lied to Zachary. Martin *had* invited her to dinner this evening, but she'd turned him down weeks ago. Even if she had changed her mind, she knew he had long since invited someone else. But Zachary, damn him, had been acting so uncaring that she'd wanted to provoke him.

And she'd gotten a response, too. She'd seen the jealousy he'd been unable to hide. It had come swiftly, darkly, and she suspected that it was still there.

But what did that prove? That he didn't want her for himself, but didn't want anyone else to have her, either?

The lamp cast deep shadows on Althea's portrait across the room. For a long time Beth looked at it, feeling sadness and loss and despair pooling inside her. "I've missed you ever since you died," she whispered, "but never as much as now. I know you could help me. You could tell me why Zachary's acting this way. You could tell me what to do."

But Althea had told her years ago what to do: live her life for herself. To be what *she* wanted to be. To care about her own opinion, not her family's and not her friends'. To be a person she could live with, a person she could be proud of, a person she could love.

Did she love herself? Not yet, but she was learning. She certainly liked herself better than she had seven weeks ago. Falling in love with Zachary had changed her. It had made her more real. More alive. More likable.

But she still needed to make other changes. She needed a life, not a career. She needed a family and friends, real friends like Sarah. She needed to feel important, not as a lawyer but as a person. A woman. A lover. Maybe even, someday, a mother.

She needed to know that she mattered. That when she died fifty years from now there would be people whose lives were better because she had lived.

Gradually she became aware of a soft sound in the hallway. Footsteps. Probably one of her co-workers coming back for a file he or she had forgotten, she told herself, although her pulse speeded up a bit, anyway. But the steps came to a halt outside her office, and the door swung silently in. It wasn't a co-worker who stood there—no one that unimportant.

It was Zachary.

He came inside and closed the door, turning the lock with an audible click. For a moment he remained across the room while he removed his leather jacket and gloves; then he slowly started toward her. "Martin Hamilton called and left a message for you," he said quietly. "He's sorry you couldn't make it tonight, but there's always next time."

She smiled, only mildly embarrassed at being caught in her lie. "You didn't have to come all the way down here to tell me that. A note would have sufficed."

He moved closer. "I was curious about where you'd gone, since it obviously wasn't to Martin." He paused, then added, "I was hoping you would be here."

She didn't swing her feet to the floor or tug her skirt down or any of the image-conscious acts she might have made only a few weeks ago. He had seen her at her best and at her worst, and he had liked her either way. He was the only man she could make that claim about.

He sat down on the sofa beside her and laid his hand just above her knee. In spite of the gloves he'd worn, his fingers were cold against her skin. But *he* wasn't cold. His eyes weren't cold. His expression wasn't cold.

In the dim light Zachary studied the dress he'd refused to look at earlier. It was black with long sleeves, and it fit like a second skin, with the skirt ending high on her thigh. It was pretty and slinky and sexy, and he wanted nothing more than to remove it and toss it on the floor, out of his sight, out of his mind. "I am sorry," he murmured, moving his fingers only fractionally over her stocking-clad leg.

"For what?"

She wasn't being coy or difficult; he acknowledged that. She truly didn't understand why he'd been behaving this way. "This case is going to the jury tomorrow. They'll probably have a verdict by Wednesday, and I'll be home by Thursday." His smile was taut and faint. "I don't want to take you home with me, Beth." He already had enough memories to haunt him for a lifetime. He didn't need to add any more. He didn't need to make love to her one last time...although he knew he was going to, again and again, before Thursday. He didn't need to focus so intensely on her...although he knew she would remain the most important part of his life for a long time. He didn't need to love her...although he knew he would. For always. Forever.

"This was just supposed to be an affair, wasn't it?"

She didn't offer him confirmation.

"But something happened. I fell in love with you, lady. And now I have to figure out how to fall *out* of love with you. Any suggestions?"

She numbly shook her head. His admission had taken her by surprise, he saw in the pale light. She had never expected to hear that he loved her. She'd made certain that he knew from the start exactly what she was willing to give him: an affair. A few weeks of passionate sex. Nothing more.

"I've always been sensible," he went on. "I understood from the beginning that there wasn't any future to this—to us. I just lost control of things somewhere along the way. But I'll get it back. I'll manage." For a moment he broke off and watched his progress as his hand moved along her thigh, now reaching the hem of her short black dress, now gliding beneath the fabric.

"I'm looking forward to going home," he said, smiling a bit as her eyes fluttered shut when his fingers intimately probed. "The last couple of months have been a great experience, but it'll be nice to let my life get back to normal—to go back to working part-time and finishing my house, seeing my family and friends. But I'll never forget this time, Beth. I'll never forget *you.*"

Beth wanted to cry at the note of finality in his voice, but her body betrayed her, shutting down all coherent thought in order to concentrate fully on the sensations he was sending through her. She gave a start when his mouth touched hers in a pure, innocent kiss, so at odds with the wicked things his hands were doing to her.

He brought her to completion using no more than his kisses and his caresses. Then he took off her clothes, removed his own and made love to her. Her tears found release then, just a few, sliding over her skin to disappear into her hair. It was the sweetest, gentlest thing she had ever experienced. It was the sort of lovemaking that memories were made of. It was almost perfect.

Only almost. Because it was also goodbye.

It was possible, Beth realized the next day, to completely shut off your feelings and still function. She'd gotten dressed this morning that way, and she'd made the trip downtown to the courthouse that way, too—perfectly functional but feeling nothing. She'd even managed to survive this morning's court session, listening to Carrie's responses to Duane Misner's cross-examination, making the proper objections the few times he made a remark or asked a question that was out of line. She had even carried on conversations with Zachary as if he hadn't said such hurtful things last night.

I don't want to take you home with me, Beth.

This was just supposed to be an affair, wasn't it?

I understood from the beginning that there wasn't any future to this—to us.

It'll be nice to let my life get back to normal.

As if being in love with her wasn't normal. As if sharing her home, her bed, her life, wasn't normal. As if he'd fallen in love with her unwillingly and now wanted only to be free of her.

Actually, she thought, toying with a gold pen, she was glad he'd said those things. If he hadn't, she might have made the mistake of telling him that *she* loved *him,* that she wanted to live with him, to help him finish his house on the mountain, to raise children with him there.

She might have made a fool of herself in ways that she had never achieved even with Philip.

She sighed for a moment, thinking about Philip. For a long time the mere mention of his name had been painful. Then, as her feelings for him faded, pain had given way to shame. She had been embarrassed by the way he'd used her, the way she had let him use her. She had been ashamed of her gullibility and her vulnerability.

Now . . . she felt nothing. It was almost as if he had happened to someone else.

Now, if she wanted heartache, she only had to think of Zachary.

"They're not going to bring a verdict back tonight."

She blinked, then looked at Zachary, seated across the desk from her. After the case had gone to the jury after lunch, they had come back to her office so she could work while awaiting the verdict. But she hadn't been able to concentrate on anything except her own problems.

But Zachary was right. By now the jury had surely been released for the night. They would reconvene in the morning and take up the deliberation again.

"What is it they say—that the quicker a jury comes back, the more likely the verdict is not guilty?"

Beth shrugged. "I haven't found any real pattern personally, except in cases where the evidence was overwhelming one way or the other. All this means for sure is that the jurors didn't wholeheartedly accept either the prosecution's arguments or ours." With a sigh, she opened the center desk drawer and dropped the pen in it. "Want to go out to dinner tonight?"

"Sure."

He didn't sound any more enthusiastic than she felt, Beth thought. Whoever would have believed that she could grow so used to home-cooked meals for two in such a short time? There was such a cozy, homey feel about eating in. But tonight she didn't want to be cozy, at least, not until bedtime. She didn't want to spend any more time alone with Zachary. She didn't want to think about last night and the things he'd said, or tomorrow night, when he probably wouldn't be around to say anything at all.

They went to a nearby restaurant, where they found numerous reasons for not speaking to each other—the menus, the waiter, the food, the other diners. They had come full circle, she thought without one bit of humor. They were back to the awkwardness and uneasiness that had characterized their relationship in the beginning. No one who saw them tonight would guess that, in a few hours, they would be making passionate love.

Or so she hoped.

Dear Lord, how she hoped.

The call came in shortly before noon on Wednesday: the jury had reached a verdict. Zachary and Beth hurried to the courthouse, where they met for a few moments in private with Carrie. She wore the green dress, but today the rich color merely emphasized her pallor. Seven weeks in jail could do that to you, Zachary thought. Maybe soon she would be free again to go outside, to hold her kids and put them to bed, to give birth to the baby she carried and make a home for all the children. Maybe.

"I just want it to be over," Carrie said, her voice pitched low. "Even if they find me guilty, even if they send me to prison, I just want the not knowing to end."

"All we're going to get today is the verdict," Beth warned. "If you're acquitted, you'll be home with your children tonight. If you're found guilty, the judge will set a sentencing date, probably in a month or so, and you'll go back to jail. During that time, the probation department will do a presentencing investigation to determine what kind of sentence they'll recommend. It could be probation, or—" her voice softened "—it could be a long time in prison."

"But at least today I'll know," Carrie said stubbornly. "I'll know whether I'll get to spend Christmas with my kids." When the bailiff tapped on the door, she stood up, then faced both of them. "I want to thank you for all you've done. I know this has cost you an awful lot of time and money, and I can never begin to repay you, but... thank you." Gravely she shook Zachary's hand, then enveloped Beth in an awkward embrace. Then she walked out and joined the bailiff who would escort her to the courtroom.

Zachary watched Beth. For a moment she seemed to have forgotten him, and selfishly he didn't like it. "Any headaches? Heartburn?" he asked, circling the table to stand beside her.

"Headaches?" she echoed.

"You said before that by the time the verdict comes in on a case, you usually have a long-term case of heartburn and a world-class headache. What about this time?"

She considered it for a moment, then smiled. "Other than a minor case of nerves, I feel fine."

"I wonder why that is. Maybe because you chose a case based on the facts and not on the billable hours or the partners' recommendations?"

"Maybe. Or maybe it's because I had a good partner of my own this time," she replied.

Maybe, Zachary silently agreed, but he didn't think that was the only reason. Maybe it was because in addition to long hours of work on this case, she had also spent long hours relaxing. Unwinding. Forgetting about the trial. Making love.

Like last night.

As Carrie had done only moments earlier, she offered her hand to him. "It's been a pleasure working with you, Zachary. Thank you . . . for everything."

He accepted her handshake and resisted the urge to pull her into his arms—just barely. He held her fingers long after he should have let go, and for one crazy moment he considered asking, begging, *pleading* with her to let him remain a part of her life, to see him on weekends, to give him even the slightest hope that someday they might work something out.

Then she pulled away and said, "We'd better get to the courtroom."

And the moment passed, leaving him with an abrupt feeling of emptiness. Of despair. Of hopelessness.

He followed her to the courtroom and to their table at the front. Court was called to order, the judge took his seat at the bench, and the jury filed in in two somber rows. The formalities passed over Zachary's head as he suddenly realized that this was it: the goal he and Beth had worked toward for the last seven weeks. Had they succeeded, or were they going to lose big? Was Carrie going to lose?

The judge instructed the jury foreman to read the verdict. First came the case number, then the reading of the charge, then the verdict itself. At the sound of the word "guilty," followed by gasps and murmurs in the crowd, his heart sank in his chest. Somehow he had hoped, had believed, that everything would work out all right for Carrie, that just this once life would be fair to her.

But the foreman continued reading, and he realized that he'd reacted too soon. They had won. He needed only to look at Beth's face to see it and at Duane Misner's to confirm it. Carrie had been found guilty not of first-degree murder, the charge the prosecution had aimed for, but of manslaughter. The lesser charge brought with it a lesser penalty, maybe a few years in prison, maybe even simple probation. It was possible that these weeks awaiting trial and sentencing would be the only time she would have to serve.

After Carrie was taken away, Misner came to the defense table. "Not bad, Beth," he said, his tone a tad ungracious.

"Not bad at all," she agreed. "I hope you watched us closely. You might have learned something, Duane."

With a scowl, he returned to his table for his briefcase, then left the courtroom. Zachary leaned against the table and watched him go. "Looks like there's quite a crowd out there," he remarked before the door swung shut. "Are you finally going to give the reporters something besides 'No comment'?"

"Let Misner play with them. He thrives on the attention." She picked up her own briefcase and fiddled with the clasps, then set it down again and looked at him. "This calls for a celebration, don't you think? There's a place here in town that has the best steak and homemade rolls and . . ."

He shook his head, and her invitation trailed off. "I'm sorry, Beth, but I can't," he said, his voice thicker than he wanted it to be with emotion he didn't want to feel. "I've got to head on home."

For a moment she looked disappointed, and he knew that if she asked him again, he would accept. He would stay for one more evening with her, one more night with her. But the disappointment changed to cool reserve, and she smiled her best ever-so-professional smile. "I understand. Well . . . be careful. Have a safe trip. And good luck on your house."

She stuck out her hand, and he took it, and this time he didn't resist the urge to pull her closer. He simply did it, sliding his arms around her waist, nuzzling her head back, leaving a sweet, lingering kiss on her mouth. Then, wearing a smile that he didn't feel, he released her and, without looking back, walked away.

Beth heard the heavy door close behind him as she sank weakly into her chair. She was alone in the courtroom now—and alone in so many other ways, too. How could she bear going home and knowing he wouldn't be there? How could she spend even one night in her bed without him beside her? Every place in her life held intimate memories of him, even—after a few nights ago—her office.

How was she going to survive?

That night she delayed going home as long as she could. When she finally gave in, she walked into a cold, empty, unwelcoming place. There was a hall lamp burning, because Zachary had been considerate enough to turn it on for her when he'd picked up his things. On the marble table where it sat were the extra keys she'd given him to the house and the office and, beside them, a single rose. It was red, and it still bore its thorns. She picked it up, breathed deeply of its scent and sternly warned herself not to cry even as the first tear slid down her cheek.

Upstairs the ice-blue bedroom was untouched, as if no one had ever been there. Her own bedroom seemed that way; even the closet that had held his clothes was now empty. She walked into the room, hating its stillness. Clutching the rose in one hand, she pulled the white comforter off the bed, grasped hold of the black sheets and yanked them free of the mattress. She shook the pillows from their cases, gathered the pile of linen together and carried it to the wastebasket downstairs in the kitchen, dumping it into the empty container.

As she passed her office, she thought about the answering machine and wondered if he'd left anything behind besides the rose. Even just a tape-recorded goodbye would mean something.

There were messages, but all three were from her mother. The first was a simple, "Call me," followed by a longer message about Christmas. The last told her more than she wanted to hear. "Christmas dinner will be served at two o'clock Friday. I want you here no later than one so you can help me with the guests. And wear something pretty, Beth— maybe in blue? No black, please. It *is* a holiday, after all."

"Yes, ma'am," Beth muttered with a mocking salute as the machine shut off. She would show up not one minute after one, and she would be wearing blue, even if she didn't particularly care for the color. Even if there was no place on earth she wanted to be less on Christmas Day than at her parents' house.

She curled up in a chair in front of the cold fireplace and sighed. It sounded so loud and *lonely*. Yes, she was already lonely. How was it possible to miss someone who didn't want to care about you? Didn't she have any pride, or had she lost that along with her common sense when she invited Zachary into this house and into her life?

Lord, how it would help if she could simply talk to someone. But there was only one person she could talk to about love, and it was far too late to be waking Sarah just so she could cry on her shoulder.

The phone rang, and she wearily unfolded her legs, going to sit at the desk and listen while the answering machine picked up the call. It was her mother again—it was too late for *normal* people to be calling, Beth amended her earlier thought. In the middle of Francine's message, she pushed the button that would stop the tape and picked up the phone. "Hello, Mother, I'm here."

"Did you get my message about Christmas dinner?"

"Yes, I did."

"And you'll be here at one to help." This time it was a statement, not a question. Her mother was so sure of her, Beth thought with a sick little smile. And why not? Except for her one brief rebellion regarding her education and career, she had always done what her parents wanted.

But not this time.

"No, Mother, I won't," she said quietly. "I intend to spend Christmas in my own way this year." *Alone.* She couldn't go to Sarah and Daniel's, because they would be celebrating with the Adamses, and she couldn't handle that. But she didn't have to spend it with her family. She didn't have to be miserable and tense on what should be one of the most joyous days of the year. She didn't have to let her parents ruin one more holiday for her.

"What do you mean—spend Christmas in your own way?" Francine asked. "Don't be silly, Beth. You're coming over here, and—"

Her hand trembling just slightly, Beth replaced the receiver in the cradle, disconnecting the call. She felt a little shiver of relief at her daring. Never had she spoken crossly to her mother or walked out on a conversation or done anything that a well-mannered child wouldn't do. Now she had not only defied Francine, she had hung up on her. It was a first step, and she was proud of herself.

Zachary would be proud of her, too.

Monday morning found Beth in her office, all ready to work—but not on business. She was going to find a solution to the mess her life had become. After moping for an entire weekend, she knew what she wanted to do: quit the firm, sell her condo and say goodbye to Nashville forever. Of course, that was her number two list. Her priority wish list included the same items, but was topped by marrying Zachary and living happily ever after with him on his mountain.

She had called Marian Vega on Sunday and told her that she would soon be available for cases similar to Carrie's. The psychologist had been pleased. Who wouldn't be pleased, Beth admitted honestly, to get an attorney of her caliber for free?

She had begun going through her files, estimating how much time she needed to complete or transfer her open cases and composing letters to the clients who'd been with her from the beginning. She would give them time to retain new lawyers—but not too much time. Now that she was finally taking action, she was eager to start making new friends.

But where? The only place she had ever considered was Sweetwater, and now it wouldn't exactly be fair to Zachary for her to move in on his territory. After all, hadn't he as much as told her that he didn't want to care for her? That he was actively trying to *stop* caring for her? *And now I have to figure out how to fall out of love with you.* That was what he'd said. Moving to his hometown after he'd told her that, forcing her way into his life, would be less than generous.

She'd repeated his words to herself so often in the last week that the sting was gone. Now there was just sadness. Acceptance.

And now I have to figure out...

Suddenly she frowned. Flipping to a clean sheet on the pad in front of her, she wrote the sentence down, word for word, the way he'd said it. She studied the words, then read them out loud.

And now I have to... Have to. Not want to. He *had* to find a way to stop caring. As in against his will. As in having no other choice.

Reining in her excitement, she tried to recall his next words, something about being sensible, followed by something about the future. *I understood from the beginning that there wasn't any future to this—to us.*

Was that what he'd meant? she wondered, her hands trembling so badly that she had to clasp them together. That there were so many obvious differences between them that they could never work out any way to be together, and *that* was why he'd felt forced to stop loving her?

She reached for the phone and dialed the first three numbers, then stopped, her fingertip poised over the number pad. Was she reading too much into his choice of words? People were rarely precise in their language; as a lawyer, she understood that all too well.

But Zachary was a lawyer, too, and he had no problems saying exactly what he meant.

Slowly she hung up. She needed to know the truth. She needed to know how he really felt—about her, about them, about a future. She needed to tell him that she loved him, that she was willing to do whatever was necessary to be with him.

But not yet. This wasn't something that could be done over the phone. She would go to Sweetwater. She would look into his sweet blue eyes. *Then* she would know the truth.

And it wasn't something that could be done until her life was in order. Until she was free of all her old obligations, all her old responsibilities.

Until she was free to offer him anything.

Until she was free to offer him everything.

And if that wasn't enough? If he really didn't want her?

She smiled bleakly. As Carrie had said on the last day of her trial ... at least she would know.

It was a cold, clear Saturday, the kind of winter day that made Zachary thankful he'd been born in these Tennessee mountains and not somewhere else. The sky was startlingly blue, the clouds thin and wispy. The temperature was in the high thirties, but it wasn't warm enough yet to melt the last patches of snow that blanketed the shady areas around the house.

It was the middle of January, over three weeks since he'd seen Beth. He'd had the opportunity just a few days ago, when Carrie had been sentenced, but he'd declined to tag along. He certainly didn't need to be there to hear that she'd been sentenced to a year in prison. With credit for the time she'd already served and for good behavior, she would be out and home with her children in a matter of months— maybe even before her baby was born.

He had been tempted to go, though. He'd wanted to see Beth—just see her, not touch her or kiss her or make love to her—so badly that he'd ached with it. But seeing her would just stir up the pain that had finally become manageable. It would disturb his nights when he'd finally found some peace in them again.

And so he had stayed away, and he'd heard the news about Carrie from the Morrises. And he'd gone on with his life the way he had the last three weeks: one day at a time.

The way he was afraid he would have to live it for months—years—to come.

Behind him he heard the French door open, and he picked up the stack of two-by-fours that he'd just finished cutting. Daniel and Tyler were working on the laundry room that opened off one end of the kitchen. They knew his mind was elsewhere these days and that he was working more slowly because of it—Daniel had even suggested that maybe he shouldn't use the power saw until he could concentrate more clearly—but they were being patient with him. They must have figured they'd been patient enough in waiting for this wood.

Grinning, he turned, ready to respond to whatever remarks they might make; then he stopped suddenly, and his grin disappeared. The lumber fell from his arms, clattering to the deck, one piece missing the small, booted feet there by only inches.

Beth.

All he could do was stare at her, wondering dimly if he had conjured her up with the intensity of his thoughts, and why, if that was the case, it hadn't happened three weeks ago when the pain around his heart had been strong enough to make him sick with it.

Her expression was uncertain, a curious little smile that threatened to vanish any second now and an uneasy shadow in her green eyes. Those eyes had haunted him every night, asleep and dreaming, and awake, too. Lovely eyes. Eyes he'd gotten lost in and even now couldn't find his way out of.

"Hey, Zachary." Her voice was unsteady, and she cleared her throat to strengthen it. "How are you?"

"Okay." God help him, he couldn't stand here and exchange pleasantries with her as if they were no more than casual acquaintances. It would destroy his soul. "How are you?" Waiting for her answer, he bent and began picking up the wood he'd dropped. What he saw froze him in place as surely as what she said.

"Lonely."

He stared at her boots—not the expensive, low-heeled leather boots that she'd worn before, but hiking boots, virtually identical to his own, only smaller and newer. And jeans? Beth Gibson wearing *jeans?* They were dark indigo and pressed and creased, but they were undeniably jeans, and they fit her undeniably well, from her long legs to her slender hips and narrow waist.

He stood up again and stacked the wood on the sawhorses beside them, then dusted his hands. "You came to see Sarah?" he asked, having to swallow hard to get the words out.

"No. Actually, I came to show you something."

He waited expectantly, and she smiled that nervous little smile again.

"It's out front."

Rather than cut through the house where he might run into Daniel or Tyler in this addle-brained condition, he gestured to the steps at the end of the deck. He followed her down them, around the corner and to the front of the house. There he stopped abruptly. Parked next to his Jeep on one side was Daniel's truck; on the other was another pickup. This one was brand new. It was flashy and more than fast enough, he thought with a slow grin, and it was definitely fire-engine red.

"It's not a sports car," she said quietly. "But a sports car couldn't clear the ruts in your road."

These things—the boots, the jeans, the truck—weren't just things, he thought as he walked closer to the pickup. They were Beth's declaration of independence. She was turning her back on the life that had stifled her for so long and reaching for something new.

And could that something new include *somebody* new? he wondered, feeling a measure of hope for the first time in weeks. Turning around to look at her again, he asked, "What about your condo?"

"I turned it over to a real estate agent to sell."

"And your career? Did you simply walk away from the partnership?"

"That job didn't suit my needs anymore. But I have another. As soon as I get settled, I'll be working part-time with Marian Vega, handling cases for women who can't afford legal counsel. It will mean some travel. I'll work hard for a couple of months, then my time will be my own for a couple."

He took a step closer to her. "Get settled where?"

"Zachary—" She swallowed hard. "I don't need the city. I don't need the career or the firm or the people or the parties. I can live without those things. I can live..." She faltered, then started again. "I can live without you, too, if I have to. If that's what you want. But I need to know."

He glanced at the truck again, and this time he saw the suitcases that filled the passenger seat. That was all she'd brought with her from her old life: a few suitcases of clothing—although he would bet Great-Grandmother Althea's portrait was stored somewhere, waiting for a new address.

She really was looking for something new, he thought, more than a little surprised. But not *somebody* new. No, she'd come to somebody old, somebody who cared. Maybe somebody she loved?

He moved again, until only inches separated them. "I already told you that I love you."

She wet her lips with the tip of her tongue. "But you made it sound like goodbye."

"I thought it was. I thought those other things—the condo, the firm, the social standing, the money—were more important to you than me."

Beth blinked away the moisture that filled her eyes. A month ago she would have blamed the tears on the cold, but today she was being honest. She was about to cry because she'd never felt so many emotions, all so strong and all at once. "Nothing is more important to me than you are. I love you, Zachary." More than ten years had passed since she'd said those words to a man, and she had sworn she would never say them again. But they came so simply, so easily, and they were so true.

He slipped his arm around her waist, then brushed his hand over her hair. "Are you sure?" he asked softly. "Our nearest neighbors will be more than three miles away. It could get awfully lonely up here sometimes."

Our neighbors, she thought with a smile. And it would be our house, our friends, our family. That one three-letter word could certainly make a big difference. "I'm sure, Zachary."

He studied her face for a moment, his eyes searching hers. Once, not too long ago, he had done that, and she had worried about what he'd seen. This time she didn't worry. She knew what was there, and when he slowly smiled, she saw that he'd recognized it, too. Promises. Love. Forever.

"I love you, Beth," he said, his voice throaty and hoarse. "Will you marry me? Will you be my lady?"

"Yes," she whispered, and then he kissed her. It was a gentle kiss, sweet and undemanding, but with a hint of something more—of passion, pure and lasting. Of soul-deep hunger. Of love.

Silently, deep in her heart, she repeated her answer. Yes, she would marry him. Yes, she would be his lady.

Zachary's lady.

*   *   *   *   *